D1572391

Betty King lives in Hertfordshire; she is the mother of three grown-up children and regards her writing as a luxury in a busy home life. It was this absorption with family life that drew her to the lives of the Beauforts. THE LORD JASPER is Betty King's third novel centred around the Beaufort family and she is working on a fourth. She has become a specialist in fifteenth century history and spares no effort in ensuring historical accuracy. She has always been interested in writing and planned to make a career in journalism, but the war intervened. Her hobby is painting.

THE LORD JASPER

Jasper, Earl of Pembroke and later Duke of Bedford, was the brother of Lady Margaret Beaufort's first husband, Edmund, Earl of Richmond. This is the story of Jasper's early life and of his fateful meeting with Margaret on the day of her betrothal to his brother. When Edmund died tragically soon after his marriage, Jasper's love for Margaret took on a new poignancy. Unable to marry her, he devoted his life to the care of her fatherless son; and it was he who was largely responsible for Henry VII's success in wresting the Crown from Richard III on the field of Bosworth.

Books by Betty King
Published by The House of Ulverscroft:

WE ARE TOMORROW'S PAST
THE FRENCH COUNTESS
THE ROSE BOTH RED & WHITE
MARGARET OF ANJOU
THE LADY MARGARET
THE CAPTIVE JAMES

BETTY KING

THE LORD JASPER

Complete and Unabridged

ULVERSCROFT
Leicester

First published in Great Britain in 1967

First Large Print Edition
published 2001
by arrangement with
Robert Hale Limited
London

British Library CIP Data

King, Betty, *1919* –
   The Lord Jasper.—Large print ed.—
Ulverscroft large print series: romance
1. Love stories
2. Large type books
I. Title
823.9′14 [F]

ISBN 0–7089–4419–1

Published by
F. A. Thorpe (Publishing)
Anstey, Leicestershire

Set by Words & Graphics Ltd.
Anstey, Leicestershire
Printed and bound in Great Britain by
T. J. International Ltd., Padstow, Cornwall

This book is printed on acid-free paper

For My Husband

Acknowledgements

I wish to thank the following people for their kind assistance in the preparation of this novel:

Lord Salisbury; Miss Clare Talbot, Librarian of Hatfield House; the Staff of Enfield Central Library; the Staff of the British Museum Reading Room; Colonel R. O. Dennys, O.B.E., Rouge Croix Pursuivant of Arms; The Reverend D. Hywel Davies, Vicar of Monkton Church, Pembroke; Mrs Booker, Curator of Tenby Museum; the Syndicat D'Initiative, Vannes; Mons. Albert Degez, Architect, Vannes; Mons. Jean Texur, Tours D'Elven, Brittany; and my family.

Bibliography

Main Sources

E. F. Jacob: *The Fifteenth Century.*
Sir J. Ramsay: *York and Lancaster.*
J. R. Lander: *The Wars of the Roses.*
A. H. Brodrick: *The Peoples France.*
  Brittany.
Ed. J. Gairdner: *Paston Letters.*
C. H. Cooper: *Memoir of Margaret.*
Halsted: *Life of Margaret.*
A memoir. E. A. C. Routh:
  Lady Margaret.
Dictionary of National Biography:
Lodge: *Illustrious Portraits. Vol I.*
A. Strickland: *Lives of the Queens of
  England.*
Nicholas Harris: *Testamenta Vetusta.*

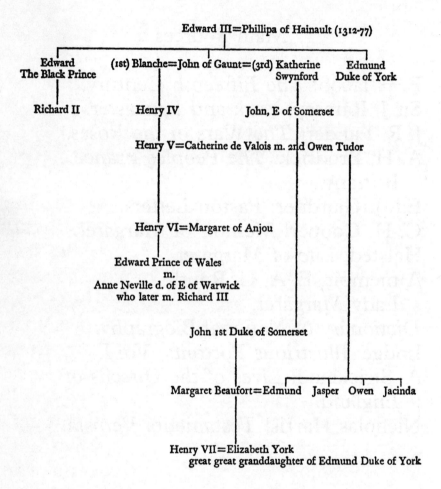

Edward III＝Phillipa of Hainault (1312-77)

Edward
The Black Prince

(1st) Blanche＝John of Gaunt＝(3rd) Katherine
Swynford

Edmund
Duke of York

Richard II

Henry IV

John, E of Somerset

Henry V＝Catherine de Valois m. 2nd Owen Tudor

Henry VI＝Margaret of Anjou

Edward Prince of Wales
m.
Anne Neville d. of E of Warwick
who later m. Richard III

John 1st Duke of Somerset

Margaret Beaufort＝Edmund   Jasper   Owen   Jacinda

Henry VII＝Elizabeth York
great great granddaughter of Edmund Duke of York

1

'Jasper! Jasper!'

The small boy, perched high on an accommodating branch of one of the oaks in the gardens of Hatfield Palace, recognised in the ascending tone of his nurse's call a querulous note that would not brook disobedience.

With a last, lingering look towards the distant hills, palest grey in the evening light, he climbed down reluctantly and ran as fast as he could towards the woman who stood in the shadow of the buttressed wall.

'There you are!' she cried. 'Just see your hands and clothes, and your hair does not look as if it has felt the brush since morning.'

Jasper ruefully spread his fingers through his untidy locks and tugged his doublet into place. Hopping behind his nurse, who was now hurrying across the square courtyard to the small house where they lived, he straightened his hose and made unsuccessful attempts to rub off some of the patches of green acquired in his climb.

When he came into the parlour he found

the rest of the children already in their places.

Edmund greeted him with a quick smile and indicated the empty chair beside him while Owen clapped his fat hands and Jacinda banged the table from her high stool. From the large number of his mother's ladies, who were also seated, he understood this to be one of the evenings when his father and she preferred to sup alone.

He slipped quietly as possible into his place next to his elder brother, acknowledging swiftly the kindly glances that came his way. He bowed his head as a priest of the Bishop of Ely's household said grace.

The two boys ate the food put before them without speaking, carefully minding their manners as they had been taught, for the thought of their gentle mother being worried with tales of their misbehaviour when she was near her time with another child was unimaginable. The penance was no real hardship for they knew once the meal was finished they would be put to bed in the room they shared with the small Owen and would be free to talk until they fell asleep.

They had also learnt, with the wisdom of their six and seven years, that if they were quiet they heard more of what was said about them. This, they had discovered with the insight of the very young, was necessary in a

2

household such as the one in which they lived.

Surrounded as they were by the love of their parents, their days were filled with happiness. Just to watch their handsome father as he looked with tenderness on their mother was enough to convince them of the world's goodness; and to be thrown high in his strong arms or be cradled to her bosom was to know bliss. Yet, despite this pervading atmosphere of delight, or perhaps in some subtle way because of it, they knew their life was different from that of other people.

Neither Jasper or Edmund were five years old when they realised the messengers, who came frequently to the house within the confines of the Bishop's Palace, wore the livery of the Royal Household. It greatly interested them that, when Lancaster Herald or Garter King of Arms headed the party of visitors, it was their mother who received them while their father was absent hunting in the surrounding forest or about the manifold business of their large household.

Of late, their mother had been paler than usual and sometimes they came into their parent's chamber to find her pillowed in their father's arms while large tears dropped down her cheeks. Their father had explained to them that mothers awaiting the birth of a child were often given to fits of melancholy. This information he had given them as man to man confidence and their chests had swelled with pride in the knowledge of his awareness of their understanding.

Be this as it may, they were still uneasily conscious the name of Gloucester seemed to be curiously intermingled with the tears, and it was often after the visits of the messengers from London that their mother was sad.

Supper finished, when at last their nurses were satisfied with their washings and had heard them repeat their prayers, they tumbled into the bed they shared. Owen, their smallest brother, was already asleep in the cot at the other side of the room.

A little of the day's fading light still lingered as they talked together in whispers.

'Did you catch anything when you went hunting with Father today?' Jasper asked.

'No,' answered Edmund. 'We saw no deer and I was glad — '

'Glad?' interrupted Jasper.

'Yes,' said Edmund hurriedly. 'I would not have liked to see the poor thing killed.'

'Oh,' said Jasper slowly, thinking over this new aspect of an every day occurrence. 'Somehow, when I look forward to going out with Father as you do, I never think of the animals in peril of their life.'

'I try not to think of it at all,' Edmund went on. 'I just enjoy being with Father and riding the new pony he gave me.'

'Is he easy to manage?' Jasper asked.

'Very; besides that there is no need to be frightened when you do go because Father keeps you close by his side.'

'I would never be frightened,' said Jasper quickly. 'Are you?' he asked, in wonder.

'Not really,' Edmund replied. 'Sometimes perhaps when I feel how strong the horse is beneath me and how much I am in its power. But Father is there and I know he will not allow any harm to befall me. What did you do this afternoon?'

'Sat up in my tree.'

'Could you see Wales?'

'I don't think so,' Jasper said with a little sigh. 'It was so hot that the hills looked shimmering in gold. Perhaps I could just see the towers of Pendragon's castle, but I am not really sure. Do you think we shall ever go to Wales and see the places we hear about in Father's stories?'

'I hope so!' Edmund answered sleepily.

'When?' Jasper asked eagerly.

There was no reply, and, although there was still so much he wanted to say to his brother, Jasper could not bring himself to do more than shake his arm in a half hearted effort to awaken him.

He contented himself with curling up and drifting off into a happy state midway between sleep and dreaming awareness where he was living in his parent's own castle somewhere in the remote country of his father's birth. Here he was no longer a small boy subjected to the ministrations of the womenfolk who plagued his life but a knight astride a horse with flowing mane and tail. Dragons came vaguely into the fantasy, but they were not enemies, while helpless damsels called to him to rescue them from unnamed perils.

A little smile of pleasure curved his mouth as he relaxed into the sleep of secure childhood.

In the room across the courtyard, at right angles to that of his sons Owen Tudor lay unsleeping, cradling in his arms the heavy body of his wife. She lay on her back, her head against his shoulder and her hand trustingly in his. As the moon sailed higher in the sky its light filled the room and he could see her face almost as if it were day.

How long had he loved her? Surely it was since that day when he had first seen her at the court of her father in France. She had only been a girl then, tremulous and shy, afraid for the destiny her mother was preparing for her as the future Queen of England.

It was not long after the battle at Agincourt, Owen remembered, that he had accompanied the English King's train to Paris as a very humble and young knight and had witnessed the meeting between the victorious Henry and his future bride.

In the fullness of his great success in the field and his abundant promise as a leader of diplomacy in Europe had Henry ever really had time to love the Princess Catherine? In his lifetime there had not been much opportunity to discover the truth of the matter, but Owen had been among those who rode off with Henry two days after his marriage to Catherine to besiege Montereau, and had wondered then how any man in his senses could put the waging of war before the loving of a new-found wife.

With the campaign in France throwing more and more glittering prizes into the English King's hands, Henry had thought it the right moment to return to England and present his wife to his subjects. Together they had made a triumphant tour of his realm.

Catherine had been crowned with the traditional pomp of the monarch's consort and had received the loyal protestations of the peers of the realm. In the Hall of Westminster afterwards, a great banquet of Lenten fare was given in her honour and the King's brother had stood in respectful courtesy at the side of her chair.

Owen threw out his arm as if to ward off some obnoxious presence at the memory of Gloucester making a show of his loyalty to the new Queen. Hypocrite, Owen thought. Oh, the hypocrite. Catherine stirred as if she sensed his disquiet and he soothed her with gentle words until she slept again.

Humphrey of Gloucester was the last remaining son of Henry IV. More the pity. The brave Clarence and the valiant Bedford, with their brother Henry V, had all died in France and left Gloucester in gloating triumph to exert his influence on the fifteen year old nephew who was Henry VI.

Since Bedford had died, almost a year before, Catherine's position as mother of the King had worsened considerably. It had been Gloucester who had insisted upon the passing of the Act which forbade Dowager Queens to remarry, and since that day their love had taken on a new poignancy.

Owen thought again of Catherine's coronation feast and her beauty as she had sat enthroned on a raised dais while minstrels sang her praises. He had gazed at her from one of the furthermost trestles, comforting himself with the knowledge that she still possessed an almost virginal air and conversed as often with James the young King of Scotland as she did with Henry.

When the King returned to France to continue his campaign Owen accompanied his train but the Queen did not. Owen recalled his sick jealousy when he learned the reason.

He remained with Henry's army, earning himself a reputation for valour as he hurled himself into fighting in an effort to forget the pain in his heart. He recalled there had been great need for bravery for the campaign had been bitter and dogged with ill luck. The bloody flux, aggravated by wet weather and water logged earth, claimed more victims than the enemy. Not even the birth of an Heir revived the spirits of the men, who until now had clamoured to follow Henry in his punishment of their hereditary foes.

Worse was to follow, for it soon became obvious the leader of the expedition was suffering with his troops. Bedford, hastily recalled from an expedition to relieve the young Duke of Burgundy, who was besieged near Lyons, was only in time to hear his brother appoint him Regent as he lay on his deathbed. Owen remembered the wave of depression which now hit the already disheartened army and the guilty lift of his own spirits when he realised Catherine was a widow.

She arrived in France too late to see her husband alive and so never heard him condemn her for allowing their child to be born at Windsor where there had been portents of disaster for a Prince who first saw the light of day in that place.

She had followed the bier through its weary journey across France and into England, and Owen had followed her at the necessary respectful distance. She had looked strained and ethereal and was much in the company of the exiled King of the Scots. Owen, watching with the eye of a closely guarded love, hopeless by virtue of their completely different stations, was strangely not made jealous by this friendship, for he could see that passion played no part in it. He was glad rather that she had someone on whom she could call for comfort and advice.

It was a pity that before long the Council decided the time had come for the King, James Stewart, to be allowed his freedom to return to Scotland after spending eighteen years as their captive. This meant Catherine would be without his help in the strangeness of the English court, but she repaid James for his kindness to her by supporting his suit when he fell in love with Jane the niece of the Bishop Beaufort of Winchester and took her to Scotland with him as his Queen.

Thank God for Beaufort, for without him Catherine's lot would have been more dismal than it was. She had fallen out of favour with Gloucester, who was acting as Regent while Bedford remained in France, for reasons Owen could only surmise. He had made her miserable in a thousand intangible ways, undermining her authority and counter-manding her orders; it was a blessing Henry had recognised his brother's devious nature and entrusted the upbringing of the infant King to the Duke of Exeter, brother of Bishop Beaufort and half-uncle of Henry.

Owen grimaced in the moon-lit room as he remembered that one of the explanations for Gloucester's unkindness to the Dowager Queen had been her rebuttal of his amorous advances, for Gloucester was well known as a tireless womaniser who had twice openly disgraced himself with scandalous matches. Be that as it may, he had not tried to help his widowed sister-in-law in any way and had been largely responsible for the decision to take the baby King away from her at a very tender age. The Beauforts had succeeded in delaying the parting as long as they were able, and it was only because Catherine knew

11

Exeter would treat the child as his son she finally consented to him being taken from her.

It was at this sad juncture of her life that miraculously Owen was appointed to her household. He never knew to whom he owed gratitude for this ascendant step in his fortunes. It was not long before he was able to ease some of the petty miseries she suffered. He would enquire from her ladies her taste in food and wine and would ensure that she had them included in her diet. If he heard a minstrel singing in another part of the castle in which they were staying he would ask the youth to go to Catherine's chambers to repeat his song.

He dared not linger with her when she sent for him, but made himself pleasant with her and spoke lightheartedly to the ladies who attended her. He did not know if she noticed him particularly, but he saw, before long, she had regained a little of her former gaiety and youth.

He had been in her service for about a year when Beaufort summoned him and told he had been made Master of the Wardrobe to the Lady Catherine and that he would now be responsible for the management of her accounts and her personal wellbeing. Owen could not believe his ears, but could only thank God for his good fortune.

It was Christmas soon after this and the Court came to Windsor bringing the little King with them. Catherine's happiness was increased when she found her son had not forgotten her and had asked her at once to tell him some of the stories she had told him long ago. The little boy was rather quiet and apt to sit for long periods lost in his own day-dreams, but he seemed healthy enough and spoke with pleasure of his uncle Exeter.

One evening before Twelfth Night snow began to fall and cover the castle in an enveloping veil of white. There was no wind and the flakes fluttered down in an uncanny stillness. In the Hall the servants brought dried logs to push under the smouldering Yule log and hung fresh cressets in the iron brackets on the wall.

When the supper was over, the boards were cleared away and musicians played for dancing. Owen found himself pulled into a circle of merrymakers by Joanna Coucy, one of Catherine's ladies. He enjoyed dancing, his athletic grace suiting the swaying movement and he soon forgot Catherine was sitting at the side of the room on a heap of cushions surrounded by some of her other waiting women. This was not to last, however, for the girl in front of him tripped as she passed the

Queen's place and Owen, going to her assistance, fell almost into Catherine's lap. For a moment he lay in shocked silence, then leapt to his feet, stammering incoherent apologies for his carelessness, but he had stayed long enough to see the widening of her eyes and hear her quick intake of breath.

Bowing he went out of the Hall as quickly as manners allowed. Once in his chamber, he fought to control the wave of longing her nearness had aroused.

Waking from a troubled sleep, his man came in to tell him it was already morning and that the Dowager awaited him. He went quickly, his heart beating in anticipation of the rebuke she would undoubtedly administer.

Catherine was sitting in her customary chair by the fire and she looked up as her page admitted him. Across the room their eyes met and she smiled in a way he had never seen before. Suddenly he knew she was not angry with him, and going to her side he knelt to her and took her hand to his lips.

So began the happiest years of their lives. Exercising the greatest caution and discretion, they were secretly married a little later when Catherine had been sent to Hatfield to take up residence there. Only the ladies of her bedchamber and some of the most trusted servants knew of their marriage and they were sworn to secrecy. If others suspected the liaison went further than a mutual attraction Gloucester had enough enemies to make them avert their eyes. By the nature of the risk they ran they were safeguarded for no one would have thought they dared flout the law of the land to such an extent.

Owen, loving her so well, made her safety his first concern and tried not to show, by thoughtless word or gesture when officials of the Council were present, the depth of their happiness.

When Edmund was born, and later Jasper, they suffered many anxious days; but when their secret remained hidden they could only count their blessings that Gloucester was so involved with his mounting quarrel with Beaufort that he had no time to spare for Catherine and how she passed the days of her virtual imprisonment in the Palace of the Bishop of Ely.

They lived from day to day, thanking God for the joy He heaped upon them; Catherine knowing the contentment of family life which before had been denied to her, Owen revelling in the delights of their mutual affection.

He was, however, never lulled for a moment into any sense of false security and had friends at Court who passed on to him as much as they dared of the movements of Gloucester and his Council. Now that the birth of their fifth child was imminent he was especially concerned on her behalf. She had been strangely distrait and quiet during the past weeks and had hardly allowed Owen from her sight. When he pressed her to tell him what ailed her she could only reply she had had bad dreams.

Now, lying in their bedchamber surrounded with the peace of the Hertfordshire countryside, he recalled suddenly the astrologer who had told their fortunes long ago one Christmas when the court was at Windsor. What had been his name? Paniloni — Panini. Yes, that was it. What had he told them?

Owen cast about in his mind trying to recall the mutterings of the dark little Italian as he had bent over his cauldron and told them of the future. It had been he who rightly foretold the deaths of Clarence and, later, his brother Henry V. What had he told them? Wasn't it that he would accomplish his heart's desire and that she would never have a moment of unease?

Comforted, he bent over her and gently lifting some damp tendrils of hair from her forehead kissed her and settled back into the pillows to sleep.

16

2

On the following morning Catherine stayed in bed and, propped on pillows, watched him dress.

Warm sunlight filled the chamber and she experienced a peaceful sense of well-being as her eyes dwelt on the familiar shape of his head and the supple grace of his back. Turning, he smiled as he saw her watching him and, coming swiftly to her side, took her in his arms. She nestled against him, relaxed and trusting.

Later, she dressed slowly and went to sit beneath the trees in the sweeping meadow outside the Palace wall. Here the children were brought by their nurses and played happily until a red-faced, perspiring messenger hurried from the house to tell her Owen wished them to come in from the fields as his look-out on the Church Tower had seen dust rising from a party of horsemen approaching by the London road.

Her pulses quickening, Catherine helped the women round up the small boys and retrieve Jacinda from the rug where she had been kicking contentedly, and returned to the Palace.

A little breathless, she seated herself in the dim parlour and listened with strained ears until the childish voices were lost in the distance as the children were hurried away to their nurseries.

Joanna Coucy brought her some embroidery but, although she spread the wools on her knee and threaded a needle at random, she found it impossible to concentrate. She was more than usually apprehensive of any contact with Westminster and ascribed her anxiety to her condition which she had always found heightened her fears for her family.

Catherine picked up the needlework and forced herself to make a few stitches but the poor light did not help her and after a few moments she laid it down. Agnes Guillemote, who had been damsel of the bedchamber since she had first come from France, saw her distress and taking a small silver chalice filled it with wine and brought it to her mistress. The girl knelt at Catherine's feet and watched as she sipped slowly.

'Some more, Madame?'

'No thank you, Agnes; should our unlooked for visitors be from Court it would not do for me to be tipsy. Of late but a small quantity of wine is sufficient to make my head swim.'

Her ladies exchanged glances, for none of them were happy about her condition. They clustered about her all speaking at once as they hastened to comfort her.

It was thus her chamberlain found them as he came to announce Lancaster Herald who has arrived with greetings from the King to his mother.

Catherine almost fainted with relief as the full meaning of what she heard came to her.

'Have him brought to me at once,' she said, pulling a gauze scarf more tightly over the fullness of her bosom.

Lancaster Herald crossed swiftly to her and dropped on his knee.

Catherine proffered her hand and motioned him to take the stool Joanna brought for him. He smiled his thanks and sat down facing the window behind Catherine's head. Like this, she was able to catch and note any expression, however fleeting, on the face of her visitor. She saw her women make their curtesies and steal away to the nurseries where they could be of more service in keeping the children occupied in case spies from the Council were nosing out any possible scandal to relate to Gloucester.

'Well, my Lord,' Catherine said more brightly than she felt, 'what news do you bring me of my son?'

'He is well, my Lady, and my Lord Exeter sends word with me to say His Grace applies himself with diligence to his lessons and has already signed his first document of State.'

'Indeed!' Catherine exclaimed. 'Then he is growing faster than I imagined. Would that I might see him, even if it were for a short time only. Is there any mention of a visit at St. Michael's mass or Christmastide?'

'I did not hear of any, my Lady, but His Grace asked me to give you this as a token of his affection and wish that you should know you are always in his thoughts.'

Lancaster Herald opened the pouch hanging from a belt at his waist and brought out a small leather purse.

Catherine took it from him with trembling hands and fumbled to open the strings as her eyes filled with tears. She was glad when Lancaster Herald rose and went to look out of the window.

She pulled from the bag a ring set with a great glowing ruby. Slipping it on to her hand she stood, holding her head on one side to admire it.

'See, my Lord, is it not beautiful?'

'Yes, indeed, and becomes you well,' Lancaster Herald told her in a kindly tone. 'His Grace asked me to give it to you and say he inherited it from his uncle Bedford whom he was certain would be delighted for you to wear it.'

'Poor John,' Catherine said softly as she remembered with difficulty the face of her dead brother-in-law. 'Thank my son for his kindness and tell him his gift has given me great happiness.'

'Thank you, my Lady. What else shall I tell him of you?' For some reason Lancaster Herald found himself unaccountably concerned for the woman before him. 'Shall I tell him you are well and your needs are taken care of?'

'Tell him all is very well with me and I am happy and contented. My only prayer is that I shall be allowed to remain here in peace and tranquillity.'

'With great pleasure, my Lady.'

Catherine offered him the hospitality of the Palace for the night but he declined saying they had further business in Hertford. Hiding her relief, Catherine sent for wine and when her ladies returned drank it while the talk became general.

Later, when the messengers had ridden off through the narrow lanes for Hertford and the children had been brought by their nurses to say evening prayers in the chapel with Owen and Catherine, these two sat in the parlour as the day's light faded in a magnificent apricot sky.

Despite the warmth which had crept into the room as the sun touched it, Catherine had shivered and Owen had sent pages for tinder to light the fire. The sweet-smelling apple wood crackled and leapt into life and Catherine smiled her gratitude. She had shown him the ruby ring and he had been glad for her pleasure in the token of her first born's continuing respect and affection. Owen knew she grieved secretly for the child of her first marriage, suffering for him in that she had never been allowed to shower him with the motherly love of which she had later been proved so abundantly endowed.

He was glad, also, she had been distracted sufficiently for his own anxiety to have escaped her notice. This was rare indeed, for they were so mentally and physically attuned to feel, sometimes when apart even, a change of mood in the other.

His concern now stemmed from one of Lancaster Herald's staff who had served with Owen at Agincourt and had made it his business to tell Catherine's husband of Gloucester's return from Flanders, where he had been absent in an endeavour to invade the country.

'So that is why a more peaceful vein had been apparent in communications from the

Council during the last few weeks!' Owen had said as he heard the news.

'Yes,' his friend had told him. 'During his absence Beaufort has been drawing Suffolk further and further into his influence and convincing the young Henry of his worth compared with that of Gloucester.'

'Gloucester would not be pleased with that,' Owen cried.

'No, indeed. It is common knowledge he was incensed when he returned and found what was toward. Since then, nothing has escaped his wrath and he has looked for any source to discomfort Beaufort and Suffolk. I hesitate to speak of this, although I should be no friend if I did not, but it is believed at Westminster he had become aware of your alliance with the Queen Dowager.'

The man paused, embarrassed by the magnitude of what he had said.

'God alone knows how it has escaped his notice before this. He has always had his suspicions, for the Act forbidding dowager Queens to remarry was an expression of his spite,' Owen said evenly. For a moment his mind boggled at the thought of a breaking up of the idyllic happiness of the Hatfield menage.

'Perhaps he has been so caught up in his own advancement and sordid affairs that he could not imagine others pursuing their own path to happiness,' his friend was continuing. 'He is a strange mixture, this Gloucester, for he has a very real interest in the advancement of knowledge that sits oddly with his power-seeking. Who knows, if he had not been so possessed with wresting power from his uncle Beaufort's capable hands he might have become the greatest patron of learning England has ever known.'

'More's the pity he did not,' Owen said grimly. 'What think you I should do now? In his present mood he is capable of anything and I hesitate to contemplate the lines his vengeance would take if he found his suspicions correct.'

'There seems no reason why he should discover your secret now than at any time before, but extra care would not go amiss.'

Owen fell silent.

'Thank you,' he said at last, 'for your timely warning. I shall be permanently on my guard.'

In the following weeks he gave as much time as he could possibly spare to his wife and children.

The September days were settled and filled with sunshine. Owen organised easy expeditions into the outskirts of the forest surrounding the Palace. Servants carried

Catherine on a litter, while the boys led ponies bearing panniers of food.

When they had eaten, Edmund and Jasper would lie back in the bracken and watch lazily as the sun sparkled through the overhanging boughs. Now and again they would run off after a butterfly fluttering among the grasses but would return swiftly and throw themselves down close to their parents.

They were days of perfect happiness.

Towards the end of the month, messengers from the manor at Hadham, where Edmund had been born, arrived with letters from the bailiff asking for Owen to settle some dispute which had arisen.

Very reluctantly Owen agreed to accompany the men to Hadham. Before he left, he gave the strictest instructions to the Steward of the household to keep a double guard on duty night and day. To reassure himself no harm would befall his family during his absence, he took only a small escort and spoke to each of the soldiers who made up the company of the Queen Dowager's retainers.

Jasper and Edmund were in their mother's bedchamber when Owen came to bid her farewell. They watched, solemn-eyed, as she clung to him and moved with one accord to her side as Owen went to the door.

'Take care of your mother while I am gone and see you give her no case for concern with your behaviour. You do understand you are not to go beyond the wall while I am at Hadham, don't you?'

'Yes, Father,' Jasper answered quickly. 'We shall protect our Mother — with our lives, if need be!'

'I pray that will not be necessary.' Owen cried, cursing the fate that made it necessary to inflict the young with the need for caution against a calamity they could not encompass.

He left hurriedly and seeking out the men from Hadham, told them he was ready to depart.

He rode throughout the day, unable to appreciate the beauty of the ripening year. At any other time he would have enjoyed the swift movement of the horse beneath him but now his mind refused to be diverted and he could think only of Catherine's face and her eyes, enormous with unshed tears.

At Hadham he found the Bailiff confined to bed with a sickle cut on his leg. Although his wife was washing the wound with wine and water, it was slow in healing and during his absence the hands were obtaining beer in excess of their daily ration and spending most of the vital harvest time in a state of befuddled intoxication.

Owen saw he would have to spend a few days at least at the manor while the Bailiff recovered.

With thoroughness and much personal courage he set about restoring law and order. He was driven on by a steely determination to go back to Hatfield at the earliest opportunity. Each evening, when the farm men and women were returned to their cottes and quarters, he wrote a brief letter to Catherine and sent a man to the Palace with it on the following morning.

After almost a week the Bailiff was sufficiently recovered to hobble with the aid of a stick and, professing real gratitude for what Owen had accomplished on his behalf, stood at the house door and waved them on their way to Hatfield.

Owen turned in the saddle as they rode off and noticed for the first time the purple clusters of the fruit of the elderberry trees nestling against the house. With a shiver Owen recalled that the superstitious planted them thus to protect the inmates from the evil eye.

Digging his heel with unusual ferocity into his horse's flank he made all haste for home. God forbid any harm had befallen his loved ones while he had been gone from them!

He was beset with nameless anxiety during

all of the day. Only his innate care for those in his command made him stop for a snatched midday rest. He walked off, unable to eat, while the men ate slices of dark bread and hunks of cheese.

The air had become very still and seemed to press on him with a great weight. He noticed with surprise the sun was hidden by a huge bank of copper-rimmed clouds. The fair weather had been with them so long it was apparently never-ending. By the time he had mounted to the saddle again, his shirt clung to him and his limbs felt heavy and disorientated.

As they came into the small hamlet of Essendon, thunder rumbled from the distance and grew louder as they approached Hatfield. Breasting the rise to the house a great clap broke almost above their heads and large drops of warm rain spattered their heads and shoulders. By the time they had gained the gateway they were soaked to the skin.

Owen noted with relief the guard was wellknown to him and only opened the heavy doors when he was certain of the identity of the bedraggled troop.

Owen flung himself to the ground.

'All is well at the house?' he asked quickly.

'All is as you left it, Sir Owen.'

'Thank God!' Owen breathed and throwing the reins to his groom went into the house.

Catherine rose uncertainly to her feet as he rushed into her parlour.

'Owen! Owen!' she said with joy mingled with disbelief. 'When no messenger came from Hadham this morning I prayed it meant you were returning — '

'You had no letter from me this day?' Owen asked, holding her away from him and looking down into her face.

'No,' she replied. 'Should I have done?'

'I sent messengers at first light with word to say we were returning.'

He saw a slight frown between her brows and went on quickly. 'Perhaps one horse went lame and they were kept on the way. But do not let us think of it for the moment, for we are together and you are well. That is all that matters. The men will be here before long and we shall find out what has kept them.'

With Catherine he went to the nurseries where their children were being put to bed. He stayed with them, telling them of his stay at Hadham and listening to their small adventures of the past week.

Thanking providence they were reunited, he kissed them goodnight and promised to take them to the woods on their ponies if the rain had stopped on the following day.

Catherine and Owen enjoyed a solitary and prolonged supper. Eating little and stopping often to talk and look at one another. Once or twice Catherine spoke of the messengers who had still not arrived, but Owen spoke of other matters and took her early to bed.

However, when she slept peacefully beside him, he found his own mind refused to give him rest on the subject, and although he told himself that at worst the men had been set upon by footpads, a nagging anxiety would not leave him. When he slept it was fitfully and with tormented dreams.

At midday on the following day he was considerably relieved when the couriers arrived at the Palace, footsore and bearing the unmistakable signs of having been in a fight. They readily poured out to Owen the story of the band of ruffians who had lain in wait for them in a hedged hollow and who, knocking them from their horses, set about them with heavy sticks. When they were senseless, the thieves had made off with the mounts and departed.

Obviously feeling very guilty at this confession of their defeat at the hands of undisciplined louts, they apologised to Owen with much shuffling of feet and downcast eyes.

Owen dismissed their defensive excuses

and sent them to the apothecary at the Bishop's Palace for salves and bandages for their wounds.

He hurried to Catherine to put her mind at rest and, when he saw the tenseness leave her face, wondered why it was he was still possessed of a certain unease.

It was not until nightfall he remembered he had not asked the men to hand over to him the letter he had given them to deliver to Catherine.

He sought them out as soon as the household was astir on the following day. When he asked for the roll of parchment he knew at once what had caused the sheepish looks he had been given on the previous day. The letter had been taken with the horses and the small amount of money they had had with them.

All day he comforted himself with the knowledge that letters meant nothing to footpads who could neither read or write and who would quickly dispose of any incriminating evidence. But the small coil of unaccountable fear refused to leave the deep recesses of his brain and he tortured himself with the stupidity of committing his feelings for Catherine to paper as he had done.

A week went by and he began to breathe again. Once more he picked up the threads of the ordinary day to day business of the Hatfield household, seeing to the replenishment of food and firing for the winter ahead of them, and arranging as well for Jasper and Edmund to receive tuition from the monks in the other part of the Palace.

Catherine seemed to recover her spirits and he was persuaded into believing all was as it had been.

One morning, early in October, taking his usual groom with him he rode out as far as Bell Bar. Here they startled a small deer and gave chase, more for the pleasure of watching its graceful movement than with any thought of capturing it. Exhilarated by the crispness of the morning, Owen exulted in the exercise, crashing through drying ferns, oblivious to low branches whipping across his face.

So lost was he in the moment, both he and the groom were unprepared for the shock of being suddenly thrown from their horses by men who had concealed themselves along the length of overhanging boughs and who fell upon them as they rode beneath.

Owen fought with all the power of his strong frame as his assailant was supported by other men who came quickly from their hiding places in the surrounding thicket. Strive as he might, he knew within a short space of time it was hopeless and, although he kicked with fury at those who sought to pinion his legs, he had no chance against the six ruffians set against him. He mercifully lost consciousness as a sack was pulled over his head and tied about his waist.

Bundling Owen and his groom unceremoniously across the saddles of their own mounts, Gloucester's men led them to the highway and turned towards London.

At the Palace, Catherine was just beginning to feel slightly anxious that Owen had not returned when the household was shocked by the continued ringing of the bell at the Great doorway.

'See who it is,' Catherine called to Joanna Coucy.

She waited impatiently for the woman to return, but was startled when a man burst into her chamber, while others clustered about the door.

'Madame, prepare yourself to leave immediately!'

'Leave?' Catherine cried. 'What do you mean? By whose authority do you come bursting into my apartments?'

'By the authority of the Duke of Gloucester, my Lady, who gives orders you are to be conveyed at once from here for your own safety.'

'I am safe enough here,' Catherine retorted

bravely. 'Where is Sir Owen?' she asked desperately.

'If you mean he who is called your husband, Madame, he is now proceeding towards London, as you will be very shortly.'

'We are to be reunited then?' Catherine said swiftly.

'I know nothing of that or anything else. My orders from his Grace were to bring you to Bermondsey Abbey — '

'What of my children? What has my son, the King, to say to this outrage of my privacy?'

'I am merely the Captain of the Duke's guard, my Lady, and am not able to speak for those who sent me. My orders are to escort you and your children to the Abbey in safety. Shall I call your women to come and help you?'

'Please,' Catherine said faintly. Her head throbbed with fear, and every fibre of her being called out for the comfort and wisdom of Owen.

Jasper and Edmund were breaking their fasts in the parlour when their nurse came and handed them their cloaks.

'We are going on a journey?' Edmund asked slowly.

'Why?' Jasper demanded fiercely, as the woman nodded without speaking. 'There are tears in your eyes,' he said wonderingly. 'Are you not coming with us? Is our Mother? Where is Father?'

'Sir Owen has not returned from his morning ride, but do not fret, from what I can hear he is also being taken to London.'

'To London?' Edmund echoed. 'Who has called us there?'

'My lord Gloucester, so I believe,' the nurse replied.

Jasper and Edmund exchanged glances and involuntarily moved closer together, elbow touching elbow. Suddenly the room was very cold and still.

3

The New Year was ushered in, and the monks came out from the Church of the Abbey of Bermondsey and pulled their cowls tightly about their heads, almost afraid to breathe the biting cold air of the January night. They hurried across the cloister and made for the dormitory, where they could hope for a few hours sleep before they were roused again for matins.

As they passed the lodging where the Queen mother was housed they saw subdued lighting and they crossed themselves and murmured a prayer. All knew the Lady Catherine had been delivered of a stillborn infant and was grievously ill.

In her chambers, Catherine's ladies sat huddled over a meagre fire. Now and then one of them moved from its scant warmth and took up her position next to the bed of their mistress. A bowl of water stood on a stool and from time to time the waiting woman dipped a cloth and applied it to Catherine's forehead.

She lay very still, her face, once so fair, ravaged with the pain and suffering she had borne. Occasionally she murmured, and the watching woman leant to catch the breathless whisper. When they could make out what she tried to say, it was always the same thing.

'Owen. Owen. My babies!'

Joanna Coucy, when she took her turn beside the inanimate form, thought for the hundreth time how they had come to Bermondsey with the real hope of Owen being with them before long, only to have their faith in the future dashed when news had at last filtered through to them that Owen had been cast into New Gate gaol.

During all the months since they had been so cruelly parted, no word had been allowed between the two of them. Catherine was dying from a broken heart as surely as her life blood was seeping away from her.

Gloucester's merciless revenge in persecuting her in this manner seemed unforgivable in the light of his own degrading misdemeanours, and his inhumanity had reached its peak when he had summarily sent to the Abbey and removed Edmund, Jasper and the little Owen to the nunnery at Barking.

Joanna could still hear Catherine sobbing as she had cried all the night when her sons had gone. Surely no happiness had ever been paid for with such suffering.

Now, only Jacinda remained at Bermondsey; and, when she had been brought to visit her mother and had stood wide-eyed at her bed, Catherine had only been able to smile wanly and touch the small hand proffered for her comfort.

With the morning, Catherine seemed somewhat easier and some of the waiting ladies stole softly from the room to rest. Joanna was sitting at her side when the Prior sent to enquire if a messenger from his Grace the King might have access to the King's mother.

Joanna looked quickly to where Agnes Guillemote knelt to stir a potion at the fire.

'Let him come,' Agnes said. 'She will not know who it is and she is beyond being hurt further.'

Joanna nodded to the messenger and turning to Catherine, smoothed the pillow and pulled the covers higher over her shoulders. Catherine stirred and the monk returned to usher in a priest of Henry's household. She opened her eyes and looked with difficulty at the stranger.

Joanna put her hand over Catherine's.

'It is someone come from the King,' she said soothingly.

The priest, hiding his distress at the condition of the woman he had come to visit, knelt briefly at the bedside.

'I have brought this New Year's gift from his Grace,' he said softly.

Catherine closed her eyes and Joanna took the tablet from the man and placed it between her palms.

'My Lady,' she said quietly. 'See it is a most beautiful crucifix made of gold and set with sapphires and pearls.'

For an instant the eyes flickered and the mouth made an effort to smile.

'Thank him for me. God bless him — '

With a helpless shrug, the priest moved away from the bed. Joanna followed him to the door as Agnes came to the Queen's side.

'His Grace will be deeply shocked to hear of his Mother's illness. He has no idea that she is near death. How came she to this sorry state?'

Briefly Joanna told him of the course of events leading up to the Queen's decline.

'So it was true the Lady Catherine took Sir Owen as husband? She has led the life of a recluse for so long that it has been difficult to make difference between truth and falsehood. Are there other children of the marriage?'

'Yes,' Joanna replied, quickly assessing the wisdom of speaking openly to this man of the Church. 'As well as the child born dead there is another little girl and three boys who were sent to Barking Abbey to the Abbess there.'

The priest looked at her incredulously.

'The King does not know of their existence,' he said. 'It requires much thought if it would be wise to tell him or not.'

'May I beseech you to do nothing to hurt my Lady further. The Duke of Gloucester is merciless and it is said he has the King much in his power.'

'Of late the King has shown he has a will of his own. But rest tranquil, I shall do nothing impetuous.'

Joanna thanked him and returned to Catherine's side.

The short day drifted into night and from the Church came faint chanting as the monks made their evensong.

Catherine had roused sufficiently during the afternoon to take a few spoonfuls of milk with a little beaten egg and now lay propped high on the pillows, breathing with difficulty.

Her ladies had returned and were once more grouped about the fire, burning brighter than before with the extra wood Agnes has begged from the lay brother who saw to their daily needs. The service in the church had ceased and a peculiar stillness had fallen over the Priory when a knock sounded on the chamber door.

'Enter,' Joanna said quietly.

The door did not open and another, more gentle knock tapped the heavy oak. Joanna arose and went to see who was outside. The others heard her gasp as she raised her hand to her mouth and went quickly from the room.

In the corridor Owen stood, thinner and pale with the months he had spent in New Gate. Behind him in the shadowy corridor, Joanna recognised John Boyers, Catherine's Confessor, and a servant from Hatfield whom she thought had been with Owen when they had last met.

'How have you come here?' she asked swiftly, looking beyond them with anxiety, in case Gloucester's men should be on their heels.

'John Boyers and this man of mine helped me to escape from New Gate. But that is of no account. It is of my Lady I want to know. I did not rush straight into the room for the Prior told me, when I asked permission to see her, that she is ill. Oh, God, I have gone nearly mad with the frustration of being cooped up in that stinking hell of a prison without news of her and our children! Will it cause her harm to see me now?'

'Sir Owen,' Joanna said summoning courage into her tired body, 'your lady is dying — '

'Oh, no, that cannot be!'

John Boyers moved to his side.

'May we go in?' he said quietly to Joanna.

'Please,' she answered, and led the way into the chamber.

For a moment Owen could not see for the tears filling his eyes but he brushed them away with an impatient hand and walked to the bed where he threw himself on his knees.

'Catherine!' he said in a groan. 'Catherine!'

She opened her eyes at the sound of the well-beloved voice. Tremulous hands sought his and he caught them up and cradled them against his mouth.

The waiting women turned away and several of them cried unashamedly.

'Let us go,' Joanna said. 'She is safer with him than any of us.'

They hurried to the small solar which had been set at their disposal and Agnes went to find food and drink for Catherine's confessor and the servant. She returned with two of the monk's servants, who carried food and wood for the fire.

John Boyers told them as quickly as he was able how he and the servant had disguised themselves as pedlars and gained entrance to New Gate. It had taken several visits to discover where Owen had been imprisoned but, this done, they had bundled some women's clothing in their packs, and Owen, dressed in these, had come out with them on their last call.

'Bent almost double to hide his stature,' Boyers recalled. 'He had been kept in abject misery with no creature comfort and was denied all news of his wife and family.'

'How wicked!' Joanna cried. 'When one remembers the happiness of the household at Hatfield all this seems unbelievable.'

'Tell me of the Lady Catherine,' the priest asked, and shook his head in disbelief when he had listened to all they had to tell him.

'It will be a blow to him to discover his boys are not here.'

Joanna returned to the Queen's room. Owen and Catherine remained much as they had been when she left them and she stole quietly to the fireside.

She must have slept, for she awoke with a start to hear her name.

'Joanna, will you go and summon Sir John, please?' Owen said to her.

She stood quickly and gathering her senses went to the bed. A glance told her Catherine was dying. She hurried to fetch the priest, who was nodding in a chair in the parlour. He awoke as she touched his shoulder and followed her without a word as she led him back to the chamber.

Later they led Owen, dumb with grief and shock, to the cell made ready for him and forced him to drink a mixture of poppy juice prepared for him by the herbalist.

A monk stayed with him until he was overcome and covering him with blankets made the sign of the cross and went out.

Towards evening, Owen awoke and found John Boyers sitting in the corner of the cell. The priest came at once as he heard Owen rouse.

'Stay there until you have eaten,' he said and went to the door and spoke to a passing monk. 'Food will be brought to you.'

Owen shook his head.

'You will have need of it,' John said. 'We must leave here immediately for the Prior has sent word to the King of his mother's death and the danger increases as each hour passes.'

'I shall not desert my family again,' Owen said thickly. 'Is it possible for you to have my children brought to me?'

As gently as he was able, the confessor broke the news to Owen that his sons had long since been removed to the Abbey at Barking.

'Not here?' Owen said incredulously. 'My poor Catherine; no wonder she despaired unto death.'

He raised himself from the narrow bed

44

with difficulty, stretching the once magnificent frame and grimacing at the pain in his limbs.

'My daughter?' he asked.

'The little Jacinda is here — '

'But you doubt the wisdom of seeing the child for only a brief instant?'

'It would seem unkind to revive her memory of you only to have it snatched away again,' John said softly.

'Perhaps you are right,' Owen agreed despondently. 'Perhaps I had no right to such perfect happiness,' he said almost as much to himself as to Boyers, 'but surely what I did, if it were a sin, did not merit such absymal hell?'

'Most of us query Divine purpose at sometime during our lives and one prays a revelation will be forthcoming to enlighten our doubts.'

They were interrupted by a servant who brought large bowls of broth and pieces of black bread. Owen forced himself to eat.

'When I leave, would it be asking too much of you to stay and look after things here?' Owen asked the priest.

John Boyers regarded him gravely.

'If that will help you most I shall remain.'

'Thank you. I shall know then someone with our interest is close to my family. If only

I might have a sight of my sons!'

'Go now and save your own life. Perhaps later, when the King comes of age, he will be able to exert his influence over his uncle and restore you to favour.'

'We shall see,' Owen said. 'I think my best plan is to make for Wales and seek out friends in the Midlands who will aid me should it ever be necessary to come to my children's succour. I have failed them so dismally in the past I must make sure I am ready to help them in the future.' He fell silent.

Turning away from Boyers he rested his head against the stone wall of the cell.

'Will you shrive me and ask for a measure of peace from my torment?' Owen said quietly.

'Of course, my son. But surely you are taking your guilt in this matter too seriously? The blame lies with Gloucester — '

'But Gloucester would not have had proof of my marriage with the Lady Catherine had not that accursed letter fallen into the hands of those footpads who waylaid the messengers from Hadham.'

'I wish I had not told you of the matter, for you cannot now change the course of destiny. If the footpads had not recognised the royal seal and sent the letter to the Council, in fear of their lives, you may rest assured Gloucester would have trumped up some other charge to take you from Hatfield.'

'I must try and believe you,' Owen answered.

He fell on his knees and with bowed head waited for the priest's blessing.

After he received Boyer's benediction he visited the chapel where Catherine's body lay, and gazed on the well-loved face now, miraculously, restored to its former beauty.

Then, with hurried gratitude to Boyers and Catherine's ladies, he rode off into the cheerless January evening.

As he took the road on the south side of the Thames, to avoid meeting up with any possible envoy from the royal household, great waves of misery hammered at his brain and he put spurs to his horse in an effort to quieten his distress.

He slept the night in an alehouse, oblivious to both the drunken noise of the revellers in the room below and the lice crawling in the dirty straw.

His last thoughts as he slept were of the astrologer Panini whose words he suddenly remembered with startling clarity. He had said of Catherine that she would not have a moment's unease at the death of he whom she loved more than life and that he would accomplish his heart's desire, encompassing at the same time the eventual doom of his life.

In the height of his happiness he had thought only of the fulfilment of his desires but now, as the meaning of his joy was removed from him, he recalled only too clearly the underlying tragedy the horoscope had foretold. He cursed himself for not taking more heed of the warning he had been given.

4

'It hardly seems possible we shall be leaving here on the morrow,' Jasper said, as he and Edmund came in from the fields.

They stopped at the stile before the pasture surrounding the Abbey's wall, and Jasper sat on the topmost pale while his brother leant companionably at his side.

Now almost seventeen and eighteen years of age, they had inherited the good physique of their father and the subtle features of Catherine. Edmund was slightly taller than his brother, while Jasper was sturdier and stronger limbed. They were both dark, their faces tanned with the fresh air the Abbess, Katherine de la Pole, insisted they had each day as they did their stint of the menial duties of the Abbey.

'How much has happened since that terrible day!' Edmund said. 'Do you remember how poor Owen cried for days for our Mother?'

'It was only seeing him cry that kept me from doing the same thing,' Jasper said grimly. 'It was he who reminded me I was older than he and able to take care of myself as Father had tried to teach us. It is strange he is different from you and me and has chosen the monk's life already, but then he was always quieter than we were and of all of us had the least of our father's robust strength.'

He fell silent.

'Can you recall our Mother's face?' Edmund asked suddenly.

Jasper thought for a moment.

'Sometimes I can see her as clearly as if we were still together at Hatfield and sometimes it is difficult to recall even the colour of her hair. I know she was very pretty.'

'Do you think we shall have an opportunity of seeing Father?' Edmund asked.

'It might be possible,' Jasper answered. 'Since that loathsome Gloucester died — or was murdered as some people say — his life has been easier; but he does not come often out of Wales, does he?'

'No, but when he learns we are to live at Court he may seek permission to come to us.'

'Surely that will not be necessary,' Jasper cried. 'The King — Henry, that is — has always treated him honourably and with great favour since he discovered he was married to our Mother and he does not need to crave permission to visit us. I must confess it would be wonderful to see him. I think it was the

50

uncertainty of our life when we first came here that was the most difficult to endure. If we had not been such a loving family it would, perhaps, have not been the blow it was to be reft apart as we were. I remember the kindness the nuns heaped upon us was nothing compared with the happiness which seemed to flow round us in those early days.'

'Yes,' Edmund agreed softly. 'Whenever life became more than I could bear I would comfort myself with the memories of those happy days and think there were thousands of people dragging out miserable existences who had never shared in such love as we had known.'

'Holy Bones!' Jasper said, jumping down from the stile. 'We shall all be wanting to be monks next and electing to stay here rather than take up the glittering promise of the giddy court held out to us by our good half-brother.'

He talked rapidly all the way back to their cell pushing away from him the longings provoked by their conversation. It was not difficult, even after all these years, to remember how appalled he had been at the events which had torn their mother from them and eventually caused her death.

It was only during the last few years he and Edmund had begun to piece together the jumbled fragments of Owen's, Catherine and their own lives.

The Abbess had told them, kindly, of Catherine's death, but it had not been until quite recently John Boyers had been able to visit them and they had learnt from him the true significance of Gloucester's hatred for all the Tudors.

It was following this shattering visit that they had been further startled with an emissary from the King.

Lancaster Herald brought with him a letter, written in Henry's own scholarly hand addressing them as 'My brothers'.

They had been prepared for this intimacy since learning of their kinship with the King, but they stared amazed at the contents of the scroll.

Henry told them he had but just learnt of their existence and his conscience was troubled by his lack of knowledge of his mother's other family. With great humility he spoke of his failure to discover how Catherine had fared and how he now intended to redress any suffering or wrong done to them. It would please him if they would continue their studies at the Abbey of Barking and, when the Abbess thought fit, he would be happy to receive them at Court.

This time had apparently arrived, for the

two boys were to leave Barking on the next day and journey to Westminster, where the King was holding Court.

They both felt a slight uncertainty for what the future might bring for they had grown accustomed to the guarded lives they had led at Barking where they had been brought up by the Abbess, and later educated by the priests of the Abbey. Their sister, Jacinda, had joined them shortly after the death of their mother and it had been decided she was to remain at Barking for at least some time to come. She was approaching her fourteenth year and, as she had not shown any particular desire to take the veil, it would be necessary to find a husband for her. This, the Abbess had told her brothers, would be a difficult task, as a girl without a dowry was a doubtful asset in the marriage market. The boys had not needed to be reminded of their penury which became, as the day approached for them to go out in the world, a recurring nightmare.

It was, therefore, a very pleasant surprise to be summoned to the parlour of the Abbess to make their adieus and to find waiting for them a selection of simple but elegant clothing, and a purse for each of them filled with sufficient pennies and rose nobles to constitute a fortune to those who had never before handled money.

'You may consider yourselves very fortunate indeed,' Katherine de la Pole said, a little tartly; her impending loss of their company after more than ten years putting an unaccustomed edge to her tongue. 'It is a well known fact the King dresses with no care for fashion and saves his money to build colleges and schools.'

Edmund coloured slightly, but Jasper looked the Abbess in the face and smiled with so much obvious pleasure that she was unable to keep up her severe expression, and smiled back.

'Well, I am sure you have learnt here how to conduct yourselves in a seemly manner and will not go out into the world and disgrace either the Abbey or your father. Is there anything you might like to ask me before you go?'

'There is so much,' Edmund said, 'we do not know where to begin.'

'That must be so,' Katherine replied. 'And I have not been in the outside world for so long I am not au fait with the currents lying beneath the surface of political life. Since the deaths of the Duke of Gloucester and his old enemy, Cardinal Beaufort, and the noble Warwick, who had had with Beaufort so much influence over your half-brother Henry,

54

it is told me my own brother, William, Duke of Suffolk together with Edmund, Duke of Somerset are his constant advisers.'

'Was it not the Duke of Suffolk who secured the hand of the King of Anjou's daughter for Henry?' Jasper asked.

'Yes, it was,' the Abbess replied, looking down momentarily but quickly meeting again the candid pairs of eyes watching her so closely. 'It was seen at the time, and now also, as a stroke of momentous good fortune, for England was staggering under the continuing losses in France and needed such a marriage to restore a little of the prestige that was fast ebbing away.'

'Has it been a happy choice for Henry?' Edmund asked. 'There is as yet no heir, which must be a source of anxiety for his wife and him.'

Katherine closed her eyes and suppressed the smile that threatened.

'They have not been married so very long,' she said. 'Now,' briskly changing the subject, 'would you care to have a supper brought here and I will see if it possible for your sister to join you?'

They set out on the following morn, cool and misty with the promise of Autumn in the September air, with mingled regrets and eager anticipation of what life held in store for them. They had put on their new garments, vainly trying to appear unconcerned as they paraded before Jacinda, and were secretly delighted when she pronounced them very pleasing. The soft feel of the silks and velvets after the coarse, home-woven wool and linen to which they had been accustomed was sufficient to tell them the life they were about to enter was to be totally different from that at the Abbey.

They talked intermittently as they made their way through the shut-in lanes of the countryside, following the two servants sent to guide them, and hardly noticing the familiar sights of the ploughman and the milkmaid about their daily tasks.

'Do you realise,' Jasper said, 'we shall be in women's company for the first time since we were infants?'

'By the sound of your voice you are looking forward to the experience,' Edmund retorted.

'But of course!' Jasper cried. 'Is it not the same with you?'

'Why, certainly!' Edmund said. 'But are you completely discounting the nuns with whom we have spent the better part of our lives?'

'No, Heaven forbid,' Jasper answered. 'When I said women I naturally meant those who have chosen to remain at Henry's court rather than seek their soul's contentment in the closed cloister.'

'Do you not agree with the life of the monk or the nun, then?' Edmund asked with amusement.

'I agree with it all right,' Jasper said, 'but it is most certainly not for me. I have seen enough of being shut away to last me a lifetime. God be praised I never have to spend any more of my life incarcerated!'

'Amen!' Edmund said.

'As they approached the White Chapel they could see the Conqueror's Tower looming high above the river, and they stopped talking as the crowds thickened around them.

Coming to the mean houses outside Ald Gate they watched, fascinated, the empty carts, some smelling strongly of fish, trundling homewards, their wares already sold.

At the gate they exchanged pleasantries with the crowds milling around them, fending off pedlars and beggars alike. Cheapside held them spellbound, its booths decked with striped awnings and eyecatching displays of exotic fabrics and jewellery. St. Paul's, with its throng of worshippers, they thought beautiful but familiar, while they stared at the rich merchant's houses crowding Lud Gate Hill, vying with each other in elaborate decoration. They craned their necks to see the sky peeping through the built-out storeys.

'You best not look up too much!' one of the servants told them. 'You're more than likely to get an eyeful of slops!'

Jasper and Edmund hastily looked down and spurred their horses towards the Lud Gate.

They reached it with relief that their new finery was not bespattered, and trotted past the Temple, Baynard's Castle and the site of the Savoy Palace.

'What is that?' Jasper asked, pointing to the blackened ruins, half-covered with trees and ivy.

'That's the Palace of old John of Gaunt. It was set on fire during the Peasant's revolt and has not yet been rebuilt.' One of the servants replied.

'Does it belong to the King?' Edmund said.

'Yes,' the man replied. 'It was the town house of the Duke of Lancaster, and when John of Gaunt married his daughter he became possessed of the Palace and willed it to his son, who passed it, in turn, to the King's father and so down to him.'

'He doesn't choose to live in it?'

'No. The place has not happy memories for the house of Lancaster and they prefer the Palace of Westminster when they hold their court in London.'

When they saw the fair walls of the royal dwelling they could understand Henry's preference, for the palace was a graceful and well laid out collection of buildings. Close by, they saw the Abbey Church of St Peter with its sprawling mass of ecclesiastic houses and, beyond, the river. The sun had cleared away the mists and sparkled on the waters, half way to flood. Barges and ferry boats thronged its surface and the boys would have liked to remain on the banks watching the day's commerce.

Reluctantly they followed their guides to the Steward's office, where they were received with courtesy and shown to the chamber they were to share.

'I am afraid it is rather small,' the Steward told them. They hastened to assure him it was most acceptable and when he had gone rushed to the window and saw, to their great delight, it faced onto the broad sweep of the Thames and they could see almost as far down as the overgrown Savoy and upstream the same distance.

'The Steward is obviously not acquainted with the cells of an Abbey if he thinks this room is small,' Jasper said wonderingly, as he walked round fingering the curtains and bed hangings.

'I can hardly believe it is happening to us!'

Edmund said. 'Henry will probably not send for us today but we had better be prepared.'

A servant came to tell them he had been told to wait upon them and show them round the Palace when they had partaken of the midday meal. He led them to places on a side table, where they were able to watch the full panoply of Henry's court. At first, the noise in the Hall was deafening for they were used to living in the priest's house where the refectory was small and intimate.

The food was lavish and well-prepared but they paid it scant attention as they watched the high table where their half-brother sat with his Queen, his Chancellor and other Officers of State. They had tried to catch the names as the Herald had announced them, but it had been difficult to their unaccustomed ears.

Henry was in every way as they had imagined him. Slightly stooping, spare of frame and dressed in a robe resembling a monk's rather than a king's.

'He is rather like you,' Jasper said in an undertone to Edmund. Adding hastily, 'only in the shape of his head and some of his features; he wouldn't stand a chance against you if it came to hand to hand tactics.'

'One would imagine that would be near impossible,' Edmund said, 'I cannot think of him enjoying a scuffle or anything of that nature. He looks as if he spends much time at his books.'

'No wonder he kept us at our studies, then!' Jasper said. 'Let's pray he doesn't insist upon too much schooling while we are here.'

'You may rest content we shall not escape that,' Edmund assured him. 'We may know something of Greek and Latin and mathematics, but we are ignorant of the law and courtly graces.'

'That's true enough,' Jasper said, somewhat gloomily, but brightened as he added, 'we don't know much about tilting or the chase either. What do you think of the Queen?'

'I would rather you answered that question,' Edmund replied, quickly.

Jasper looked at his brother with affection tempered with amusement.

'So you do not trust your own judgement?' he queried laughing.

'Not when it comes to assessing Henry's wife.'

Jasper pondered over this for a moment, leaning back on his bench and subjecting Margaret of Anjou to a long appraisal.

'She is cast in a strong metal,' he said eventually. 'And judging by the number of glances she makes down the table to that rather florid man at the further end she is not satisfied with the bedsport doled out to her by our aesthetic brother!'

'Jasper!' Edmund said, in mock dismay. 'You'll have us returned to Barking without further ado if you are overheard.'

'They don't know who we are discussing,' Jasper said, smiling round the board at which they were sitting. 'And I warrant the most of them could tell us a story if we asked.'

They were presented to Henry later in the day and found him sympathetic and most kindly disposed towards them. He melted their shyness and dispelled their gaucherie by asking them to be seated while at the same time dismissing his attendants.

On closer inspection, the King had fine features but was pale and too thin. He handed wine to his half-brothers but did not touch it himself.

He seemed pathetically anxious to be told about their mother and questioned them in detail about their life at Hatfield. It was obvious he was well acquainted with how they had come to Barking, but did not spare himself as he probed into the story.

He shook his head over his uncle Gloucester, while a faintly bewildered look shadowed his eyes.

'I trusted him so well,' he murmured.

'When uncle Beaufort told me he had the soul of a viper I could never bring myself to believe it, but apparently he knew what he was talking about. It was so difficult to come to one's inheritance while still in the cradle and it is natural for the young to put their faith in those of their own blood. I hope you will find it in your hearts to forgive the Duke and accept the hospitality I offer as a sincere retribution.'

The boys assured him of their gratitude and the absence of rancour at their treatment now Gloucester was dead and their father restored in honour.

'Our mother,' Edmund said bravely, 'was at least happy for a few years before we were taken away from her and her health was not good after the birth of our little sister.'

Henry winced. Of a sudden Jasper and Edmund felt as if they were the older and that the King stood in need of their care as much as they of his.

Rousing himself, Henry stood.

'The Queen is holding a small court this evening and it is her wish I take you there to be presented to those who are with us in Westminster.'

They followed Henry down the steep, winding stairs from his sparsely furnished chamber to the stone flagged corridor below and thence to the walled garden running down to the river's edge.

The sweet scent of gillyflowers and the melodious voice of a luteplayer greeted them. Henry beckoned them to follow the sound.

'Are you not coming with us, your Grace?' Edmund asked, as Henry turned for the doorway.

'No,' he replied, 'I do not care overmuch for singing and dancing and I have my confessor coming to my room before long.'

The young men bowed over his hand, thanking him for his great kindness in bringing them to Westminster. He waved away their gratitude and went inside.

For a long minute they stood, thinking over what had happened in the short interview and then, their eyes becoming used to the soft dusk, made their way towards the gathering.

In the garden, pleached with apricots, a fire was burning brightly in a brazier. Here Margaret of Anjou was seated on a stone seat while clustered around her were men and women of all ages. The luteplayer, in the azure and silver of the house of Lancaster, finished his song as Edmund and Jasper diffidently made their way towards the Queen.

She rose as they approached, tall and proud of carriage. In the firelight her tawny dress reflected the colour of her eyes. She was full breasted, her dress cut daringly low over her bosom and her arms were rounded and strong. Edmund had time to think Jasper would admire her obvious animal attraction before she was calling them by their names and drawing her companions to meet them.

'May I present my lord Suffolk,' she said, catching hold of the hand of the florid man Jasper had noticed at the midday feast, and leading him forward.

Edmund and Jasper bowed.

'And his wife, Alice.' Was there a slight indrawn breath as she said this?

The Countess of Suffolk, pale and elegant, curtsied to them stiffly. Before the boys could think further about it, three young men stood before them.

'Humphrey Stafford, heir of my lord Buckingham. Henry Percy, Northumberland's eldest son. This young man, Henry of Dorset, is the boy of Edmund, Duke of Somerset. He is the King's Lieutenant in France, as you know.' She smiled on them all. 'They are all cousins, but I confess it is beyond me to work it out for you now. You will doubtless unravel the tangle before you have lived with us for any time.'

Other ladies and gentlemen clustered round, anxious to meet the sons of the Queen

65

whose last years had been so shrouded in mystery.

'Lady Roos, Lady Salisbury, Lord Clyfford and Sir Richard Ocle.'

Margaret of Anjou wandered off as Edmund and Jasper were encompassed in a laughing chattering group. Jasper had a brief glimpse of her walking away with Suffolk who was looking down at her radiant, upturned face.

'Poor Henry,' he thought, before he was caught up in the animated conversation around them.

When at last they stumbled, weary and heady with the spiced wine they had drunk, to their chamber they found their new servant awaiting them. He jumped to his feet from the corner where he had been dozing and hurried to fetch them water and towels. They quickly stripped and fell into the beds, cool with lavender-smelling linen sheets; a luxury they had not known since their childhood. Rather contrite they dismissed the man and told him not to awaken them too early.

'Heavens!' Jasper said on a long whistle when the door closed behind him. 'Suffolks, Buckinghams. Salisburys, Somersets, Beauforts. There is no end to the lot of them!'

'My lord Suffolk is not much akin to his sister, is he?' Edmund said.

'Most definitely not. It is a very good thing the Abbess is *not* au fait with the political scene for she would not rest at all if she could see how her brother and the Queen are besotted of one another. What think you of that, Edmund?'

'I can only think how Henry must suffer.'

'Do you think he notices?' Jasper asked musingly. 'He seems to me to have his head rather in the clouds and to have his mind on higher things than we ordinary mortals.'

'Let us hope that is so,' Edmund laughed.

They talked together until they had exhausted most of what they had observed during the day.

'We must find someone who will give us insight to what the lady Abbess called the 'political scene',' Jasper said drowsily. 'That young Dorset looked as if he might be able to help us. We'll try and run him to earth tomorrow.'

Edmund sleepily agreed.

5

Making the most of what they described as a few days grace before resuming the studies which Jasper at least had hoped to avoid, but which Henry sent word to say he was preparing for them, the two boys wandered down to the wild gardens at the river side.

Here they found the young Dorset earnestly applying himself with a home-made rod to the task of catching a salmon.

He looked up, rather annoyed at having his sport interrupted but, seeing who it was, put down his tackle and offered them a sweetmeat from a crumbled heap tied up in a 'kerchief.

Edmund and Jasper threw themselves beside him and they chewed in companionable silence as they watched the traffic on the river. The tide was once more making and the broad barges, sorrel-sailed and laden to the gunwales with straw and timber, went past them to tie up in the Chelsea reaches.

'Will you help us?' Edmund asked diffidently. 'We must confess we find meeting so many new people confusing to say the least.'

'Gladly,' the younger boy replied. 'It must be different indeed from an Abbey. Although it must be an interesting experience to live with a host of nuns.'

'Great Heavens!' Jasper shouted. 'We had not lived among them since we were ten years of age. The Abbess sent us to the priests to be brought up and taught by them. We had to have some kind of a home.' His face clouded momentarily. 'So she always acted as a foster mother to us, especially when our sister Jacinda came to the Abbey as well. Lord,' he said, turning to look at Edmund, 'I do hope it is not mooted around we are convent weaklings. That would be the crowning insult.'

Henry Beaufort hastened to apologise for his ignorance.

'What would you like to know?' he said, smiling disarmingly. 'To begin with, as the Queen told you I am the son of Edmund Beaufort who in turn was a grandson of John of Gaunt — '

'But so is the King!' Edmund cried.

'Well, you perhaps have forgotten, or do not know, John of Gaunt had three wives. Blanche of Lancaster, who brought him the enormous Lancastrian inheritance, Constance of Castile, whom he thought would bring him the throne of that country, and our great grandmother the lady of Sir Thomas Swynford. This last lady he had loved since the death of Blanche, who was the mother of Henry IV — '

'Oh,' said Edmund, 'now I understand. But do go on.'

'He loved the lady Swynford, and she him, but unfortunately he had contracted to marry Constance before he realised this fact and four children were born to them out of wedlock. The eldest was my grandfather.' He was silent for a moment. 'Cardinal Beaufort was his brother and it was because of this family relationship the King's father commanded that the mighty Beaufort should be a guardian of his son, as he lay dying.'

'And you will be Duke of Somerset one day?' Jasper said.

'If I survive,' the boy laughed. 'Although I should not have been had my uncle John Beaufort's heir been a boy instead of Margaret.'

'Margaret?' said Edmund. 'Who is she?'

'She is my cousin. Her father, my uncle, was killed when he fell from his horse. He was Captain-General of France at the time and a pretty influential man with the King. My father inherited from him and took over his responsibilities. Not that they have brought him much fortune. Never have things gone so badly for us in France before. Much to the delight of the Duke of York who was jealous of the Beauforts being given power in France — or anywhere, for that matter.'

'York?' Jasper echoed. 'He is not at court, is he?'

'As little as he can possibly be. He hates Suffolk as much as he hates my father and hated Margaret's father.'

'Was Suffolk a friend of your uncles, then?'

'Yes, he trusted him so much he made him guardian of his baby daughter. I doubt if he would have had the same confidence now if he could see how power had corrupted his friend.'

'How's that?' Jasper asked.

Dorset glanced over his shoulder and lowered his voice.

'There are stories,' he said. 'East Anglia lives in terror of bands who are said to be under his captains, while his wealth exceeds that of the King.'

'This could be all hearsay,' Edmund said uneasily.

'It could be,' Dorset agreed. 'But his influence with the King — and the Queen is real enough.'

'Yes,' Jasper said, 'the Queen seems almost enamoured of him.'

'Almost!' Dorset exploded with precocious

candour. 'She has been enamoured of him ever since he stood proxy for Henry at their betrothal at Beaumont-les-Toures. They spent eight days feasting, with great jousts and tournaments, to mark the occasion. Suffolk had not run to seed then and she was a most attractive girl.'

'Do you not think she is attractive now?' Jasper asked.

'Do you?' Dorset parried.

'Yes,' said Jasper to Edmund's dismay. 'But it has a repellent quality, quite lacking in charm.'

Edmund breathed again. Life at court seemed complicated enough without his young brother becoming a competitor for the hand of the Queen.

'You spoke of rivalry between the Duke of York and the Dukes of Somerset and Suffolk,' Edmund said, glad to steer the conversation away from the Queen's attraction.

'Yes. Henry's advisers have always been divided into two camps. I suppose it was because he was only a baby when he came to the throne and his father's wishes about the Regency were not faithfully carried out. Gloucester — ' Jasper looked quickly at his brother and as quickly away, 'never did agree with Beaufort; and when that controversy was ended with their deaths it was taken up by the Somersets — my father and uncle as I have just told you — with the Duke of Suffolk as their supporter, and York in opposition. It has grown of late since my father received the Lieutenancy of France, which York coveted, and it is said he is stirring up trouble for Suffolk to oust his position as chief adviser to the King.'

'Is the Duke of York royal blood that he should seek such eminence?' Edmund asked.

'He also claims direct descent from Edward III, as do the King, the Beauforts and the Earls of March, and he was kindly looked upon by Henry V. It was not until he threw in his lot with Gloucester's party that a shadow was thrown on his loyalty.'

'You do not suggest he would seek the throne for himself?' Jasper cried.

'Oh, there is nothing as dramatic as that!' Dorset said laughing.

'Poor Henry,' Jasper said. 'It all sounds to me as if a throne can be a hazardous place. Thank you for all your help. I am going to find a mug of ale. Will you come with us?'

Gathering his rods Dorset returned with them to the Palace.

In the months to Christmas the Tudor boys had ample opportunity to observe the truth of what they had been told. Henry moved his court about the country when plague threatened the capital in the summer warmth and they accompanied him to Winchester and later, much to their delight, he took them to the Marches of Wales.

At Ledbury, they recognised the true depth of Henry's generosity when he summoned them to sup with him and found their father awaiting them.

Speechless, they stood gazing at the dimly remembered well-loved figure. Still, they saw in the timeless moment, magnificent of stature, although stooped somewhat and grizzled at the temple.

Owen came towards them with arms outstretched and they fell on their knees. Henry motioned to his gentlemen and they went out leaving the Tudors alone.

'I still can't believe it,' Jasper said, when the evening was eventually over and he and Edmund were alone. 'To really see our father again is like finding out, after all, that fairy tales are true.'

'Did you find Hatfield was only as yesterday and the years between faded out?'

'Yes, it seems exactly like that to me. And yet what Father has been through since those days is incredible, isn't it? To think he was twice shut up in New Gate prison and twice escaped. Do you remember John Boyers?'

Edmund nodded slowly.

'I remember a priest who was always with us at Hatfield, but had you asked me his name I doubt if I should have been able to tell you.'

'Was he not our mother's confessor?' Jasper asked.

'I believe he was and that probably accounts for his willingness to help father to escape. He would have been the one to warn father not to trust the Council when they promised him safe conduct to the King after our mother died.'

'It was fortunate he took Sanctuary in Westminster instead; and when he came out at last and defended his cause the King gave him fair hearing and allowed him to return to Wales.'

'But did you not hear him say the safe conduct was violated and he was brought back to Wallingford!' Jasper cried.

'Yes, I did,' Edmund agreed. 'But when Henry came of age and was no longer responsible to anyone he insisted father should be allowed to go in peace.'

'Well, all I can say,' Jasper said, yawning, 'is that Henry may have a reputation for piety and staidness but he is generous without limits.'

Before they took leave of their father to go to Windsor, they were able to tell him Henry was to knight them before Christmas.

They spent the vigil preceding the receiving of the accolade in Henry's private chapel at Windsor. Clad in simple tunics they knelt on the unrelieved stone flagged floor throughout the night. They watched, almost hypnotised as the weary hours progressed, the red and green painted candles burning in their ornate holders on the altar.

Jasper, stealing glances at his elder brother, was overcome by the devout expression on Edmund's face. During the years they had lived together he knew without doubt Edmund had qualities he found lacking in himself. He admired him for his simple acceptance of right and wrong, his lack of conceit and his ability to meet temptation with a calm knowledge of his own competence to withstand it.

Since they had become part of Henry's court they had learnt many things beside the undercurrents of the opposing factions. Both of them, grown more polished as the gangling days of the monastic life faded behind them, had not failed to realise the women found them attractive. It was almost as if their untouched chastity was a challenge to the waiting-women and other ladies they met in their daily lives. Edmund received their advances with an engaging grace so appealing that the would-be bestower of favours hardly realised she had been repulsed.

With Jasper it was otherwise, and he had spent several languorous and passionate hours in well-chosen bowers and hedged gardens which would undoubtedly have resulted in further and deeper indulgence if he had not been conscious of Edmund's unspoken, but nevertheless very real disapproval.

However pleasant the dalliance was, it paled beside the thought of displeasing Edmund. Their relationship was closer because of the circumstances of their childhood and Jasper would not endanger the one continuing link of their lives.

Fighting off sleep through the hours after midnight, they gained fresh strength as Henry came with Bishop Waynefleet and his chaplain, John Langton, in the first chilly light of the December dawn to touch their shoulders and invest them with the honour of chivalry.

At the feast later in the day, he bestowed on them gift of several manors, thus ensuring each of them a modest but certain income. They found themselves unable to express their thanks but were rewarded by Henry's obvious pleasure in their gratitude.

They were glad they were able to give their

brother this measure of happiness, for the affairs of his state were far from smooth running. Each day brought fresh rumours of discontent against Suffolk and his growing influence with Henry.

Only the celebration of Christmas kept the charges being brought into the open in London, but in Norfolk and Suffolk the Duke's supporters were asked to account for their actions against the countryside.

Just before Parliament was due to be recalled a plot was discovered for the murder of the Chancellor and all signs pointed towards the implication of Suffolk.

Henry steadfastly refused to hear ill of the man on whom he relied implicitly and, backed by the Queen, would not give ear to those who wished to blacken Suffolk's name.

The king was forced into action when a minister named Moleyns was murdered by discontented sailors, and it came to light he had accused Suffolk of treason while under duress. Reluctantly, Henry informed Suffolk he must prepare to defend himself in the Commons.

The court seethed with rumours as Suffolk fought to clear his name by recalling to the parliament the long list of his services to the throne and the country. These did not, however, outweigh the overwhelming numbers of charges brought against him from all sides, and Henry, was compelled to accept his guilt but managed to reduce the sentence the lords and Commons wished to pass on the offender to one of life banishment.

On the evening following this shattering blow to the Queen and Henry, the court retired early, glad to escape to their chambers from the stifling atmosphere of gloom.

'Great heavens!' Jasper said, as the two young men stood on the winding stairway to their chamber. 'Just come and look at the mob out there.'

Edmund craned through the aperture to the narrow slit and stared amazed at the large crowd milling in the court below. Raucous shouts and intermittent snatches of songs broke the usually tranquil night while torches were thrown in all directions with total disregard for safety.

'They look ugly,' Jasper said. 'I hope we get a chance of going down and dispersing them!'

'Not much hope of that; there have been trained bands quietly coming into the Palace all day by the river and they will be called upon should the need arise. Let us go to bed.'

Once in their chamber the noise diminished and finding their servant absent they hurried into bed, for the room was chill with the brazier burning low.

'What a day it has been!' Jasper said. 'We shall see some changes now, no doubt. What do you think will become of the Queen without Suffolk at her elbow all day?'

'Perhaps she will be able to devote more of her time to looking to Henry's welfare,' Edmund said. 'Henry Dorset told me the King was overcome with distress and has taken to his bed. Nor was he the only one to be upset by the day's occurrence.'

'How do you mean?' Jasper said.

'Do you remember Dorset telling us Suffolk had a ward?'

'Yes, I do have a hazy recollection about some little girl. Wasn't she his cousin?'

'That's right; the Lady Margaret Beaufort. She had been at court, apparently, for about three months and I happened to be passing through the solar when the news of Suffolk's disgrace was brought to the Queen and her ladies, and in the general confusion that followed the child heard the women discussing Suffolk's plan to make a bid for the throne by marrying his son to herself.'

'Great God!' Jasper cried, sitting up in his excitement but hastily retreating beneath the covers as the cold struck him. 'That's a nice way to hear about your future matrimonial arrangements. What happened?'

'Well, of course, in the outcry which followed the child was forgotten and I came upon her crying as if her heart would break and picked her up and returned her to her Nurse.'

'Did you, indeed.' Jasper whistled. 'Quite the knight parfait. How old is she?'

He turned to watch his brother in the dim light of the pottery lamp at their side, but rolled on to his back again as Edmund said:

'About nine years old, as near as I could judge.'

'That is a little young for you,' Jasper said reluctantly. 'I thought perhaps at last you might have found an interest of the heart.'

'Go to sleep you amorous paramour, it's a pity you don't apply yourself to your studies with as much aptitude as to your thoughts of the fair sex!'

6

There was not much time in the months which followed Suffolk's banishment for dalliance of any kind.

Henry began to lean more and more on his half-brothers and he excused them from studies and drew them into the workings of his household and Council.

The King had seemed to recover from the shock of finding his trusted councillor had played him false although the Queen went through the motions of living as if she was partly paralysed and had lost all sense of feeling but a further blow fell upon them as Suffolk was murdered making his way to France.

Henry did not need this further demonstration of the unrest growing in his country to prove to him he wanted another Cardinal Beaufort to help him govern with a strong hand. His lack was sharply underlined when other murders of responsible citizens took place and a band of rebels called together under the banner of a certain Jack Cade began to march on London.

Jack Cade professed his crusade was to

protect the King from the machinations of his evil lords and their grasping ambitions, and it seemed this was true when Henry hastily amassed a large army and rode out to parley with Cade on Blackheath.

It appeared, as the mob slowly dispersed, as if he had persuaded the rebels to retreat, but once the King had retired to his manor of Greenwich the Kentish men reformed and stormed onwards into London, killing and destroying as they went.

The King's army, dispersing to the various nobles houses from which it had been assembled, hastily met up again and eventually caught Cade in the Weald of Kent. As an example to other miscreants who sought to take the law into their own hands his naked body was dragged through the streets of the City of London and was hung, drawn and quartered in New Gate.

This action probably did deter the common man from flouting the monarch's sovereignty, but in Ireland, when word was brought to the Duke of York of the extraordinary events taking place across the Irish Channel, he thought this was the moment for his return to his native land. He quietly landed in Wales and went to his castle of Ludlow.

Henry, distracted by the revolt, sent to

France for Edmund Beaufort. Even if the Lieutenant of Calais was not of the same mettle as his uncle, the great cardinal, at least he was loyal and versed in the intricate matters of government.

When Beaufort arrived the King relaxed as a more peaceful aspect settled over his court. The Queen, with Suffolk's friend to encourage her, retrieved some of her lost looks and, guided by Beaufort, turned her flagging interest to the college she was founding in Cambridge.

In this she was encouraged by Henry, who, whatever the political situation, was always deeply involved with his own college and the almhouses and school he was building in the water meadows of Eton close to Windsor Castle. He was delighted to see a flicker of returning spirit in his wife.

Jasper and Edmund were sent at fairly regular intervals to the low-lying town on the edge of the fens where the two colleges were gradually taking shape.

In the autumn of this eventful year Jasper set out with Sir Joseph Wenlock, Margaret's chamberlain, armed with a roll of papers from Henry and a similar sheaf from the Queen. Coming to the Cross marking the intersection of the Icknield Way and Ermine Street at Royston, Wenlock told Jasper of the hermit who lived in a bell-shaped cave beneath the site of the cross. Jasper, impatient to reach the end of his journey, agreed somewhat reluctantly to visit the holy man and climbed down the rope ladder to the small chamber hollowed out of the chalk.

Once inside the extraordinary cell, he was glad the chamberlain had suggested the halt, for the room and the chapel below were such as he had never seen before.

The Augustinian monk, frail and aesthetic, who inhabited the cold chamber received them with pleasure and took them to the chapel to say a prayer for their safety in travelling. This completed, he showed them, with pride, the carvings of St. Christopher carrying his Saviour across the water and St. Katherine with the wheel of her martyrdom in her hand. Afterwards he climbed with them into the dank autumnal air and waved to them until the hills hid him from sight.

Jasper spent the rest of his journey a little subdued at the thought of the holy man passing his days and nights in solitary contemplation of the Divine Will and praying — very necessary prayers as Jasper admitted — for the well-being of those who travelled over his cell.

Arriving in the University town, Jasper and Wenlock sought out Andrew Doket in the rectory of St. Botolph's. This was the farseeing priest who had envisaged the idea of the new college, of which he was to be president, and had written to the Queen asking for her patronage.

Margaret had immediately seized upon this opportunity of gratifying her pride by founding an establishment such as Henry's in her own right; and had asked Doket to allow her to share in his foundation. When he had agreed with her suggestion, she had written asking for the further favour of calling the college 'Queens' and Doket had been forced to comply with her wishes although he had envisaged honouring St. Bernard in its title.

Jasper was thinking about the Queen's conceit as he and Wenlock followed the earnest little priest while he showed them, with enormous pride, the buildings growing out of the morass of mud and piles of heaped stone. He thought it must be strangely gratifying to watch a college come to life and realise one day hundreds of young men would come here to sit at the feet of the sages and absorb their belief and theories. The only thing slightly out of context to Jasper was the Queen's own apparent lack of education. Margaret could read and write, but he thought of her as a creature of earthy sensuality rather than a woman interested in acquiring wisdom. He could only conjecture, a little wryly, that her passion for the college stemmed from her desire that posterity should link her name with the founding of a great University.

With these reflections he remembered Edmund's fear he might fall under the spell of the Queen. Knowing full well how his brother suffered for him on this account, he hastened to assure him, whenever opportunity presented itself, that he was in no danger on that score. He had, in fact, experienced a sense of relief when Beaufort had returned to England and had at once stepped part of the way into Suffolk's shoes.

Having visited the chapel of King's College where the walls were several feet high, and spoken with the surveyor and master mason, Jasper and his squire walked past the colleges of Peterhouse, Clare and Gonville Hall to the hostel where the landlord was expecting them and where Edmund would join him in the evening.

They were all glad to come in out of the raw day and warm themselves at the ample fire in the private parlour. The food, mostly of pies and puddings, was excellent and Jasper hoped the students who lodged above were as well treated.

Edmund arrived after dark, travel worn and cold to the bone.

'Are you alone?' he greeted his brother. 'No female companion to help you while away your time?'

'What, here?' Jasper laughed. 'I am quite content to sit and keep warm. Sir Joseph and Dr. Doket have gone to the house of the Chancellor, but I begged leave to await your coming.'

The landlord came in with servants carrying tureens, and pulled up a small table before the fire, setting it with trenchers and horn-handled spoons.

'I seem to have been eating all day,' Jasper said.

'Then you are more fortunate than I,' Edmund answered.

'We had food in Baldock but the road from there was dogged with mists and we have been hours getting here.'

'What news?' Jasper asked, when they were alone.

'Something quite startling,' Edmund said.

Jasper looked at him sharply.

'The Queen is not with child?'

'Nothing as amazing as that,' Edmund chuckled. 'I can't believe she ever will produce an heir,' Jasper said reflectively. 'Brother Henry doesn't really strike me as interested in bedsport. He would make a perfect monk, don't you think?'

'Yes, he is too gentle and withdrawn to make an ideal king. He must inherit those qualities from our mother, for all who knew his father say he was a true leader with the attributes necessary for that office. But you don't seem very interested in my news?'

'Of course I am,' Jasper said lifting the pewter lid from the large bowl in front of him and helping himself generously from its contents. 'This stew is very good. What do you think it is made from?'

'Eels,' Edmund said.

'They certainly know how to cook! Now, tell me your news.'

'You remember Suffolk was ward to the little Lady Margaret Beaufort?' Jasper nodded. 'Well, after you left to come up here, Henry sent for me and asked me if I would act as her guardian now that he is dead.'

'Holy Bones!' Jasper cried. 'Henry must have a pretty high opinion of you to choose you for that position. There must have been hundreds of men — Buckingham — Beaufort himself — only too anxious to have a say in the handling of her vast estates. Is it true she is as wealthy as rumour has it?'

'Quite true.'

'You'll have trouble, then, keeping the

would-be suitors at bay.'

'No,' Edmund said, shaking his head and looking into the fire. 'There won't be any difficulty there for Henry has decided that I shall marry her.'

Jasper looked at him for once speechless.

'I told you the news was surprising and you can understand now what I meant.'

'What does the Lady Margaret think about it?' Jasper asked.

'She seemed quite pleased,' Edmund said musingly, thinking back to the previous day when Henry had summoned them both with Lady Welles, Margaret's mother, to tell them his decision. He could still see the delight on her upturned face as the girl accepted him as her new guardian.

'She is an attractive child,' Edmund went on. 'Her mother is sensible and has brought her up well. I think she even has her own tutor at Bletsoe, where they live.'

'Really,' Jasper said, slowly turning over the significance of this new aspect of their lives. 'And what does she say to being married with the King's half brother?'

'Oh, Henry didn't tell her that,' Edmund said quickly. 'There will be time enough for breaking that to her in the future. Henry also told me he is making me — and you — further grants, so that we shall not appear as fortune hunters.'

'That is just as well, I would hate it to be mooted around we were to be married for money! Our brother had no plans for my future?'

'No, but he stressed to Lady Welles, Margaret's mother, that she could call upon you also for support and advice.'

'Good,' said Jasper. 'Is Lady Welles as charming as her daughter?'

'Very handsome,' Edmund laughed. 'But well and truly married to Sir Leon Welles, so you have no hope there!'

Jasper lifted his shoulders and spread wide his hands.

'Ah, well! Is there talk of when the marriage will take place?'

'Not yet, so our bachelor days are not to be ended for a while at least.'

'It will entail extra work for you,' Jasper said.

'Yes,' Edmund agreed. 'But I won't mind that. Have you left me any of that stew or is it all gone?'

Jasper took his trencher and refilled it.

'You look tired out,' he said later. 'We had best be finding our rooms if we are to make an early start for Norwich.'

During the next three years, which were heavily laden with increasing tension between

91

the Houses of Lancaster and York, the Tudor brothers were constantly at Henry's side, going with him on his extended progresses and supporting him through mounting troubles.

The Queen, still childless, turned more and more to Edmund Beaufort. There was no hint in this liaison of the passion which was rumoured to have existed between Margaret of Anjou and Suffolk, but it was as if she must have some man, other than her husband, to help and encourage her.

The Commons, and indeed the country, had been shocked when a member, Thomas Yonge, had petitioned that, as the Queen had not produced an heir, York should be recognised as the next in line for the succession.

From this moment, the Queen seemed to be possessed of a new determination to keep the Lancastrian star in the ascendant and pushed Somerset into the front so pointedly that eventually York succeeded in having him put in the Tower.

This infuriated Margaret of Anjou and she used every method within her power to have him released. When she succeeded the latent dissension was fanned into dangerous embers only too ready to burst into flame.

Henry went through this period with his

short-sighted eyes seemingly fixed on some object beyond the vision of ordinary mortals. He tried hard to act as mediator and refused to listen to his wife's wild stories of York's misdemeanours. He plunged himself more and more into his plans for his college and school and spent long hours at his devotions in his chapel.

His affection for his half-brothers was as strong as ever and they had spent several weeks visiting their father.

In March of 1453 in a splendid ceremony at Westminster he created Jasper, Earl of Pembroke and Edmund, Earl of Richmond.

'He is unbelievably generous, Jasper,' Edmund said as he came to bid farewell to his brother before Jasper rode off into Wales to take possession of the estates now granted to him.

'It is amazing,' Jasper agreed. 'I didn't think the Queen looked too happy about it all.'

'She did seem somewhat pale this morning and a little distant when I addressed her. Come to think about it, I believe I did hear she was to be granted the assignment of the Pembroke Estates. That could well account for her feeling put out.'

'That is almost certainly the cause of her coldness. She is an acquisitive lady at the best of times. I suppose that is because her father never had a full treasury and she was brought up in comparative penury.'

'How long will you be in Wales?' Edmund asked.

'Not for long,' Jasper told him. 'For Henry has given me instructions to be at hand next month to escort the Queen on a progress to Norwich and East Anglia.'

Jasper could hardly believe as he took the road out of London towards Oxford that at last he was making for Wales where a home of his own awaited him. His Welsh blood, which had invoked the dream fantasies of his childhood, re-awoke at the prospect of dwelling within the magical boundaries of his father's country. He cursed his luck that his stay was curtailed by his obligation to go with Margaret of Anjou on one of her many tours around the countryside, but chided himself for his ungenerous thought and knew these progresses were vital in keeping the loyalty of the common citizen.

Oxford, Gloucester, Hereford and then the Brecon hills. Jasper breathed the thin Spring air as it swept in from the distant Atlantic.

He tired his suite as he rode outrageous distances in a day, putting up at any doubtful inn rather than at the more conventional hospices of a well-ordered journey. There would have been more murmuring than there was among the men who followed if it had not been that he was secretly admired for his intrepid fortitude and his straightforward dealing with men of all ranks. His leadership had also been proved for, before Ledbury, a band of robbers had ambushed them as they rode between two high and narrow banks, and Jasper himself had taken on two of the assailants and scattered them with blows from a well-aimed flat sword. Surprised, the rest of the crew had scrambled for the safety of the hedgerows.

By the time they clattered into Pembroke, wind-browned and lean, Jasper had behind him a devoted following.

He looked at Pembroke Castle for the first time with delight tinged with awe. The great fortress with its high round keep towered over the river surrounding it on three sides and it seemed, at first sight anyway, to be impregnable.

The Steward — his steward — Jasper realised with a slight shock, awaited him and took him first to the apartments set aside for the new owner.

The rooms were well proportioned, most of them with anterooms and garderobes and they led out onto passages linking them with the Hall below. The hangings and curtains were old and faded but possessed a certain elegance Jasper found pleasing. He knew the castle would, from now on, always mean home to him and he relaxed in the surroundings which seemed of a sudden to be almost familiar.

Within the week he knew the layout of the place completely and had looked into the castle's defences and store of arms and foodstuffs. It did not take the Steward or his wife long to realise their new lord was young but thorough and well suited to be in command of so large an establishment.

The Stewards' wife accepted the compliments Jasper paid her on her management of the household and agreed to provide a feast at Easter for the neighbouring nobles and their families. While Jasper studied the accounts and revenues of the Estate she saw to the stocking of her larder for this event.

Most of Lent had been marked with strong south-westerly winds and prolonged rain, but the evening of the gathering was gentle, following the first day of sunshine for almost a month. Maids had been sent to gather primroses and wild daffodils and these were scattered over the new rushes on the flagged floor of the hall while the long boards were set with the silver Jasper had brought with him from London. Candles shone in their sconces and huge fires burnt in the fireplaces.

Coming to inspect the room before his guests came down from their chambers, Jasper admitted to himself he was proud of the pleasant setting and hoped the people, most of them unknown to him, who would join in his hospitality, would enjoy it.

There was no doubt of this as the evening progressed, and well cooked food was passed round the tables. Lacking a hostess, he had dispensed with a high table and had had the boards set in a square. Close to him he had put the Carew and Manorbier families interspersed with members of his suite while, at right angles, he had seated the Steward with the Bishop of St. Davids and the families of Carmarthen and Kidwelly Castles.

Facing him were the families of Llewelyn and Fychan, both of whom, he knew from his father, were distantly related to the Tudors. Among them and looking directly at him as he raised his cup to drink was a girl with raven hair and milky complexion. His heart missed a beat as she smiled; a strange smile, not really touching her mouth but creasing the corners of her enormous, luminous eyes.

During the long meal Jasper found himself looking again and again towards where she sat and each time he found she was watching him. He experienced some difficulty in concentrating on the talk around him but forced himself to pay attention, as much of what was said concerned the King, Margaret of Anjou and the trouble fomenting between the Beaufort party and the house of York. Jasper realised his opinions and views were valued for he had first-hand experience of the difficulties and what he told them now could have much bearing on future events should partisanship become more defined.

When, after midnight, the older members of the party professed they were weary, Jasper had them escorted to the rooms prepared for them and took the others to his own suite. He sent for wine and thrusting the poker into the embers of the fire mulled it for his guests. One of his squires brought out his lute and in the softly lit room the young people sang roundelays and ballads.

Jasper saw the girl with the flowing black hair sitting slightly apart in a deep embrasure at the end of the room. He joined her and she looked up, without surprise, as he seated himself beside her.

'My name is Mevanvy,' she told him. 'And yours is Jasper, Earl of Pembroke, half-brother of the King, second son of Catherine de Valois and Owen Tudor.'

'You are well-informed,' Jasper said with amusement.

'You have suddenly become the most

98

talked about man in the County,' she said. 'And when we were honoured with an invitation to visit you here, I thought it was the least I could do to acquaint myself with the heritage of our host.'

'I am indebted,' Jasper said. 'But you do not tell me who you are.'

He looked up into the great eyes which he now saw were almost black, so dark was the blue of them. She smiled the same closed-in smile he had seen during the feast.

'Mevanvy,' she said again. 'My guardian is the wife of Llewelyn ap Iorweth and since my parents died I have lived in their household.'

Jasper did not know how to express sympathy for her orphanhood for she spoke lightly, almost in jest and went on quickly to cover an otherwise awkward moment.

'Tell me about your life at court.'

'Only if you tell me about yours in this mysterious, remote part of Wales.'

'There is nothing to tell. I am taught the usual accomplishments of a daughter of a great household and have learnt them indifferently well. I can sew and spin, sing a little and will probably make some man a fairly satisfactory wife.'

'Does that prospect please you?' Jasper heard himself asking.

'Not particularly, for whoever is selected

for me will probably be old and fat and require a nurse rather than a mate.'

'You would be a mate then?' Jasper asked suddenly breathless.

'Yes,' she whispered very low. 'And I always knew when I found the man I desired I should not hesitate to tell him so.'

Jasper glanced uneasily round the room but the others were engrossed in their singing. He found himself floundering in an unfamiliar sea. The experience he had gained of affairs d'amour in Henry's court had run, almost without exception, to an unspoken code. Before his excited brain could think further Mevanvy had leant towards him and kissed him on the mouth. His pulses raced and he put out a hand to detain her as she quietly slipped away from him.

Swallowing, he rejoined his other guests as he saw her go out of the room.

Much later he climbed wearily to his own sleeping quarters, noting with a little amazement his manservant had not waited to help him disrobe.

Thinking it was somewhat demanding of him to expect the man to sit up for him until this late hour, he went into the garderobe and threw off his clothes, merely dipping his fingers in the tepid water he poured from the copper ewer in the bowl.

A single candle burned low in its holder, as rubbing his eyes which were heavy with sleep, he drew back the damask curtains of the canopied bed and saw Mevanvy lying upon the pillows.

'Great God!' Jasper croaked. 'How in heaven's name did you get in here?'

'Don't waste time asking questions,' she said. 'Just accept it that I am here and the night is passing fast.'

She threw back the covers to make a place beside her for Jasper and he had a momentary glimpse of ivory flesh before he went in and drew her towards him.

7

Reluctantly, Jasper set out for Westminster and his obligations to the Queen.

On the way, riding a little in front of his escort, he had much time for reflection of the events that had taken place during his brief stay at Pembroke.

Even now his body still retained the sentience of the passion invoked by Mevanvy. The beauty of the surrounding countryside, trembling into the full growth of Spring, was obliterated by the remembered loveliness of her limbs and bosom.

When he had woken after the night they had spent together he found she had slipped away, leaving nothing behind but a knowledge she did not intend they should not meet again.

He had bidden farewell to his guests under the enormous portcullis at the outer gate and as she offered her hand to him to kiss he caught the words.

'Visit me.'

This had presented no difficulties for Jasper had been asked to come to Narberth Castle where the family of Iorweth were at present in residence. Curbing his overwhelming impatience to see Mevanvy again he let two days go by before he announced he was riding to Narbeth for some hunting promised him. He sent his Herald in advance to announce his coming.

He did not see the girl until the men went to the ladies' parlour after they had supped alone. Only a slight widening of her already large eyes as they met his was her greeting to him, but he knew by the care of her dress she had been aware of his arrival in the castle.

The green gown with a matching surcoate was fashioned to exploit her body without being immodest and her hair was newly washed and shone with brushing. Jasper moved away from her once the salutation had been made, for he found her proximity disturbing. He was at once caught up in discussions of the political situation and it was past midnight before he was able to snatch a few hurried words with her.

'Do you hunt tomorrow?' she asked.

'Yes. If you do.'

'I do.'

When his page took him to his chamber he half hoped she would be waiting for him, but he was not surprised when he found she was not. He smiled at her delicacy and the sureness of her fascination. He slept a deep and untroubled sleep and awoke refreshed and eager for the day's happenings.

Llewelyn's household were already assembling as he rode out into the yard and without ado they took the road for Restone Cross and made for Llawhaden.

Bright sunshine glittered on the hunting spears but a gusty south-westerly held promise of rain.

They rode out into the deep valleyed countryside, Jasper and his squires in the van of the party setting a good pace. They gained the main highway running between Haverfordwest and Carmarthen and a groom from Narberth spotted a boar racing for cover in a group of alders. As the sky in the west filled with darkening clouds scudding low across the hills, the hunters put spurs to their beasts and gave chase to the grey beast. They lost him at the same moment as the rain beat down on them in torrents.

'We'll have to make for home,' Llewelyn shouted and turning his horse bent his head to the weather.

By the time they slithered down the wet cobbles to the castle Gateway they were bedraggled and miserable but the mistress of the house sent the servants scurrying to heap on wood and heat water. She told them food would be awaiting them when they had changed their garments.

Jasper was among the first down to the long, stone hall and he stood at a deeply recessed window looking out towards Pembroke as the rain still lashed the countryside. He sensed Mevanvy come to stand at his side. He did not trust himself to look at her for a moment but kept his gaze on the desolate landscape outside.

'There is a small solar leading out of my bedchamber,' she said in the husky voice so peculiarly her own. 'If you would care to come there after we have eaten I will tell you some of the stories handed down to our people since the days of Arthur.'

'Thank you,' Jasper said gravely.

He faced her now and saw she was wearing an amber houppelande, slightly outmoded, with long tight sleeves and buttoned into the neck. He realised she was even more desirable in this gown than in the provocative attire of the previous evening.

As she moved away from him he heard with dismay her open invitation to the other young members of the party to visit her solar after the meal. Jasper lost a little of the ravenous appetite the exhilarating chase had given him but sulkily, when the long meal was finished, sought out her chamber. He found several people already present and with the briefest nod to Mevanvy plunged headlong into an account of the morning's hunt. Stopping for a moment, he glanced in the girl's direction to find her regarding him with the same secret smile she had given him in the Hall at Pembroke. Blushing, he stammered and lost the thread of his narrative, furious she should be reading his thoughts so accurately.

When all her guests had arrived she curled up on a highbacked settle and in a low and compelling voice told them of Merlin and Guinevere, Lancelot and Mordred. The chamber was very still, almost as if the ancient magic held it in thrall. Despite his chagrin, Jasper was caught up with her spell binding, transported in the sweet cadences of the verse in a pursuit of the Holy Grail and perfect Chivalry.

So carried away was he it was some time before he realised she had stopped her storytelling and the others were chattering about him. He moved slowly to the high casement listening to the unabated fury of the rain storm and did not move as he heard the young men and girls begin to drift away. It was almost dark in the firelit room as the door was firmly closed and Mevanvy said his name.

She was standing in the fading light, her demure gown unbuttoned to her waist. With a little cry Jasper came swiftly to her and her arms entwined round his neck. Hungry for her beauty he pushed the houppelande from her shoulders and it fell in glowing folds at her feet. She wore no shift and he gazed at the remembered comeliness of her body before he swept her into his arms. She strained towards him, her mouth on his, her strength as great as his own. At last she drew away from him and stooping pulled the gown over her nakedness.

'Do you desire I shall come to you when the household sleeps?' she asked him.

'You do not need to ask that question. But may I not stay with you now.'

'You have nothing better to do?' she asked half mocking him. When he shook his head she went on: 'Then why should you go. Our time together will be short enough, foreboding tells me, and it would be a pity to curtail it more than we need. Come here and I will tell you other stories than the legends of Arthur.'

It was dark now and Jasper threw on a handful of logs and when they crackled into life sat on the settle and took the girl into his arms.

The evening after supper seemed interminable but Jasper could not retire early and appear ungrateful for the lavish hospitality his new neighbour heaped upon him. His inborn courtesy and good manners forced him to make conversation and appear attentive to his host but he was filled with delight when at last the conversation began to lapse and the guests were lighted to their rooms.

Jasper found his servant huddled in the corner close to the brazier, his short cloak about his ears. He stumbled to his feet and helped his master prepare for the night.

When he was gone Jasper stretched his limbs under the coverlets and lay staring into the darkness. His ears, sharply attuned for any noise, heard the latch of his door lifted and then returned and pushed into place with the wooden bolt.

'Mevanvy.'

Her bare feet made no sound as she came towards him and slipped without speaking into the bed beside him.

The magic she had created in her tales of Arthur paled beside the enchantments she wove for him now. He had not realised such transports of delight existed and he was lost in her sorcery.

She gave herself unsparingly and Jasper realised she had spoken the truth at their first meeting when she had told him she would not hesitate to declare the discovery of the man with whom she desired to mate.

It was of this he was thinking as he set his face towards London and the life which had suddenly become alien to him.

Mevanvy's love-making had encircled him, made him forget all else until only the sight of her and the touch of her flesh was reality.

He dragged himself back to the day's routines with difficulty.

It was not until they were almost at Westminster he realised no word of love had ever been spoken between them. In his heart he knew if she had asked him he would not in truth have been able to answer her.

8

Jasper was quickly jolted out of his dream-state when he had been less than an hour at Westminster.

Edmund, after a brief glance at his brother and a remark about his exceptionally healthy appearance, lost no time in telling him of the growing tension about the court.

'I feel Henry is far too trusting where York is concerned. While you have been absent he has been to Ludlow and stayed as Richard's guest there. This has infuriated Edmund Beaufort, who backed by the Queen, has refused York admittance to the next Parliament.'

'Has he so!' Jasper said wonderingly. 'And what has been the outcome of that?'

'Beaufort, who has spies everywhere, disguised as merchants and troubadours, is discovering London filling with York's men. Also, we do not need spies to bring us the pamphlets he is circulating accusing Beaufort of the worst mishandling of English affairs ever known. I am more certain than ever that bloodshed will be the inevitable outcome of these two men's jealousies.'

'It would seem as if my journey with the Queen to Norfolk is more necessary than before,' Jasper said. 'I was half hoping she would have changed her mind.'

'Talking of Margaret,' Edmund cried, 'I am almost forgetting the most important news of all! The Queen is with child.'

'After all these years of marriage? It seems hardly possible. How long have they been wed? Eight years, isn't it?' Edmund nodded. 'No wonder York is doing his best to placate Henry and at the same time taking no chances with the citizens of London.'

When Jasper met Margaret of Anjou he was struck with the change in her looks for she had regained some of the animal properties that had been hers while Suffolk lived. She glowed with health and had lost a little of the restlessness acquired over the last three years.

His progress with her to Norwich was easier than he had anticipated and she enjoyed the brief stay they made in Cambridge on the return journey so that she might inspect the advance made in the building of Queen's college. Since Jasper had been to the college the site had taken on a tidier and more orderly appearance and the summer weather was more suitable for viewing than the November mists in which he had last made a tour of inspection.

The Queen made herself most agreeable to Andrew Doket and they parted the best of friends, enthusiastic for the completion of their joint enterprise. She returned to Windsor, where the court had taken up residence, in excellent spirits.

These were rudely shattered when she discovered Henry had been unwell most of the time she had been absent. A group of anxious physicians sought an audience of her immediately she arrived and left her in no doubt of their concern for the King.

'His Grace has been subjected to too many disquieting perplexities and his gentle mind is not able to withstand them.'

'What ails him?' the Queen asked bluntly.

'We are not able to say, Madame,' the spokesman told her.

By the middle of August, however, neither they or she were in any doubt about the nature of Henry's illness for the King went completely out of his mind.

He lay, his tall frame limp and lifeless, throughout the day and night while he stared with unseeing eyes into nothingness. Only with great difficulty could he be persuaded to swallow broth or goat's milk to keep him alive.

Jasper and Edmund were dismayed in the change in their half-brother and tried everything they could think of to restore him to health. When they spoke to him it was if he heard nothing.

'All we can do to help is support the Queen to the best of our ability,' Edmund said.

'I confess I find that difficult,' Jasper replied, 'for she seems possessed herself these days.'

'Perhaps it will be easier once the child is born.'

'Let us hope so.'

This did not appear to be the case, for when a son's birth was announced on 15th October and later the Queen took the infant to show him to Henry, the King made no sign of recognition of either his wife or of the baby.

'Buckingham told me it was horrible,' Edmund said to Jasper. 'Time and time again they tried to penetrate Henry's shell but he just lay and stared into space as he does and made no answer to their pleas to look at his heir.'

'Since then, Margaret has been constantly closeted with Edmund Beaufort and it is my opinion she will seek either to become Regent herself or support him in that office.'

In this Jasper was proved correct for when parliament met in the November Margaret made an impassioned speech in which she asked for the rule of the land to be made over to herself with full powers for spending the King's money and filing offices as she desired.

Promising to give the matter proper consideration, the Commons dispersed for the Christmas festival. It was no secret they were divided between the Queen and York, who had been quietly working to further his own cause.

Several times during the next months abortive attempts were made to speak with Henry on the matter and the Lords sent representatives to Windsor to find out for themselves how severe was Henry's illness.

At length, to Jasper's surprise, York was made Protector of the Realm, although with severely restricted powers. Richard of York and his friends were jubilant, while Beaufort's and the Queen's supporters slunk off to the country to lick their wounds.

Jasper had other matters besides the King's health and the Queen's disappointment to concern him for he had received word from Narbeth of Mevanvy's pregnancy.

He had returned to the new quarters assigned to him in Windsor Castle one evening to find a messenger arrived from Wales.

Jasper had received him in private and

listened to what he had to tell. The man had left at once for Pembroke with instructions for Lady Scudamore, the Steward's wife, to prepare chambers for Mevanvy and care for her with every possible kindness. It was typical of the girl she had not bothered him with her plight until the birth was almost imminent and he knew he would not be able to reach his home before the child was born.

Later, without giving him the reason, Jasper told Edmund he was going to Pembroke but would return as soon as possible to share with his brother the burden of Henry's prolonged illness. Edmund said nothing but that he hoped he would have a safe journey; and suddenly Jasper wished he could bring himself to confide in him his liaison with Mevanvy.

Since he had left her he had longed to possess her again with a passion that gnawed at his loins. He had several times sought the company of women who were known to dispense their favours cheaply but had discovered on each occasion he had been unable to progress further than a preliminary skirmish. Mevanvy possessed more then the physical attraction of a beautiful body. She held within herself the mysterious magic of the country of her birth and was to Jasper a personification of the dreams he had had since his childhood. But he knew he did not love her.

Riding to Wales, more than a year after his first visit to Pembroke, he thought much of the reason for this lack. Although he examined his feelings as unemotionally as was possible he could reach no conclusions and would not have admitted to a strange fear of her hold on him had he realised it was true.

He went, as before, at a great pace and came to the towering castle on a still May evening. He reined in his horse and sat gazing at the stronghold Strongbow had built more than three hundred years before. For a moment he dreaded his second coming to his home but, shaking off the apprehension, waved his entourage forward.

As before, the Steward and his wife awaited him under the Gatehouse and he called greetings to the many inhabitants of the place who had come to see his arrival. He knew at once Mevanvy was not of their number.

The Steward led him to his private parlour and Jasper noted the improvements which had been carried out to his instructions. Ornamental plasters and new hangings had been added to the room and it had an air of restrained luxury. He complimented the Steward's wife for her part in the restoration and said there were doubtless many things

116

she would wish to discuss with him on the morrow.

'Now,' he said, slightly aghast at his own blatancy. 'I would know where you have housed the lady Mevanvy.'

'We have given her the South rooms of the Gateway,' she told him, without a change of expression. 'She is well content with them and has proved quite invaluable to me in the preparation of your apartments.'

Jasper experienced a sense of relief that Mevanvy had helped both of them by making friends with this important member of his household. He declined the woman's offer to escort him to the South rooms and after an interval left her to find them alone.

Climbing the stone stairway, he realised the Steward's wife must have thought him without feeling as he had made no enquiry about the child. In truth, he wanted to know about his son or daughter only from Mevanvy.

He went into the antechamber of the suite and asked a girl who came from within, her arms full of clean linen, the whereabouts of her mistress. The girl made as if to return whence she had come but Jasper forestalled her and, thanking her, said he would go unannounced.

He stood for a moment outside the heavy

oak door fighting a mass of emotions but lifted the latch resolutely and went in.

Mevanvy was sitting on a footstool at the fireside with the child at her breast. She looked up, wide eyed, as he came in and then, in a graceful movement, stood and with upturned face waited for him to kiss her. Crushing the child between them he held her to him, mouth to mouth.

At last, with a breathless laugh, she disengaged herself.

'Do you not want to see your daughter?'

'Daughter?' Jasper echoed looking down for the first time at the baby. He looked swiftly back at her mother.

'Who is she more like? You or me?'

'Most people think she favours you with your determined chin and me about the forehead and — '

'Eyes,' Jasper said for her.

Mevanvy went over to the casement and Jasper followed. In the dying light of the day he could see his daughter better and she him for as he bent over her she smiled at him a contented, replete grin. Jasper felt an absurd sense of pride.

'We have done rather well,' he said laughingly. 'What have you called her?'

'Helen,' Mevanvy said. 'I hope you approve.'

'I do. With your eyes, she will be stirring up the men of Wales to fight for her even as her namesake did nearly two thousand years ago.'

'Her namesake?' Mevanvy queried.

'Helen was the wife of Menelaus. They both lived in Greece, where she was the daughter of a king. While her husband was away fighting in one of the innumerable wars of the time, Paris, son of King Priam of Troy, carried her off. This insult to Menelaus resulted in yet another battle to regain possession of Helen.'

While Jasper had been speaking, Mevanvy had gone to the door and called the child's nurse to take her to her cradle. For a moment Jasper thought she had not heard the story he told her, but coming back to the casement she stood in front of him.

'Would you fight for me, Jasper?'

'Yes.'

'But you would not marry me,' she stated in an even voice.

Jasper shifted uncomfortably from foot to foot.

'You do not need to answer. Had you wished to make me your wife you would have sent word by the messenger.'

Jasper started to speak but she interrupted him.

'There is no need for explanations. None

are necessary. I am content to remain your leman. I do not think there is place in our relationship for marriage.'

She turned away from him.

'There are many people who will be wishing to talk with you. Go you and return to me when we may talk in peace.'

'I should rather remain here,' Jasper said. 'May I have supper prepared for us both here?'

'There is nothing I should like better.'

Going close to him, she put both arms round his neck. Almost as tall as he, motherhood had not thickened her waist or coarsened her in any way. As Jasper kissed her he thought she was in no way different from when he had left her and her appeal was increased rather than diminished.

He tore himself away from her with difficulty.

It was some hours before he was able to return, for the Steward and the Captain of Arms had many improvements to show him. He was secretly pleased with the way his orders for strengthening the defences and rebuilding the Oriel had been carried out and expressed his satisfaction.

The Steward would have him come to his room to check over some accounts, but Jasper laughingly protested he was famished. The man was contrite and apologised for forgetting this important item. Jasper left him and promised to be with him early to take up the matters of the Estate.

He went to his own chambers before going to the South rooms and changed from his leather jerkin and breeches into doublet and hose.

Telling his squire and manservant not to wait up for him he went to Mevanvy.

Her room was warm and lit with many candles. A table, set with cold fare, was near the fire and she sat on the same stool she had occupied when he came in earlier in the evening. This time she did not rise to meet him.

'I have sent away the servants,' she told him. 'I shall wait on you.'

He knelt beside her and gathered her in his arms.

'I have lost my hunger for food,' he said huskily and carried her to the bedchamber.

This room was dimly lit with small lamps filled with oil which gave out a sweet scent. The curtains of the bed were closely drawn and Jasper threw them back as he put Mevanvy down on the bright blankets. Unhurriedly, she slipped the velvet chamber robe she was wearing off her shoulders as she waited for Jasper to come in with her.

'Where are you going?' she asked as he returned to her parlour.

'I am bringing some candles, for I want to feast my eyes on you.'

She laughed and lay back among the pillows.

He returned with the sconces, the flickering light adding to the lustre of his eyes.

'You look very comely like that,' she said.

'Mevanvy! God only knows how I have longed to be with you like this.'

'And I with you,' she replied softly.

They ate when the watch had long since called the hour of midnight and a breathless hush hung over the castle. It was as if they were alone in the world. For the past hours it had seemed as if this was indeed so. She had pleasured him with all the arts she possessed and he had lost himself in the beauty of her body.

The robe loosely round her she carved him the most succulent portions of duck and poured wine into a goblet. She sat at his feet and took small pieces of food from time to time and drank from the goblet.

They were both quiet, speaking only a little. He finished eating and wiped his hands on the napkin she gave him.

'More wine, please,' he said laughing.

She refilled the beaker and came close to

him and he ran his hands over her hair, hanging in a dark veil down to her waist.

'Take off the robe,' he said softly. 'Your hair is cover enough and my eyes will never tire of you.'

'Don't speak like that!' she cried with more agitation than he had ever heard in her voice.

'But they can't,' he assured her. 'There is no other woman in the world as you are.'

She smiled and kneeling up caressed his face.

'You are very young, my Jasper,' she said. 'But I would have you no other way.'

After a moment, the wine finished, he lifted her chin and looked into her eyes.

'Are you really quite content to stay here? Do your guardians not think it strange — '

'To have borne a child to the great Earl of Pembroke and not marry him? It has happened before, Jasper.'

A momentary uneasiness filled him as he remembered his half-brother had thought it necessary when he conferred the earldom upon him to state publicly he and Edmund were of legitimate birth.

'You are too generous,' he said.

'It is not generous to give in the sure knowledge of return. In all the dull years I spent at Narbeth after the death of my parents I was only able to carry on because I held with myself a conviction of the existence of a man who would possess the power to give me such happiness it would annul all other miseries. When I sat across from you more than a year ago in the Hall downstairs I knew you were this person.'

'You are a witch, Mevanvy. Did you have second sight bestowed on you by fairy godmothers at your christening?'

'Doubtless,' she said quietly.

She stood up.

'Take me back to bed, Jasper.'

He stayed almost a month at Pembroke, finding all manner of urgent business of the Estate needing his immediate attention and left only when he had a letter from Edmund saying he was setting forth from Windsor to visit their father, and needed Jasper's support to try and win over the loyalty of the powerful Herberts who lived close by Owen's manor.

'Edmund is betrothed, isn't he?' Mevanvy asked as they walked on the battlements on the evening before his departure.

'Yes, he is to marry his little ward, the Lady Margaret Beaufort.'

'She is only a child, then?' Mevanvy said.

'I think she is about nine or ten years of age,' Jasper said vaguely.

'You have not met her?'

'No I think not, I was absent from court most of the time she was there.'

They walked in silence her cloak flowing out behind her in the stiff breeze blowing up the Haven from the sea. Saluting a man at arms who kept watch at a slit in the stonework, they came in the lee of the curved wall and he pulled her towards him kissing her passionately. She responded by holding herself tight against him and he was surprised to find his cheek wet with her tears. He had never seen her cry.

'I wish you were not going,' she said.

'Where is my brave Mevanvy now?' he asked softly. 'I shall soon return to you, for in truth I cannot bear to be apart.'

He loosed himself gently, wiping away her tears with his fingers. He began to walk again, rather quickly.

'When I have gone, the Steward will tell you of the financial arrangements I have made for you and our child. Do not protest you do not want to take money from me. It is necessary you should be independent and under obligation to no one. Where would you turn if you wished a new gown to wear?'

'You are kind, Jasper and I thank you. I expected nothing else from you but the shelter you give me here. That is enough.'

He supped with her as he had done on his first night at Pembroke and he was delighted she had chosen a dress and surcoate of crimson, for he had had made for her a necklace of gold found in the Welsh hills, set with garnets

When the servants had cleared the food and they were alone she sat on her favourite stool which she had placed to catch the dying warmth of the sun near the casement. The rosy glow coloured the ivory of her neck and bosom and he knelt before her, burying his head between her breasts. She cradled him to her, her strong hands in his hair, murmuring his name. He stayed like this until the sun's last rays faded from the sky and the room darkled.

'See what I have for you,' he said, with a lightness he was far from feeling and drew the necklace from the pouch at his waist.

'Oh, Jasper, it is quite beautiful.'

She held the lovely thing while the gold glowed dully in the dimness.

'Put it on for me.'

She bent her head and Jasper fastened the clasp at her nape.

'It will lie there,' he whispered. 'Where I would fain lie always.'

A discreet knock at the door startled them both, and Jasper went to open it. Mevanvy's maid stood with a red-faced babe in her arms.

'I am sorry to disturb you, Ma'am, but although I have tried everything she just will not be quiet.'

'Give her to me,' Mevanvy said. 'She is hungry, poor little mite.'

Jasper took the child from the girl.

'I will feed her and bring her to you to put in her cradle. You need not wait now, except to bring candles,' Mevanvy said.

These brought and placed on the wall, Jasper handed the babe who was fretting and breaking out into wails of despair, to Mevanvy.

As the child was put to suckle he threw himself down and watched the homely sight. Why do I not ask her to marry me? he thought. Was it because he did not want to pin down her wild delights in the staleness of marriage contracts, or did it go deeper than that?

What ever it was he knew she had never looked more desirable than now. Her hair was braided and half hidden under a caul and it displayed to the full the sweep of her neck and chin. He savoured her beauty to keep with him as he rode to Trecastle and promised himself he would not long delay before returning to her. He began to be impatient for the child to finish suckling, for his time with Mevanvy was ebbing.

'I will not think of tomorrow,' he said aloud, not realising he had spoken his thoughts until she looked up at him quickly. She did not answer but gently disengaged the now sleeping babe from her breast and, covering herself, wrapped the child in its shawl.

'I shall not be long,' she said.

As she shut the door, Jasper went quickly to her bed-chamber and throwing off his clothes climbed into her bed.

In a few moments he heard her return to the parlour.

'Jasper?' she said anxiously. 'Jasper?'

'Mevanvy,' he answered.

She came with haste into the room, holding aloft a light.

'I thought you had gone,' she said, leaning against the door and closing her eyes.

Instantly contrite he told her he had only wished to show her his eagerness for her return and was rewarded with a smile.

'Come here,' he said, 'and I will help you to bed.'

She sat beside him and he took off the new necklace and undid the points of her sleeves and the fastening of the dress. She folded them and carried them, almost as if she did not know what she was doing, and laid them on a chest.

Then, naked, she ran back to him and threw herself into his arms in a paroxysm of weeping.

9

Edmund rode out from Trecastle Manor to meet him as he came, wearily, through the last of the mountainous passes he and his troop had traversed from Pembroke. His brother leant forward eagerly to grasp his hand and Jasper found himself almost unable to speak.

'How is our father?' he asked, when they had followed the Usk for half a mile.

'He is well and looking forward to your visit with some impatience. He sits a horse with as much skill as ever and hunts most days.'

Before going down to greet Owen the two young men went to Jasper's rooms.

'Are you well?' Jasper asked Edmund.

'I am,' he replied. 'But how is it with you?' He took Jasper by the shoulders and steered him towards the small casement. 'You look thin and worn to me.'

'Nonsense,' Jasper said lightly. 'It is the grime from the roads we have travelled and you know it is not my custom to waste time on a journey.'

'I know that well enough,' Edmund said.

'But it is something other than that. A woman?'

'Yes,' Jasper answered, unusually abrupt. 'But I would not speak of her now. Another time. Tell me instead of the news from Court.'

'Queen Margaret appears to have accepted the arrangement of York as Protector and so long as his power is not extended she has no real cause for complaint. But I do not trust him and neither does Beaufort — or Margaret for that matter. I wish to God Henry would recover his wits and could take up again the reins of government.'

Owen greeted his young son with open arms, kissing him on both cheeks. Jasper thought his father bore his fifty odd years lightly and had lost none of his magnificent carriage and handsome looks. If Owen in his turn thought Jasper haggard and on edge he waited until he and Edmund were alone before he commented upon it.

A feast had been prepared for the first visit he had made to Trecastle and Jasper met the members of his father's household. Among them he was delighted to find the groom and some of the other servants who had played with him and taught him to ride at Hatfield. There was a marked absence of women but a round cheeked motherly dame saw to the managing of the household and sent pages running to replenish Jasper's trencher as often as he emptied it. When the others had retired the Tudors sat talking until the dawn was breaking. Jasper rose unsteadily to his feet and realised he had drunk too deeply of the wine his father had provided but declining Edmund's tactful offer of assistance made a tremendous effort not to fall flat on his face in front of his father and walked out to the yard where he was horribly, and rather messily, sick.

He went round to the stables with his head spinning and filled a leather bucket from the pump. Having sluiced away his vomit he went back to the stalls where the horses were quartered and with some difficulty found his own stallion.

There was no sign of a saddle and he imagined they were kept in another place close to where the grooms would be sleeping.

With great care he led his horse out and after two abortive efforts gained its back. Not quite sure of his intentions he rode out of the yard, calling to the startled watch and rode westwards away from the new rising sun.

Edmund, giving his brother time to slip into bed, went quietly to his chamber and found to his dismay the bed was unoccupied. He ran down the circular stone stairway and out into the yard, where a cock flapped and crowed loudly, searching in every possible nook for Jasper. Coming to the newly washed paving he went at once to the stables and looking into the stall where Jasper's horse had been stabled he found it gone.

He shouted loudly for a groom and several men in various stages of undress came running and were sent for saddles and horses. Edmund curbed his impatience until his horse was led out.

Owen's own man came up to Edmund.

'Which way shall we search?'

Edmund gave him a swift look of gratitude.

'You come with me and two others and we'll take the Llandovery road while the three over there can go east to Brecon.'

White mist hung in the rocky valleys but the sun was gathering warmth as they set out at a good pace.

Edmund led the way and had not gone more than a mile up the road he had traversed with Jasper only the evening before when he came upon his brother's stallion and at no distance Jasper lying still with his right leg twisted in an odd way beneath him. Edmund jumped down and put his hand over Jasper's heart. Although it was beating fast it was strong and regular.

'He lives,' he said briefly to the men who

clustered about him. 'Two of you had best return to Trecastle and bring a door or table board and send others to bring in the searchers who were making for Brecon.'

When the board came Jasper was lifted gently on to it. He stirred but did not regain consciousness until nightfall.

His face grey with pain his first words were contrite.

'Please give my apologies to Father,' he said weakly. 'What a disgrace to conduct myself thus on my first night in his home.'

'Father is not angered,' Edmund replied. 'He is only concerned with the condition of your leg. The physician thinks you have cracked the knee cap. Nothing more,' he added hastily.

'What a curse,' Jasper cried. 'I shall not be much use to you when we set out to woo the Herberts.'

'By the look of you an enforced rest will do you no harm. Do you feel like some food?'

Jasper shuddered and turned his head to the wall.

'Drink this, then. It is an opiate to help you sleep.'

With a groan Jasper propped himself on his elbows and took the horn cup filled with milky white liquid. He grimaced but drank and fell back on the pillows.

His strong constitution swiftly reasserted itself and in less than a week he was walking with the aid of a crutch. He came down to the hall one morning to find Owen and Edmund reading a bundle of letters newly arrived from Westminster.

'What news?' he asked.

'Somerset is in the Tower!' Edmund told him.

'That will not please Her Grace,' Jasper exclaimed. 'And he even less.'

'And that is not all. The Archbishop of Canterbury is dead also.'

'She will be bereft of Counsellors. Once we have completed the matter of Sir William Herbert we best return with haste. Buckingham and Westmorland are with her, no doubt?'

'Yes, these despatches came from Buckingham. The young Prince Edward thrives, although his father still does not know of his existence.'

'There is no change in Henry, then?'

Edmund shook his head.

'Will you come with me to look at your stallion?' he asked Jasper. 'Will you come with us, Father.'

Owen smiled.

'No, you two go alone. I have some work to do on the letters which came for me.'

As they made for the stables Jasper turned to Edmund.

'I hope Father will not let himself become embroiled in any of this business between York and the Queen.'

'Why do you say that?' Edmund asked quickly.

'One of the letters he took up had Margaret's seal and it would be just like her to play on his debt to Henry.'

'Surely that is too far fetched to think about,' Edmund exclaimed.

'Nothing is too fantastic where support for Margaret of Anjou is concerned.'

Having inspected the horse, who had had a slight cut on one fetlock contracted during Jasper's fall, but was now recovering, the brothers left the confines of the manor and walked slowly towards the stream. Here Jasper protested that he could go no further and threw himself onto a flat topped boulder.

'There has not been word for me from Pembroke?'

'None.' Edmund said quietly. After a pause he went on. 'Was she very fair?'

For a moment he thought Jasper would ignore the question.

'Not in the accepted sense,' he said, at length. 'Perhaps you would not even think her beautiful but I can only tell you for the past month it is as if I have been living on another planet.'

Edmund regarded him gravely.

'And you are finding it difficult to return?'

'Yes,' Jasper admitted, turning his head away.

'She must have you beneath her spell! I wonder if it will be my fortune to be in thrall to a woman as you are to this enchantress.'

'You have never been so?' Jasper asked curiously. Edmund shook his head. 'You have not lived then,' Jasper continued. 'But you must! Although with you it is different for you are to be married and any liaison such as mine would necessarily hurt the little Lady Margaret.'

'You do not intend to marry your paramour?'

'To tell the truth I am torn with perplexity, for I do not see the relationship between Mevanvy and myself as wedded bliss and yet there is the child to consider — '

'The child!' Edmund exclaimed.

'Yes, we have a baby daughter, born six months ago. I did not tell you before,' he went on hastily, 'I wanted to have time to think more deeply on the subject, but this stupid accident has — ' his voice trailed off.

'It would be best if we set out for Llvanapley as soon as you feel you are able to travel,' Edmund interrupted. He stooped over Jasper and proffering his arm helped him to his feet.

Within a few days Jasper pronounced himself capable of sitting in the saddle sufficiently long enough to reach the home of the Herberts and they set out.

He had forced himself to recover, for lying idle he had been prone to the most agonising desire to be with Mevanvy again. He was haunted with her beauty and the delight of their mutual passion. His days were filled with the memory of her fragrant hair and the depthless mystery of her eyes while his restless sleep was disturbed with the remembrance of her body's exquisite ardour.

Riding, in some pain, through the rains which had spoilt the new come summer, he gave much thought to the problem of winning over Sir William and his brother Sir Richard to the Lancastrian cause.

Buckingham, who had sent further despatches before they left Trecastle, told them he hoped to meet up with them in Monmouthshire and begged them to make their headquarters in a manor of his Newport estate. He was awaiting their arrival and when they had dined talked with them for long hours of the mounting tensions of the court. Henry still showed no signs of recovering from his madness.

With Buckingham were his sons, Humphrey and Henry Stafford, fair haired and upright of carriage with an unmistakeable Plantaganet cast of feature. They were slightly younger than Edmund and Jasper but Humphrey was already married to Edmund Beaufort's daughter and he told them she was expecting her first child in the new year.

'I have brought you letters from your ward at Bletsoe,' he said to Edmund. 'Henry and I were there before we left Kimbolton to join our father and when Margaret heard we were to meet with you she gave me these for you.'

'She writes to you?' Jasper asked his brother.

'Yes,' Edmund said. 'Her mother has new ideas about the education of girls and encourages her both to read and take an interest in her estates. It is for this reason she writes now. She has visited her manor at Collyweston and tells me of some improvements she thinks necessary.'

'She sounds a somewhat precocious child,' Jasper said.

'Hardly a child,' Edmund replied. 'She must be almost fifteen years old now.'

'Marriageable,' Jasper said musingly, and quickly changed the subject to the impending visit to Llvanapley.

Buckingham and his sons rode with them and were received courteously but evasively by the Herbert brothers.

'They are more than unwilling to commit themselves,' Buckingham said grimly when they were once more on the road returning to his manor. 'I am convinced they have much sympathy for York but are not pledging it fully until he has gained more convincing support from the rest of the country.'

'Is it not so,' Jasper said, 'they were offended by Margaret of Anjou's omission to grant them higher honours?'

'Yes, that is the case. As you know it is extremely difficult to convince the Queen she must use tact and diplomacy in her dealings with those about her. I am sure she antagonises many more men than she need.'

'I have heard it said she is unjust also,' Humphrey put in.

'Unfortunately you have heard aright,' his father replied. 'She is hasty in her judgement and too proud to recant when she realises she has made a mistake.'

'But to be fair to her she is a source of strength to Henry and her loyalty to his cause is undoubted,' Jasper said.

He felt detached from their conversation and heeded only what they said with half his mind. With his knee now mended his returning vigour filled him with determination to go to Pembroke, even if it were only for a few short days, before he and Edmund set out for Westminster. With this decision made he almost enjoyed the ride to Buckingham's manor and the two days hunting which followed.

He and Edmund came to Trecastle as the evening sun filled the western heavens with a glowing apricot light that mantled the earth with a peaceful warmth.

'Some of Father's good food and wine and early to bed,' Jasper said as they dismounted and handed the reins to a groom.

'It won't be easy to retire too quickly for we shall have to tell Father of our progress with the Herberts,' Edmund said laughingly.

But one glance at Owen's face as he came to greet them at the house door was sufficient for them to realise he had news to impart to them of more import than their stay in Monmouth. He looked, quite suddenly, old and defenceless.

'Jasper,' he said quietly, 'come to my private parlour — '

'What is it? Have you news from Pembroke?' Jasper asked with anxiety.

'My son,' Owen said, as he closed the door of the panelled room behind them, 'you did not tell me of the lady Mevanvy. I attach no blame to you for that — '

'Oh, Father!' Jasper implored, 'tell me the news! Something is wrong, isn't it?'

'Yes,' Owen replied. 'Lady Mevanvy died three days ago of a miscarriage.'

'Oh, God. Oh, God!' Jasper cried as he sank on to a stool and buried his head in his hands.

Owen came to him and put his arms about him.

'I am sorry, my son. I know what it is to suffer as you do.'

Jasper looked up at him quickly.

'Forgive me,' he said simply. 'I should have a more manly bearing but I can think of nothing except I have killed her with my selfish lust. Why did they not send for me? Could they do nothing to save her?'

'The child's nurse, who came with the messenger from Pembroke tells me the Steward's wife fetched physicians and mid-wives but it was of no avail.'

'I can't believe it,' Jasper said in a strangled voice. 'She was so vital and seemingly so strong. Oh, what have I done?'

'There, Jasper. Do not reproach yourself too severely. In the gratification of passion it is usually necessary for two people to be agreeable and it does not sound to me as if

142

you had to force the Lady Mevanvy to your will.'

'No,' Jasper said sadly. 'But it was still my fault. She had but recently recovered from the birth of our daughter and I should have known more wisdom.'

'The child is here,' Owen said going to the door.

'Here?'

'Yes. It was Mevanvy's wish she should be brought to you. You will have opportunity to make amends to the child's mother by accepting your responsibilities and caring for the baby.'

'There is no question of any other course. Is the girl in the house?'

'Yes, I have given her two rooms and she is awaiting you now.'

Jasper thanked his father and made his way to the stairs. He was filled with a desolate sense of loss underlaid with self-repugnance. He kept close to the wall on the stone steps afraid to meet anyone who would recognise his abject dejection.

The nursemaid from Pembroke opened the door to him and he went in and followed her to the cradle without speaking. Helen lay sleeping in the trusting abandonment of childhood, one clenched fist above her head. Jasper's eyes filled with tears and he turned away as the nurse busied herself with folding clothes and putting them in a chest.

She went out of the chamber and returned with a flask of wine and a goblet. Jasper sat and sipped the wine, swallowing it with difficulty as it mingled with the salty saliva in his mouth.

The girl took a velvet covered box from the chest and he saw at once it was that which had contained the necklace he had given Mevanvy. He took it from her and snapping it open took the delicate gold and crushed it in his hands.

'Lady Mevanvy asked me to give it to you,' the nurse said. ' "Take the Lord Jasper our child and my necklace and tell him the gaining of one's hearts desire will always call for future payment and I paid it willingly." '

'Did she suffer very much?'

'No, it all happened so quickly. She had not been very well after you left and her milk dried and the babe would not take to goat's milk at first. This worried her. Had she but told us she was with child again we should have been able to comfort her and say this was quite natural.'

'You did not know then?' Jasper asked.

'No. She confided in no one and it was not until the Steward's wife sent for the physician that he told us what ailed her. Midwives came then but it was as if she could summon no effort to help herself.'

Jasper winced.

'Did she say nothing else?'

The girl hesitated a moment.

'When I took her hands and tried to rub some life into them I implored her to make an attempt to rally herself but she just smiled and whispered something — very low I could only just hear her — about it being better to die now than to recover and live to lose one's heart's desire.'

Jasper bowed his head and stood up.

'Thank you.'

At the stairhead Edmund awaited him and together they went down.

'We shall leave for Westminster the day after tomorrow. There is much needs our attention and we best go while the weather holds fair.'

Jasper nodded.

'At this moment I hate Wales, but that is nothing compared with the loathing I have for myself. I wish it were as easy to lose oneself as it is to journey from place to place.'

'Come,' Edmund said gently. 'Father has had our supper made ready in his parlour and you will feel better when you have eaten.'

10

By Christmas Henry had completely recovered from his temporary madness and was restored to health and strength. He was overjoyed at the birth of his baby son and sent gifts of thanksgiving to Canterbury and the Priory of St. John.

It was not difficult for Margaret of Anjou to sway him to her will at this juncture and, as soon as Parliament met, York was divested of his powers as Protector and Edmund Beaufort was released from the Tower.

York made no comment on the change in his fortunes but it was widely rumoured he had gone to his northern estates to see the massing of an army. The state of unrest, generally, in the realm could have been excuse for this, but his enemies read deeper meaning to his preparation. They looked secretly to their own armies.

One of Henry's first acts was to call Edmund to him and give him his blessing for the early celebration of his wedding to the Lady Margaret. The house of Lancaster had not sufficient heirs and the Beaufort heiress was now ready for marriage.

Edmund went to Bletsoe and made his formal declaration to his future bride. Jasper received word his presence was desired at the betrothal feast and at the appointed time he went into the gentle countryside of Bedfordshire to give his support to Edmund.

In the year that had gone by since the death of Mevanvy he had devoted himself to the raising of sympathisers to the King and had spent hours in the saddle riding the length and breadth of Wales. He had lost the haunted look of guilt he had acquired and had grown in stature and strength of character. He was popular with the men he commanded, who recognised in him a man of his word, unfashionably slow in self advancement and unusually sympathetic.

The story of the mistress who had given him a daughter and died in the miscarrying of another child had been impossible to suppress and had in some mysterious way added to his standing.

Edmund had helped him in a thousand unspoken ways and only when he tried to interest him in womankind did his consideration go awry. Jasper could not bring himself to tell his brother he had not been able to look at a woman without seeing Mevanvy and recalling the desire and pain she invoked.

Now, clattering through the Town of

Bedford and crossing the Ouse, he realised the betrothal feast was one of the rare social festivities he had attended since the previous year and he found he looked forward with something almost approaching pleasure to the company of his fellow men and their ladies.

He met the Lady Margaret as they were going in to dine.

Edmund brought his betrothed ward to his brother and Jasper was struck at once with her unspoilt charm. When he had recovered from the small shock of finding Margaret a desirable young woman, rather than the studious child he had always pictured, he took in the beauty of her oval face and graceful figure. She was dressed in some shimmering robe of blue green and it became her perfectly, revealing the rounded bosom and enhancing the colour of her candidly clear eyes.

As she sat next to him at the table Jasper was conscious of two things; Margaret was very deeply in love with Edmund while he, Jasper, was able to be near her and enjoy the existence of womankind without the revulsion from which he had suffered for so many months.

Throughout the elaborate meal she talked with unrestrained ease to both Edmund and

148

Jasper, and he found her intelligence matched in looks. She listened when they spoke to her and her comments were well considered, while her quick sense of humour discovered laughter in the unexpected.

Jasper went to bed happier than he had been since Mevanvy died.

Only later, when Edmund joined him did he learn he had unwittingly caused his future sister-in-law some moments of disquiet.

'Do you remember saying to me just before the loving cup was passed round, how fortunate I was Henry had chosen such a bride for me?'

'Yes, I do,' Jasper said puzzled.

'Margaret overheard you, and as I had not yet told her Henry had wished this as well as my guardianship she was thrown into confusion — '

'She did not show it!' Jasper cried. 'I would not have hurt her for words.'

'You did not,' Edmund said quickly. 'It was I who was at fault for delaying telling her both this and that I love her as much as she loves me.'

'Yes,' Jasper said relaxing and lying back against the bed-head. 'You are a blessed man, Edmund. It is not many who can say love is given them with marriage.'

The wedding was arranged for October,

and Jasper accompanied Edmund to Windsor on the following morning to report to Henry and set in motion the complicated legal side of the marriage settlement.

At Windsor, the court was in a great flurry of preparation for the Council meeting to be held in Leicester. York had promised to be present and the Kings optimistic advisers saw an end of the differences besetting the realm.

'Do you trust him?' Jasper asked Edmund on the night before they set out.

'Unfortunately, I cannot say I do. I should like to, but one hears too many conflicting rumours.'

'I shall take along all my followers and do you the same. Who is to go with us?'

'Buckingham and his sons, Lord Roos, Clifford and the Earl of Northumberland.'

'And of course Beaufort and Dorset?'

'The Queen does not move without them.'

When they assembled on the hill outside the castle moat Jasper made quick assessment of the number of the escort.

'Getting on for two thousand men,' he said quietly to Edmund. 'If York has entrenched himself in Leicester and aroused the midlands to his support I do not profess much faith in our chances.'

They did not have to wait for Leicester, however, to assess the loyalty of York, for coming into Watford the King's party was met by the forward platoon returning with stories of a huge army of Yorkists marching on St. Albans with banners flying.

Consternation broke out and townsfolk and peasants hid as captains rooted out every available man.

Never lacking in courage, Margaret of Anjou spurred on her husband and Beaufort and they came to St. Albans in the early morning of the following day.

Spread before them were the pitched tents of Warwick, Salisbury and York. Smoke rose from scattered fires. Henry sent his herald to York for an explanation of what he considered a direct provocation of his peace.

While York prepared his answer skirmishing broke out and his followers, unaware of the parleying, put bows to shoulder and loosed a hail of deadly accurate arrows among the King's men.

Clifford, Buckingham and Jasper gave immediate orders to their retainers to take up positions and, from better vantage points, they returned fire.

In the confusion following this treacherous outburst, Somerset became a marked man and, his bodyguard fighting to the last man, went down with a quiver of arrows piercing his body.

Buckingham became separated from his sons and Humphrey lost his life in an unsuccessful attempt to come to the support of Northumberland.

For three hours bitter, hand to hand fighting raged through the narrow streets close to the Abbey of the martyred St. Alban. Henry, bewildered and unhappy, caught a glancing blow from an arrow and was removed to the infirmary of the Abbey while Margaret of Anjou, sitting astride her horse, rode fearlessly from street corner to market place encouraging the King's party. Despite all she, Jasper and Clifford with Edmund and the other loyal leaders could do, the day was lost and by afternoon the weary Lancastrians were beaten when the Flag Bearer to the King threw down the Standard and ran off.

In the evening, Henry set off for London with York, whither the Queen had already gone, and Jasper superintended the grisly task of recovering the dead and burying them.

He was saddened by the death of Humphrey Stafford, so recently the father of a new born son, and the savagery inflicted on the naked corpse of Beaufort.

'It seems impossible so much has happened since yesterday. When I said to you I did not trust York I never thought of such indiscriminate bloodshed. Poor Northumberland, loyal and well tried servant of the Lancasters, to think he should die in a miserable snare like this,' Jasper said to Edmund as they rode wearily for Westminster.

'Civil war is the cruellest of all,' Edmund said. 'By nature of our birth we are caught up in it, but I for one could wish we were not involved.'

At length when Parliament met a patched-up peace was once more concluded and York was allowed to resume his position as Protector although Margaret of Anjou made it plain she was absolutely opposed to this.

Since the death of Beaufort she had sent several times for Jasper.

'My sympathies,' Edmund said to him as he left for Bletsoe when Parliament was dissolved. 'She is becoming more like a tigress every day.'

'Do not worry yourself,' Jasper assured him drily. 'I shall not let her eat me.'

He had much cause to remember Edmund's sympathy in the days before he went down to Bedfordshire to attend the marriage of his brother and Margaret, for the Queen grew excessively demanding and kept him for long hours in argument and discussion. Henry seemed to have relapsed into a state of mental unawareness where he was able to kneel in his chapel and become oblivious to his surroundings and the problems confronting his realms. Jasper envied him his detatchment.

He had sent word to Pembroke to prepare apartments for his brother and Margaret to occupy when they came to take up residence in the castle. It had been his suggestion, and Edmund had agreed, that the remoteness of Wales was an excellent place to harbour the Earl and Countess of Richmond as they set about the rearing of their family. Jasper had taken great care and thought in choosing the hangings for their rooms and tried not to feel envious of their future happiness. He had been to Pembroke only for brief visits of late and had avoided the rooms where he and Mevanvy had made such passionate and consuming love. He had given very strict instructions that these apartments should not be allocated to the Richmonds.

The day before the marriage he spent the night in the hospice at Bedford and, taking only a couple of followers, went to the hamlet of Colmworth where the lady of the manor had agreed to prepare chambers for the Earl and his bride. Jasper smiled as he recalled Edmund's embarrassment as he had told him of Margaret's reluctance to be exhibited in her marriage bed as she awaited her husband

and his own scheme to relieve her of this strain.

Once again he felt the stirrings of envy but stifled them quickly as being unwarranted.

Coming to Bletsoe he had a hurried conversation with Edmund and assured him he had carried out his instructions to the best of his ability.

He remembered very little of the rest of the day for he allowed himself to drink more than usual, but he saw Margaret through a crowd of guests glowing with happiness and connived at their escape during the bridal feast. It was he who broke the news of the flight to Colmworth to Lady Welles and her husband, and when he had convinced them he was still sober and had restrained Sir Leon from dashing off to retrieve his stepdaughter, he put himself out to convince Margaret's mother of the reason for the journey. He was rewarded and was later able to persuade her to join in the dancing.

Three days afterwards despatches arrived from Margaret of Anjou telling of rioting and storming of private property in Somerset and Devon. Although nothing could be proved as yet, strong charges were to be levelled against the Earl of Devonshire who was believed to be the instigator of these trespasses against private citizens. With this in mind the King and Queen begged the newly married couple to reconsider before setting out for Wales, and to leave immediately for Pembroke.

Jasper said he would ride over to Colmworth and tell his brother and his bride. He was ushered into their parlour by Lady Braybrooks, the widowed doyen of the manor, and his heart contracted as he saw them together.

Did I look like that he found himself wondering when Mevanvy and I had not slept throughout the night? Did she regard me with that utter trusting adoration? Was I so patently happy?

He pulled himself together sufficiently to explain to them the reason for his visit and they both took it better than he dared hope. It meant an almost immediate interruption of their privacy and at least two weeks travelling on roads already deteriorating with the Autumn weather.

He stayed with them to share a simple meal and he had time to study his brother's bride.

Margaret had matured in the short days since her marriage and had bound her hair in coils to reveal the shapeliness of her neck and shoulders. Although it was obvious she was utterly happy in Edmund's love she made no demonstration of it before Jasper, contenting herself with letting her hand lie in Edmund's.

He left them promising to send a servant to fetch them to Bletsoe on the day after the next.

In the meantime Lord Roos came to the manor at Bletsoe with a band of well trained men-at-arms to accompany them on part of their journey to Wales and Jasper decided he could be spared long enough from Court to go with them at least part of the way.

He saw to the packing and assembling of the baggage train and sent it off well in advance with letters for his Steward telling of the precipitate arrival of Edmund and his bride.

When the autumn mists had cleared from Bletsoe on a morning a few days later they set out for Pembroke. The cavalcade made a brave show with the colours of Roos, Richmond and Pembroke streaming out against the clear sky and the tawny trees. Margaret sat her mare sturdily enough, but Jasper could not help wondering if she would find the long journey tiring. She had taken with her a maid who had been her servant since she had left nursery days behind her and Jasper saw Betsey never very far distant. Edmund was also constantly at hand and several times she beckoned for Jasper to keep them company.

The Cotswolds, possessing the solitary

beauty of an enclosed garden, charmed him as they had never done before and he delighted in the magnificent panorama presented to them as they climbed with difficulty down into the Vale of Evesham. He began to dread reaching Chipping Camden for it was here he had made up his mind to return to the Queen.

Each evening at hospice or other resting place, Edmund and Margaret, although obviously almost oblivious of other people about them, insisted upon Jasper and Lord Roos sharing their supper with them. They talked over the day's journey and the plans for the morrow. The strife and turmoil of the realm seemed distant and unreal.

He came to Chipping Camden and took his leave of them with a gaiety he was far from feeling.

'I'll do my very utmost to be with you for Christmastide,' he promised them. 'It is high time Pembroke showed what it can do!'

Returning to Shene where the royal family were now staying, he found Margaret of Anjou reluctant to release him but he discovered in himself a new firmness and insisted he would be away for the shortest possible time.

She had not wasted the short weeks since he had last seen her and had been gathering further evidence of the murdering and pillaging taking place in the West country with which to accuse Devonshire. The Lords, hearing these indictments, were moving at her instigation towards the indicting of York for his adherent's misbehaviour and he was to be confronted with the charges when the parliament met on the 14th January.

'You must be back by that date!' she said with the haughty manner so many people found antagonising.

'I shall do my best,' Jasper told her quietly.

He had written to his father to ask him to join him in Wales but Owen had refused on the grounds of the difficulty of travel from Trecastle in the winter. He had despatched the nurse and the child to Pembroke before the worst of the weather and Jasper had received word from the Steward to say they had arrived safely.

Just before he set out he heard of the betrothal of the young Duke of Suffolk to York's daughter, Eliza. Remembering this young man had been a suitor, at his father's wish, for the hand of the Lady Margaret, Jasper could only be amazed at his present choice. Could it be the Suffolk family were changing their loyalties?

He was resolved to make Pembroke a feast of enjoyment and when he came to the castle he enlisted his squire as lord of Misrule and put him to the decorating of the Hall. Guests were already arriving and they went out into the surrounding woods with the servants and came back with cartloads of evergreens and the largest Yule log they had been able to find. A huge fire was built in the Hall and the tree trunk pushed on to it.

Edmund and Margaret had greeted him with unfeigned delight and they had talked until they were tired of the different lives they had led since they parted in October.

Margaret looked, to his observant eye, slightly thinner but still possessed of the radiance her happiness gave her. Edmund had never looked better.

In the presentation of guests, Helen's nurse had brought the child, now toddling, to meet Margaret, and Jasper had watched covertly as his sister-in-law stooped to speak to her. He knew Margaret well enough to know she would not miss the likeness and almost reading his thoughts she looked up and for a moment their eyes met.

She did not mention the incident and he admired her for the restraint she showed.

The food and the players who came to entertain them were faultless and when snow fell their enjoyment was complete.

As they took their leave of him standing

under the portcullis of the Gateway Jasper knew his guests had enjoyed his hospitality to the full. His first Christmas at Pembroke had been a success. He promised himself to make every effort to repeat it in the following years. Not even in the stillness of the snow-quiet night would he admit to himself the happiness he had created was in any way connected with the presence of his brother's wife.

On the following day, she and Edmund came to bid farewell as he left to keep his promise to the Queen. He was thrown off his guard as she took his hand. He had always feared to touch her for she was so completely Edmund's but the pleasure of her nearness prompted him to kiss her lightly on the brow and she had responded with this gesture of affection.

'Thank you for sending us here, Jasper,' she said, as he jumped to his saddle to hide the confusion of his emotions. 'And for taking so much upon yourself on our behalf. If it were not for you, Edmund would be away from me so much. You will take care that you don't get caught up in any of these disturbances you have been telling us about?'

Laughingly, Jasper promised to keep out of trouble and told her the most important thing was that she should take care of herself.

Riding away, the expression in her beautiful eyes stayed with him and he found to his consternation her safety and well being mattered more to him than her importance as a hope of the Lancastrians or Edmund's wife.

Self-disgust threatened to engulf him again and he was almost glad to arrive at Westminster to discover York encamped there with a force of three hundred men. The ensuing activity within the walls of the Palace kept him from being able to dwell overlong on the singular beauty and attraction of the Countess of Richmond.

Margaret of Anjou, omitting to ask if he had enjoyed his stay in Wales, launched a volley of suggestions for dealing with the erring York. An ugly situation was fortuitously prevented when Henry threw off the mantle of unawareness which had been enveloping him and took up the reins of government with renewed vigour.

His first act was to enlist Jasper's support and confront York with an army in battle array and an unconditional demand for the relinquishing of the Protectorship.

To the amazement of sympathisers with both sides the King won the day and York retired.

An uneasy peace returned to the land.

Riots and disturbances became part of the daily scene.

Jasper received despatches from Edmund telling of an engagement he had had with a Gilbert Suoh, whose activities became suspect when he amassed an extraordinary number of followers in his castle not far from Pembroke. The man had been routed and should not prove troublesome for some time at least.

He ended his letter with the news of Margaret expecting their child.

Jasper did not know whether to rejoice or weep.

Telling his clerk he would answer the despatches the next day he went to his rooms and decided on the impulse to find an inconspicuous ferry boat and have himself taken to the Southwark bank where he would seek out a bawdy house and lose himself in the arms of the first woman who offered herself.

Crossing by the Jewel House he fell in with Henry Stafford, grown quieter of late since the death of his elder brother in the disastrous battle of St. Albans.

His suggestions of finding a tavern outside the Palace where they might enjoy an unhindered supper and gossip made Jasper change his mind and instead of spending the evening in a manner which he would later have regretted he found he had unexpectedly enjoyed himself. He established a bond of sympathy with the young Stafford who struck him as level headed and well educated. At one moment he felt almost as if he could confide the perplexities of his emotions, but stopped himself when he remembered Edmund's wife had been a friend of Henry's since childhood. Their estates at Bletsoe and Kimbolton were within seven miles of each other.

After a few days he was able to write to Edmund tendering his sincere congratulations at the expected birth.

Later in the year, after some deliberation, he wrote to his brother to say he had heard of much movement of troops around the stronghold of York at Ludlow and would suggest Edmund should look into the matter. He was hesitant to take him away from Margaret at this time but the new young Duke of Somerset, who had befriended them as Henry of Dorset, in the first days of their coming to court, had been involved during the Council meeting at Coventry in an affray with the Watch. This had resulted in the death of several men and Somerset would have lost his own life if Buckingham had not arrived on the scene in time to prevent this disaster.

The incidence had not enhanced the Lancastrian cause and, with Henry about to make a progress through the Midlands, any massing of troops at Ludlow could be dangerous.

Jasper left for Kenilworth knowing Edmund would not fail him and praying fervently no action would be called for.

He received a brief acknowledgement of his request and the statement of Edmund's intention to set forth as soon as his men were ready.

He began to make plans for going to Pembroke for Christmas. The Queen became more demanding of his time as the year wore on and her supporters proved insufficiently willing or too young and inexperienced.

As December approached it was obvious Henry was far from well and reluctantly, and yet with a sense of relief, Jasper shelved his plans to go to Pembroke. He sent messengers with gifts at St. Nicholastide and promised himself he would make the journey in the spring to see his brother's child.

Before the gifts were acknowledged his squire came to tell him messengers were come from Pembroke. He sent for them immediately.

Their grave faces told him something was amiss. Steeling himself, he said nothing and opened the seal of the rolled documents with hands he had to force into stillness.

He was torn with a physical sense of disaster as he read his brother had died of the plague and was buried in the Church of the Grey Friars in Carmarthen.

Edmund! his life long companion and dearest friend. It was unbelievable. Swift on the heels of his own grief came the realisation of the devastation this would have caused Margaret.

'How did this happen?' he asked.

'Riding from Ludlow, the Lord Edmund called to speak some words of sympathy with the mother of a boy who had been killed in the fight with Gilbert Suoh.'

How like Edmund, Jasper thought.

'Yes?' he prompted.

'Plague was rife in the town and the Earl complained of not feeling well and the innkeeper and his wife looked after him until it was discovered he had succumbed to the disease, when they sent to the Grey Friars who came and brought him to their dispensary.'

'And the Lady Margaret?' he forced himself to ask.

'Does the letter not ask you to come to her?' the messenger asked. 'The Steward is most anxious you will come at once.'

Jasper took up the half-finished letter and read it through.

'Of course I shall come at once,' he said. 'But how is the Lady?'

'She has acted very strangely since she returned from Carmarthen. Betsey Massey has been fair distracted — '

'Went to Carmarthen?' Jasper cried. 'Why, was she with my brother when he — died?'

'Yes. She would not be stopped when she heard he lay ill at the inn and was asking for her. She took her little mare and rode there.'

'But in her condition — ' Jasper's voice trailed off.

'The babe has taken no harm as far as the physicians can tell. It is the Lady Richmond for whom we all fear.'

'Well, what are we standing here for?' Jasper cried. 'We leave at once for Bletsoe where I shall meet up with Mistress Margery St. John, step-sister to Lady Richmond.'

He found the household in Bedfordshire plunged into gloom and Lady Welles could only stammer her gratitude for his swift answer to the prayer for aid from Pembroke.

Margery, whom he dimly remembered from his infrequent visits to Bletsoe, proved a calm and soothing companion during the torturous journey they had into Wales.

The weather became appalling and the roads difficult and dangerous. With even Jasper's recklessness and the gnawing anxiety which drove them both on it was January before they saw the castle creep out of the gloom and clinging rain in front of them.

Jasper was taken into the stewards apartments, with Margery, when they arrived and listened in silence to the sad story he and his wife unfolded for them.

He was, therefore, half prepared for the pathetic sight of his brother's widow. Her face was white and drawn, her eyes enormous and overbright. She proffered her hand for his kiss, saying nothing. Straightening himself he looked up to find her gazing at him, the last vestige of colour drained from her cheeks. For what seemed a long, measureless moment, she stared at him and then quite suddenly, closing her eyes she sat down.

'Jasper, oh Jasper. You are very welcome here!'

And the tears which had refused to give her relief since the dreadful day of Edmund's death poured down her cheeks. Blinded by his own tears, Jasper stepped aside to allow Margery to comfort her step-sister and knew in that instant that he loved Margaret.

Loved her in a manner that was in no way like the passion he had known for Mevanvy but which, nevertheless, went deeper into the centre of his very being.

11

The immediate years following his homecoming — for so it proved — to Pembroke were compounded of happiness and torture. Had he been asked to define them he would have been unable to say where the one left off and the other began.

On the morning following his arrival Margery summoned him to Margaret's bedside. He had known, soon after she had received him, her labour had begun and he had spent a sleepless night, oblivious of fatigue.

The gloom which had greeted them had turned, during the hours of darkness, to snow and the castle was hushed under a blanket of white. At cockscrow a peace wrapped the stronghold and possessed Jasper. He threw himself on his bed and slept.

He was fully awake and alert when Margery told him Margaret wished to see him. He went into her chamber and found her with her new born son at her side.

In a whisper as he knelt at her bedside she asked him to protect her and the child and with a tenderness he had not realised was his own he had promised to make this his lifelong task.

During the months that followed Margaret slowly regained her health. At first it had seemed as if she would never recover, for the baby, whom she had called Henry, was slow to thrive and caused her much anxiety. But with the coming of summer the child gained a little colour and Margaret walked on the battlements and found her appetite. If Margery and Betsey were most often with her it was to Jasper she turned for advice and counsel and it was he who was able to charm the rare smile to her grave face. He went to endless trouble to revive her interest in the learning and needlework she enjoyed and he was rewarded at last when she took up again some tapestries and translations she had been making before Edmund's death.

He delighted in her learning and soon realised although he had been well taught by the monks he was an ignoramus compared with Margaret.

One summer evening in 1457 she sent word to his apartments to say she would like his company if he were not too busy. He thrust aside the papers on which he had been working and went to the Tower next to the Gatehouse where he had made a home for his brother and his bride.

She kissed him affectionately as he came in and patted the chair beside her own at the window. She was, he knew, completely unaware of his love for her. He understood this very well for it had been plain Edmund's and her marriage had been welded with passion and it recalled, almost too vividly, the indescribable sense of loss he had suffered when he had known he would no longer be able to enjoy Mevanvy's body.

She had on a dress he had not seen before in one of her favourite sea green colours and he noticed with pleasure her face was fuller and her hands had lost the blue veined frailty of the past months.

'I have been thinking,' she said, 'how pleasant it would be if your father were to come and stay with us for a short while. I do not know him, as you are aware, and it is time he saw his grandson.'

'If he can be persuaded to come, it would be excellent,' Jasper answered, glad she was showing an interest beyond the walls of Pembroke. Apart from her mother he had not heard her mention her desire to see any of her family.

'I thought too,' she went on. 'It would be a good opportunity for your baby daughter to return to her home.'

Jasper looked at her, startled.

Margaret regarded him levelly.

'I have not forgotten the little dark girl brought to me by her nurse during that happy Christmas we spent here and it seems to me as she lacks a mother and my baby has no father, you and I might help one another on this score as well as on so many others.'

So Helen and her nurse came back to Pembroke and Owen spent a month with them. Margaret had one of her rare outbursts of weeping when she met her father-in-law for the first time but she had recovered her composure quickly and she and Owen became fast friends.

He sat with her by the hour and told her stories of the far distant days when he had come as a young man to the Court of Henry V and followed him to the war in France. He drew vivid pictures of the men who had filled the canvas of the English and French households until the names of Bedford, Talbot, Beaufort and Exeter were as familiar as those who sought domination at the present time.

With Owen she went riding down to the shores of Milford Haven and he taught her the names of the birds nesting in the marshy ground and found shells for Helen to make into necklaces. Once or twice he spoke of Edmund to her but at the mention of his name she withdrew into herself and he wisely talked of other things.

Jasper thought as he and his father enjoyed each other's company how wise Margaret had been to suggest Owen should come to Pembroke. His visit had done so much to heal the grief each suffered.

'So you are to remain in Pembroke?' Owen asked his son as they rode out one morning to Monkton Priory.

'Yes,' Jasper replied. 'Margaret of Anjou can find supporters enough not to miss me so very much.'

'And your sister-in-law depends upon you,' Owen continued. 'Edmund was a very fortunate man to have married such a girl. It adds to the sadness to realise how well suited they were for each other.'

Jasper did not answer.

'It is most generous of her to take the child Helen under her wing. I hope when she marries again her future husband will accept the little girl for she has grown so attached to Margaret it would be cruel to take her away from her.'

'Marry again!' Jasper cried. 'Surely you cannot bring yourself to speak of that when Edmund has not been dead for a year!'

'I can speak of it more easily than you can, my son, for if I am any judge I can assess the

174

situation without the involvement of my own emotions, which is more than you can claim.'

Jasper was silent again.

'You will have to face the idea of her marrying again however detestable it is to you for it would not be safe for her to remain a widow.'

'She is safe enough with me here!'

'But you cannot marry her and it is only by marriage her enormous inheritance can be kept secure from fortune-hunters and thieves.'

'Well, it needn't be yet,' Jasper mumbled, controlling the anger his father had aroused.

'Does Margaret know of Mevanvy?' his father persisted.

'No, she doesn't,' Jasper said curtly and then continued more gently, 'But when she does ask me about her you need not fear I shall tell her anything but the truth.'

While Owen still stayed at Pembroke Jasper went out to the Marches for the first time since he had come home in January. He knew of no one better to guard Margaret and he was secretly relieved to be away from her and the constant reminder of his hopeless suit. He realised in his personal grief and concern he had neglected his task of consolidating support for Margaret and Henry. He soon discovered evidence of Yorkist influence and heard the name of Herbert associated constantly with Richard's cause. From Ludlow the young son of York, Edward Earl of March and his brothers Richard and George had promoted an intensive campaign for support of their father.

Jasper worked hard to revive the flagging loyalties of the people for their sovereign but he could not blind himself to the growing unpopularity of the Queen. It seemed to him that Henry's saintliness was losing ground to the scheming of his wife.

He came home to Pembroke dispirited to find Owen smothering his impatience to return to Trecastle. It was harvest time and he wished to supervise his crops. He left as soon as he had listened to Jasper's report.

Jasper found Margaret on the battlements between her Tower and the Gatehouse with Betsey and Henry's nurse.

She turned as he called her name and his heart thudded as he surprised a look of joy on her face. She ran towards him, taking both his hands in hers and offering her cheek for his kiss. He brushed it lightly with his mouth.

'Oh, Jasper, it is so good to see you home! And how well you look.'

'You also,' Jasper murmured. 'How is the babe?'

'Thriving, I am happy to say. Helen is too.

She will be so pleased to see you. Will you have supper with me?'

'Gladly,' Jasper replied.

He found when he presented himself she had kept the two nurses and their charges for him to see before they were put in their cradles. Margaret's son had filled out and crowed with delight when Jasper tickled his chin. Helen stood gravely at her nurse's side, alternatively burying her face in the girl's skirts and regarding her father with limpid eyes. When he stooped and picked her up she nestled into him and put fat arms about his neck, talking a mixture of English and Welsh peculiarly her own. At her request he carried her to her cot and stayed beside her until the dark lashed eyelids drooped in sleep.

He returned to Margaret's parlour where she had caused supper to be laid for them in unaccustomed splendour. She had had brought out from chests and cupboards some of the silver and napery of her dowry which had lain unused since Edmund's death and new candles glimmered on the boards.

Her servants waited on them and it was obvious she had hoped he would sup with her for she had chosen a simple but elegant meal mainly of fish caught in the Haven and fruit from the orchards of the town.

They talked companionably of his journey

to the Marches and the life in the castle during his absence but when the servants had cleared the board and left them an air of constraint fell.

A small fire to combat the chill of the evening burnt in the open grate and caught the gleam of gold in the tissue of her dress and the fillet she wore in her hair. For the first time since her widowhood she had discarded the severe coifs which hid her hair and Jasper noted she was wearing a rope of pearls where before her dress had been unadorned.

She leaned back in her chair, gazing into the flames, and Jasper, without speaking, watched her. Lifting her eyes she discovered his regard and smiled.

'Oh, Jasper,' she said. 'Why did Edmund have to die?'

Jasper shook his head.

'I don't know, my dear. One can only think God has a purpose and we do not always understand what it is.'

'Yes, that is how I have tried to comfort myself, but he and I were so perfectly happy — ' her voice broke. 'Too happy, I suppose.'

With difficulty Jasper restrained himself from going to her and enfolding her in his arms as she had his daughter earlier in the evening. She seemed, suddenly as defenceless as a child.

'And selfish,' she was continuing unaware of his perplexity. 'Won't you tell me about Helen's mother?'

'What shall I tell you?'

'She lived here, didn't she?'

'Yes, and died here also of a miscarriage. Helen was hardly six months old at the time so it was I who caused her death,' he said suppressing a shiver.

'Why so?' Margaret said. 'Did you have to force her to be your mistress?'

'No.'

'Then it was something between you both and no more your fault than hers.' She was quiet a moment and then looked at him directly. 'Did you love her, Jasper?'

'Love,' Jasper said brusquely. 'What is love? If you mean did my flesh cry out for hers in every waking minute, yes, yes, I did love her. But if you mean did I respect her, think for her, care what became of her and want her at my side for the rest of my life, no, I did not love her.'

She was silent so long he was forced to look at her and he saw to his amazement she was crying. In self disgust he stood up and kicked angrily at the embers of the fire. She leant forward and took his hand and cradled it to her cheek.

'My poor Jasper,' she whispered. 'I am so very sorry.'

When he left a few minutes afterwards he suggested she should come riding with him on the marshes as she had done with Owen.

'You have benefited so much from the air and exercise I wonder I did not think of it before.'

'I should like that very much.'

'Good. I'll send my squire to you in the morning to ask if you are ready. Thank you for this evening, Margaret. I hope you will forgive me for being such poor company.'

'You are never that,' she replied.

They rode out early on the following day and it became a custom with them to go as often as the weather allowed. Margaret was an accomplished horsewoman and had no difficulty keeping up with the pace he set. Grooms and men-at-arms followed at a distance but the solitary countryside and the empty haven enfolded them and their peace was not disturbed.

Buckingham kept Jasper informed of the situation at court and he reported the taking of Calais by York and Warwick. This was a severe blow to Henry for the town controlled the Staple and bereaved him of a necessary source of revenue. Margaret of Anjou was reported to be looking to Pierre de Breze, who as Grand Seneschal of Normandy, was an old friend and ally. Her unpopularity increased and brawls between King's men and York's supporters were now commonplace within the confines of the royal household.

In March, 1458 Henry made a supreme effort to reconcile the Queen and Richard and a service was held in St. Paul's to mark the occasion.

The Queen walked down the aisle with her hand poised on York's but not one member of the vast congregation was phlegmatic enough to believe either of them intended to live amiably together; indeed Buckingham was writing within a few months to Jasper advising the Earl of Pembroke to press forward with the strengthening of the forts he was supervising at Tenby and Denbigh.

' 'The Queen thinks only of enriching herself, her cause is not England's and she does not understand the meaning of justice and fair dealing,' ' Buckingham wrote. ' 'York has instigated a rumour that Prince Edward is no son of Henry's but a bastard fathered on the Queen by a paramour. Margaret of Anjou is so incensed she is riding through the Midlands stirring up support for herself. Keep your men in a state of readiness for I can see no outcome of the business but on the battlefield.' '

Reluctantly, Jasper went again to look to the defences of the Lancastrian strongholds. Margaret assured him she would be safe enough in his absence and he took every precaution for her well being. He made her promise she would not go beyond the confines of the castle.

'Very well,' she agreed. 'But when you come home again you won't forget our rides by the seashore?'

'Of course not.'

It was the summer of 1459 and she had lived at Pembroke for almost four years without once returning to Bletsoe or visiting any part of the vast estate she had inherited on the death of her father when she was barely three years old.

She had first arrived at the castle and thought it grim and forbidding, almost prisonlike in its severity, but with Edmund's love surrounding her she had come to enjoy living within its walls.

When she had been desolated at her husband's death her first instincts had been to confine herself within the castle and nurse the searing pain of her loss. She had not realised, at first, to what lengths Jasper had been to increase the comfort of her apartments but gradually his care and concern and her growing delight in her baby son began to compensate for the tragic bereavement she had suffered.

Little by little she had taken up again the daily life of a great household and employed herself with real interest in her translations and other learning until her half-sister Margery was able to tell Jasper her services were no longer necessary at Pembroke and that she would now return to England and take the veil as she had previously intended.

The invaluable Betsey hovered always in the background, ready, without seeming to be so, to bolster any melancholy in her mistress and give generously of her country-bred wisdom in the rearing of Henry and the little Helen.

Henry was now two and a half, inheriting his father's looks and Margaret's quick intelligence. Helen he tolerated but his mother was the centre of his existence and she had difficulty in keeping herself from spoiling him. Fortunately he was very fond of Jasper and his uncle always set aside part of his day to visit the child. Margaret encouraged this relationship for she knew a fatherless boy could suffer much in later life from the lack of a man's strong hand in his early days.

Despite her gradual recovery and the outwardly calm acceptance of her new life Margaret would still wake in the night and put out her arms to touch Edmund only to draw them hastily away as she remembered she was now alone. Sometimes sleep refused to return after such a rude disappointment and she would lie, cold and unhappy until the morning.

She missed Jasper during his inspections of the forts at Tenby more than she realised. A fact which did not escape the vigilant Betsey as her mistress restlessly threw down her embroidery and took up a manuscript only to discard that a few minutes later to take a cloak and walk on the ramparts.

Margaret was plainly delighted when one of Jasper's squires came to tell her, as they were about to retire for the night, her brother-in-law had returned rather earlier than expected and hoped she would accompany him on the following morning when he rode out.

As he closed the door behind him, Margaret rose from her chair and turning her back to the fire, threw out her arms and stretched luxuriously. She smiled at Betsey; the happiest look her waiting woman had seen for several years.

'Let us go to bed, Betsey. Surely I feel in

my bones Winter is over and the Spring is here!'

The next morning was alive with the earth's vibrancy; the wind blowing in, fresh and strong, from the sea.

The sun shone intermittently, casting ever-moving shadows across the stretches of wild and open country beside the Haven. Gorse glowed in the grasses and foxgloves unfolded in the dells.

Jasper awaited her and led the way down to the sward where the sea lavender bloomed. Keeping close to the wavelets breaking on the shore he spurred his stallion to a gallop. Margaret, exhilarated with the beauty of the day and the pleasure of resuming her excursions, followed him.

They rode for about a mile, Jasper glancing often over his shoulder, exulting in their freedom and breathing lungsful of the salty air.

A flight of curlews flew up under Jasper's horse and as he watched them mass and head towards the open sea he was startled by hearing Margaret cry out in distress.

Turning his horse quickly he saw with dismay Margaret's mare had stumbled and thrown her. Galloping back he found her lying half in and half out of the water. He flung himself down and knelt beside her as the accompanying grooms caught up with them.

She struggled to sit as Jasper bent over her, protesting she was quite unhurt except for a pain in her ankle. She insisted he helped her to stand. After a moment, resting within the circle of his arms to regain her balance, she tried to walk. Involuntarily she winced.

'I think it is more damaged than I thought,' she said with a breathless little laugh.

'Come!' Jasper said and, lifted her to his saddle, leaping up behind her and motioning the men to return to Pembroke ahead of them.

She was very quiet, holding herself stiffly away from him until he tightened his hold and she relaxed little by little until she lay cradled against him.

Jasper rode as fast as he dared without causing her more pain than was necessary. At one and the same time he wanted to reach the castle and give attention to her injury and to remain as they were for ever. He delighted in the scent of her hair and the warmth of her body, never before so close to him. He thought he had never loved her more than when she had stood, the folds of her surcoate dripping in sea water, and tried to walk.

Once inside the Gateway he refused assistance to carry Margaret to her chambers and lifted her with ease from the saddle.

No one answered his knock as he came to her door and he stooped to open it. The rooms were empty.

'My women are with the children — or breaking their fasts,' she said. 'Please put me down, Jasper, I can manage until they return.'

Near the chair in which she usually sat he let her slide gently to the floor. He kept his arms about her and she stayed within his embrace, unmoving, until suddenly she looked up into his face. His heart pounded as they stood thus and he gazed down at her, unsmiling, afraid to breathe and break the spell binding them in the timeless moment. Almost unconsciously he took in her heightened colour, the clear brightness of her beautiful eyes and the swift rise and fall of her breast.

Unheeding of the life of the castle going on beyond the windows of the room he looked at her until unable to exercise the control he had practised for so long, he drew her to him with all his strength and kissed the taut curve of her throat. For an instant her arms were about him and she clung to him before pushing him away and falling, with a low moan, into the chair.

Recovering with difficulty, Jasper knelt at her side and without asking permission drew off the soft, laced boot she wore and examined her ankle. It was already swollen and discolouring. He fetched a basin with water and linen from the garderobe. Tearing some strips he made a pad and bound it to the swelling.

Neither of them spoke. He returned the basin and kneeling once more beside her, took her hand and kissed it with infinite gentleness.

'Will you forgive me?' he asked.

'There is nothing to forgive,' she whispered.

They were silent again while he cradled her hand to his cheek. Her eyes, dark and strained, never left his face.

'I think I know now,' she said quietly, 'why my Confessor and other advisers have written advising me to marry again. Don't!' she said in anguish as Jasper cried out as if she had struck him.

'My father warned this was the wisest course,' he said slowly. 'But it does not make it any easier for me. It is a cruel law of the Church which forbids the union of a man with his brother's widow. No one could have your interest more at heart than I.'

'I know,' she answered, 'and I can never be grateful enough for all the kindness and support you have poured on me during these difficult years since Edmund died. I am sure he would have wished us to marry and although you are different from him, you and I are akin in so many of the ways he and I were.'

'Do you know,' Jasper said musingly. 'I believe I have heard somewhere the Jews have a strict rule that a widow marries her husband's unwed brother as soon as practical. Those strange people have some sound reasoning along with their fanatic beliefs.'

'Perhaps they have had more experience of life's problems than we have in our short period of civilisation.' Margaret said. 'But as we do not embrace their faith we are bound by our own code and cannot take solace from their customs.'

Jasper moved to the casement and looked down into the Outer Ward where men and women hurried about their daily tasks unaware of the emotional storm shaking their master.

'There are so few people who even come to my mind as possible — suitors,' he said at last. 'One hardly knows who to trust these days. To be a King's man, and therefore a Lancastrian, does not presuppose the answering of a call to arms on his behalf should it be necessary.'

189

'You think there will be war then?' she asked swiftly.

'Yes,' he answered reluctantly, 'and so does Buckingham. Buckingham — !'

He brought his disordered thoughts back to an evening many years before when Buckingham's second son had saved him from making a fool of himself when he had learned of Margaret's pregnancy.

'I must have loved you then!' Jasper said wonderingly.

'Did you?' she said in a hushed, still voice.

'Yes; and now I have said it.'

He came back to her and stood looking down at her.

'If Henry Stafford is not yet betrothed, would you take him as your husband?'

He spoke without emotion and she answered in the same manner.

'Yes. I have known him since childhood and my St. John brothers thought well of him. From what I remember he was kindly disposed.' She stopped and then continued with difficulty. 'Will you look to the matter for me?'

He nodded, suddenly unable to speak.

Jasper was barely twenty-eight years of age and Margaret not twenty and in the fullest flower of beauty.

He loved her with all his heart.

'I must go and find your women to help you. I have forgotten you are wet through. God's Bones, I hope you will not take a chill to add to my miseries!'

He stood before her like a boy perplexed with problems beyond his capacity.

She beckoned and he leant over her.

'Jasper! Very dearest Jasper. Thank you. You have restored life's meaning to me. Let us pray, with all our hearts, we are given the strength to enjoy the mutual bond and trust lying between us.'

She put her arms up and about his neck, pulling herself to her feet.

Holding his head she kissed him, without passion, on the mouth.

12

Before Christmas Margaret and Henry Stafford were married.

Jasper, bravely standing behind the couple in the chapel at Pembroke, heard Margaret make her vows through a mist of pain.

At the feast, simple and confined to the very few intimates who had made the journey into Wales, he drank steadily and retired quietly to his room before it ended.

The following morning he left for Trecastle. His main reason for remaining at Pembroke had now gone and he realised he no longer had excuse for absenting himself from active support of the King and Margaret of Anjou.

A month before the wedding the uneasy peace had exploded into a pitched battle between York, Salisbury and Warwick on the one hand and the Queen with her followers on the other. Word had been brought to the King of a gathering of Yorkist supporters at Ludlow where York was spreading false rumours of the death of Henry and his appointment as his heir.

The armies met at Blore Heath and after a

short encounter the King's forces put the rebels to flight.

York fled to Ireland and his son, Edward Earl of March, now nineteen years of age and arrestingly tall and good looking, flew into Devon with Salisbury and Warwick where they took ship for Calais.

Parliament met at Coventry in November. Jasper attended taking with him a large company of men, well accoutred and trained under his own instructions.

The meeting passed peacefully enough but Margaret of Anjou showed her vindictiveness by attainting all the Yorkist supporters present at Blore Heath.

She sent Lord Rivers, who twenty years before had been fined by Gloucester for marrying with Bedford's widow, the Lady Jacquetta of Luxemburg, and his son Anthony Wydeville to Sandwich to prevent any attack from Calais.

Audaciously the young Edward crept into the castle at Sandwich in the night and captured the two Wydevilles. In Calais Rivers called his captors traitors, and was told to hold his tongue as his lowly birth gave him no right to accuse his peers.

In the following year, now quite unhampered and greeted by no less a personage than the Archbishop of Canterbury, Edward,

Salisbury and Warwick landed in Sandwich and marched on London.

Never particularly loyal to Henry, the City was won over to the Yorkish cause. Heartened with this support they turned their armies northward.

Word of their coming reached Henry at Coventry and he and Margaret of Anjou gathered together a formidable force and waited for them in a field beside a nunnery in Northampton.

The rebel earls sent bishops to protest their loyalty but were not believed and despite several more attempts to speak were not allowed to come to the King's presence for fear of treachery.

Edward, Earl of March gave the order to commence battle giving instructions to his men to direct their attack against the nobles.

Victory was theirs as they slew Buckingham, Shrewsbury, Beaumont and Egremont. Henry was forced to sue for a cessation of the fighting and turning his eyes from the slaughter around him received the rebels in his tent.

Jasper was troubled with uprisings in his own territory and was engaged in the retaking of Tenby while this disastrous battle took place.

He met up with a despairing Margaret of

Anjou in Denbigh castle where she fled after the rout.

'Henry has gone to London and called a parliament,' she told him. 'Word has been brought to me he has named York as his successor.'

Jasper regarded her swiftly. Notoriously possessive she would not easily give up the rights to her son. Her next words confirmed his thoughts.

'Even if Henry does give up I shall never relinquish my son's birthright.'

Jasper went with her to Harlech Castle and saw her installed there with a small following and practically no money, for in her flight from Nottingham she had been waylaid and robbed of her treasure chests.

Shortly before Christmas she had gathered by divers means sufficient support to launch a counter attack and surprised the forces of York near Wakefield.

In the encounter York was made prisoner, and Jasper who had been left to guard Wales heard of Margaret's extreme cruelty when she ordered his death and had his head, crowned with a paper diadem, set on spikes on the city wall.

Margaret's army, her young son the Prince of Wales accompanying them, swept southwards leaving a train of plunder, rape and damage behind them. Any popularity she might have acquired was lost overnight.

In Wales, knowledge of a gathering of troops was brought to Jasper and he set out for Ludlow with a large force. Coming to Trecastle he planned to stay a night there and rest his men.

To his dismay he heard Owen had taken as many men as he could muster and had already been gone two days.

Before Mortimer's Cross he fell in with the Earl of Wiltshire and the next morning was engaged with Edward, now Duke of York in his father's stead and Warwick who launched an attack with a force three times the size of the combined armies of Pembroke, Wiltshire and Trecastle.

In the severe fighting that followed, where no quarter was asked or given, three thousand of the Lancastrian supporters were killed.

Among them was Owen. He fought valiantly, his great frame towering above the men about him until his advancing age told on him and momentarily off his guard was overcome and taken prisoner.

Jasper and the Earl of Wiltshire, battling against over-whelming odds, were forced to retire and seek the shelter of the Welsh Hills. Missing his father, Jasper went as quickly as possible to Trecastle, only to be met with the unhappy news of Owen being taken and forced to accompany Edward.

Keeping well out of recognition by the enemy Jasper tracked them down and followed. Coming near to Haverfordwest he was met by a crowd of townsfolk returning from a public beheadal in the market place. It did not need many enquiries to discover the victim. Something in Jasper died as he heard with sickened dismay of his gallant father kneeling to the block with courageous spirit, commending his soul to the God who had given him the blessing of marriage to the perfect wife.

Edward of York had lost no time in taking vengeance for the cruelty Margaret of Anjou had meted out to his own father. The young Duke now made his way to London where he was acclaimed King by popular vote. Henry was deposed and committed to the Tower.

Margaret of Anjou attempted to rally her flagging supporters but although Somerset, Exeter, Northumberland and Roos were at her side she suffered complete defeat and the deaths of many of the nobility accompanying her. Taking her son she fled to Scotland.

Jasper, travelling by night and sleeping by day, came at last to Pembroke. It was now Springtime. With a small band of retainers he went to Monkton Priory and asked for shelter. He was immediately admitted and the door hurriedly shut behind him.

The Prior left him in no doubt of his danger.

'You know you were attainted in Edward's first Parliament?'

'I had heard rumours of all kinds. I hope you will be able to tell me the truth.'

'Sit down my son and I shall have food brought for you while we talk.'

Jasper sat down wearily in the leather backed chair proffered him.

'Before you tell me anything,' he said, 'tell me what has befallen my family in the castle.'

'They are still there,' the Prior told him.

'Then why do I sit here?' Jasper cried jumping up.

'Be at peace, my lord. There is nothing you can do by going there except thrusting your head into the noose.'

'Why?' Jasper demanded.

'The Castle is in the hands of the Yorkists.'

'I suppose I expected that,' Jasper said. 'Who has been given my lands and estates?'

'Sir William Herbert.'

Jasper jumped up banging his fist on the table.

'This is unsupportable!' he cried. 'I must go in this night and kill the man. Is he alone there or are his family with him?' he asked as a new thought struck him.

'Calm yourself, my lord. You will help no one by senseless anger. Try to think reasonably and you will see the usurpation cannot last for ever and you will have your lands again when the King is restored to his throne.'

'Beware, Sir Prior! You speak treason and the winds of Wales may carry your words to Edward's ear. You mistake me if you think it is for my estates I care.'

The Prior regarded him keenly. It was inevitable the long association of the Countess of Richmond and her brother-in-law should be cause for speculation but he had not heeded the gossip and dismissed any guilty meaning in Jasper's words as he heard him now.

He thought for a moment or two.

'If you would care to send word to your family I shall do my best to deliver the message,' he said at length.

Jasper looked at him gratefully.

'But how may this be done?'

'Sir William, Lord Herbert, I should say — '

'*Lord* Herbert?' Jasper queried.

'Yes, he was created so for his support to the late duke of York and the help he gave in putting Edward on the throne.'

Jasper scratched his head.

'It is indeed a changed world. But I interrupt.'

'Lord Herbert has not forbidden the coming and going of monks to the castle and we still take our produce and occasionally assist the Chaplain. It would be easy enough to carry a letter.'

'But it will involve you in considerable danger should it be discovered!'

'We must risk that.'

The following morning one of the lay brothers left with the letter Jasper had spent most of the night writing. Jasper waited for his return with a fervour of impatience.

Ignoring the Prior's warning to keep within the precincts of the place, he climbed the gentle hill behind the Priory and lay in the sweet smelling grass and watched the castle. He was filled with a longing to be once again at peace inside the walls he had thought invincible. He was overwhelmed with a desolation for what might have been and knew if he had been faced at this moment with the problem of the previous year he would unhesitatingly have worked to overcome Margaret's virtue and taken her for himself.

He turned over on his back and lay looking

up at the thin blue sky. It was no use torturing himself with his mistakes. It was the future that mattered and whatever that held he must be prepared to do what he could to help those who had put their trust in him.

Thrusting the nostalgia of yesteryear away from him he went down to the Priory. The brother had not yet returned and Jasper went into the refectory of the hospice and forced himself to eat.

As he pushed the wooden platter from him the lay brother approached and signalled for him to follow him. In the privacy of the deserted cloister he brought out a rolled document from his voluminous robe and handed it to Jasper.

'I cannot thank you enough,' Jasper said.

He took the letter and went to his cell. His hands trembled as he untied the ribbon and broke the seal, still he saw, that of his brother with its quartered arms of England and France.

' 'Jasper,' ' the letter began, ' 'I cannot believe you are so near but beg of you to make no attempt to come to us. We are quite safe and honourably treated and although I am not allowed outside the castle I am permitted to walk on the battlements so can see something of the countryside and life going on below. The children are well and

Herbert is quite attached to Henry and Helen. He and his wife do not impose themselves on me often. You will have heard how he tricked Sir John Scudamore into handing over the castle to him.

' 'I was sad to hear of the savagery of your father's death. Only his gratitude to Henry could have made him take up his quarrel when he should have stayed quietly at Trecastle to enjoy the end of his days. My chief prayer is for your safety and I plead with you to exercise great caution. What a sad pass we have been brought to by the Queen's mishandling and York's greed. Henry, my husband, is not with me for he returned to Kimbolton to look to some matters of his late father's estate and has not as yet been able to come back.

' 'God bless you and grant it may not be long before you are restored to your heritage. Margaret.' '

He reread the letter until he knew it by heart then took it to the kitchens and threw it into the heart of the fire.

He attended evensong and committed those he loved into God's care before taking leave of the Prior.

'I must be on my way from here, for each hour I linger brings the threat of harm to you,' he said.

'Whither are you bound?' the Prior asked.

'I have not really thought, for my sole objective was to reach my home, but it is possible I shall go to the Brecon hills beyond Trecastle. They are practically unchartered and it will be possible to establish some base there from which to communicate with the Queen — and perhaps with yourself, if it would be permitted.'

'Of course,' the Prior told him. 'Your kindness during your occupation of the castle would far outweigh any small favour we may do in return. Let us hope,' he went on, echoing Margaret's words, 'it will not be long before you are once more restored to your rightful home.'

But his hopes and that of Jasper, Margaret and all the other Lancastrians were long in realisation for it was to be nine years before Henry was to regain his throne.

Jasper established a headquarters in Mynydd Eppynt in an enclosed valley well hidden and safe from surprise attack. He sent scouts throughout the breadth of England and Wales. Here news came to him of Margaret of Anjou seeking help from France, where King Louis was her cousin, and obtaining assistance from Pierre de Breze.

When he found her purpose was to land on the Northumberland coast he gathered together with great stealth a force to come to her aid. He arrived in the North to discover the fleet she had chartered with so much difficulty had been wrecked on the treacherous coast.

Other Lancastrian loyalists were in arms, however, and with them Jasper took Bamborough castle and remained there until King Edward beseiged it and finally captured it. When Somerset and Percy threw themselves on the Yorkist's mercy, Jasper and Lord de Roos, disgusted at this volte face, escaped under cover of the night into Scotland.

Here he stayed at the court of the Mary of Gelderland, Regent for her son, who as a niece of the Duke of Burgundy who sought to stay on good terms with King Edward, was friendly, but pleased when he decided to take himself to Anjou where the ex-Queen had set up a small court.

He found Margaret of Anjou at Saint Michel-en-Barrois, dejected, almost in rags but despite the vast number of defeats she had suffered still ready to go back to England and keep the throne for her son. With her were the Duke of Exeter, Somerset's brother, Roos and other knights and dignitaries of the Church including Morton who as Bishop, chaplained her household. She had no money except for a pittance given her grudgingly by

Rene, her father, and she occupied her time in devising means of raising more.

Jasper thought he had never seen a more pitiable sight than the once proud and haughty Queen brought to begging for her food.

At first the news they received from England was completely discouraging. Edward was having great personal success. England greeted this handsome young man as a deliverer who would save them from cruel bloodshed and the wavering rule of Henry.

Women found him irresistible until he met Elizabeth Wydeville, daughter of the peer whom Warwick found unfit to criticise him at Calais. She was lately widowed and refused to sell herself as many others had done before her and stuck out until Edward finally married her in desperation.

Now a faint ripple of trouble reached the court of Margaret at St. Michel for Warwick liked the daughter no more than he had cared for her father and he had, at the time of the marriage, — very secretly performed — been negotiating delicately for the hand of a French princess for Edward.

He came back to England in a towering rage with his protégé and set about Edward's belittlement by enlisting Clarence, the King's younger brother, to his side with a wedding to his elder daughter Isobel Neville.

Edward, lost in the clouds of popularity, did not heed the warnings and infatuated with his wife, heaped honours and illustrious marriages upon her many brothers and sisters.

The final break with Warwick came when Edward persisted, against his old friend's advice, in marrying his own sister to the Duke of Burgundy.

Warwick left England and came to Calais.

Gathering together a following he landed once more at Sandwich, but this time to war against Edward, whom he had helped to become King.

Kentish men followed him north and meeting up with Clarence he surprised Edward and took him into captivity in Warwick Castle.

Margaret of Anjou, hearing of the dissension from her court at St. Michel had sent Jasper, only too willing to return to Wales the previous year.

He had raised an army with ease and took Denbigh once more for the Lancastrians but coming to Harlech found Herbert awaiting him with an overwhelming force. Although he led his men into the fight with considerable courage he quickly realised the day was lost and withdrew before any great casualties were inflicted on his men.

Warwick returned to France and Louis affected what his advisers said was impossible and reconciled Margaret of Anjou and the dissatisfied Warwick.

Jasper, smarting under the granting of his earldom to Herbert, who had styled himself Pembroke, made his peace with Warwick also.

He landed with the Earl in Devon on 13th September, 1470.

Their supporters grew as they progressed to London. Clarence brought troops to add to those brought from France and it was a formidable force of which Edward, released from Warwick, heard for the first time as he pursued his usual course of indulgence at Westminster. Caught completely unprepared to resist any attack he raced for the East Coast and sailed for the court of his sister in Flanders.

The first task of Warwick and his followers was to release Henry from the Tower.

They found him wasted and illkempt.

When he had had a chance to reorientate himself and realise he was once more head of State, Jasper, who saw personally to the finding of clean linen and raiment for his half brother, begged permission to visit Woking.

For it was in her Manor south of the

Thames that the Lady Margaret had been granted permission to live and take her son and niece.

Jasper rode to her almost unable to believe they were to meet again after so many weary, wasted years.

13

Jasper sent his Herald ahead of him to announce his coming and dressed with especial care. His squires, handing him clothes he had not worn since he left England, thought he had not changed overmuch during his exile. His face was slightly thinner but he had lost none of the splendid physique which singled him from other men. He had not grown slovenly during his years of privation and had turned the enforced absence to his advantage.

While they had lived a hand to mouth existence in the mountain fastness of Wales he had made himself expert in the ways of wildlife and later in France had endeavoured to resume his scholastic interests. He developed a patience he had not known existed.

However, as he approached through the pleasant wooded countryside, the manor of Woking he found his fortitude deserting him. Despite his maturity he felt like a youth visiting his beloved and trembled inwardly at the prospect of finding Margaret changed towards him. He heard none of the conversation of those who accompanied him and thought only of looking upon the face that had haunted his dreams and waking hours since he had been reft from her side in 1461.

He was met by her comptroller of the Household, William Bedell and although he spoke with him had no memory of what was said. He followed the man to Margaret's parlour, which seemed at first sight, full of people. He saw none of them, his eyes drawn to her only.

He knew, as his heart lurched in his breast, she was more lovely than he remembered. She held herself with dignity and appeared poised and collected. He came swiftly and fell on one knee before her. Taking her hand it trembled in his grasp and he realised in a swift upsurge of joy her control was outward only. Unseen except to themselves he turned her palm to his mouth and kissed it, folding her fingers inward.

'My husband,' she said as he stood.

Henry Stafford greeted him warmly. He seemed to Jasper slighter and more aesthetic than before but he was obviously pleased to see Jasper.

'We are delighted you are able to return to England. Will you be able to retrieve your inheritance?'

'Yes. My brother has seen fit to restore me to my Earldom and remove the attainder placed upon me by Edward.'

'That is good news indeed. Let us pray England may now enjoy a time of peace.'

'Let us hope so,' Jasper said, although the remembrance of his frail half-brother did not encourage his optimism. He turned as Margaret touched his arm lightly.

'This is my son,' she said.

At her side Henry, Earl of Richmond, stood gravely regarding his uncle. He was a tall boy, fair haired and blue eyed.

He bent his knee to Jasper who put both hands on the child's shoulders and helping him rise, kissed his cheek. Henry smiled and Jasper saw, with nostalgic affection, the resemblance to his long dead brother. Glancing at Margaret he knew she understood for she closed her eyes momentarily.

'And this,' she said, as she once again put her hands on his sleeve, 'is Helen.'

Her grasp tightened as a young girl came towards him and curtseyed. Straightening, she presented her upturned face for his salute. He stood almost paralysed as he was flung back over the years to the haunted passion of his youth.

'Father!' the girl said gently as he continued to stare at her.

'My child!' he murmured embracing her.

Margaret's pressure on his arm relaxed and he looked towards her with gratitude. She turned away quickly but Jasper saw the glimmer of tears. Suddenly he wanted to shout at all those crowding the room to go and leave them alone so that he could take her in his arms and feel her tears on his face and the warm comfort of her body against his own. He restrained himself with difficulty realising he was under her roof with her husband beside her. Stafford's devotion for his wife was plain and Jasper pitied him and envied him in one savage moment.

Curbing himself he spoke to each man and woman as they were presented to him, remembering some of them from Pembroke. Betsey Massey greeted him with deference touched with something he could only define as a faint sense of relief. There were several priests and learned men of the company who he assumed to be tutors to the young people of the household.

He went through the motions of the evening in a state approaching torpor. It was as if he stood aside and watched his actions performed by someone else. He made polite conversation and forced himself to concentrate on what was said while he longed to be with Margaret or failing that, alone in his bedchamber where he could assess the day's events.

At any other time he would have been deeply interested in all that had transpired since he had gone to France but nothing seemed as important as speaking with Margaret.

He had begun to think he would have to return to London before he had an opportunity of talking with her when, on his second day at Woking, she sent a page to him, asking him to accompany her on her usual evening walk through the formal gardens of the manor.

He followed the boy to the hedged path where he found her, well wrapped against the cold, accompanied by Betsey Massey.

As they met the woman excused herself and returned to the house saying she had much needing her attention. The page went with her.

Without speaking Margaret took his hand and led him to the boundary of the garden where a bonfire smouldered in glowing embers. He stood looking at her in the firelight, her eyes luminous, her mouth slightly parted.

With a low exclamation Jasper turned away from her and leant on the parapet of the stone wall marking the garden's end. She came to his side and without touching him rested her arms beside him.

'I have dreamed of this moment through all the miseries and discomforts of the years since I went away and now when there is so much to ask you I do not know where to begin or what to say,' he said helplessly.

'It is enough you are returned,' she said quietly. 'What has happened is past and can wait for retelling.'

'I would speak to you as a lover and that is denied me, but must ask you — are you happy, my dearest Margaret?'

'Happy?' she echoed. 'How does one measure happiness, Jasper? Is it even necessary to appraise it? Is it not enough to have experienced it and keep it in your heart? Edmund made me happy enough to last all my life and you have heaped the richness of your affection upon me. That was sufficient to help me while we have been apart. I have always felt surrounded with the comfort of your — love.'

He was silent, then leaning back against the wall he took her hands and drew her towards him until she stood facing him but apart.

'And Stafford?'

'Stafford is a devoted husband. I am fortunate to have been married to a man of his gentle and kindly disposition.'

'And your other children?'

'Other children?' she said slowly. 'Other children? Oh, Jasper, I have no other. Henry is my only child!'

He stared at her in astonishment.

'I should have known!' he shouted in exultation. 'I should have known.'

She smiled at him, shaking her head slightly at his impetuosity. He tightened his grip on her hands and pulled her nearer.

'And you?' she asked softly. 'Helen has no brothers and sisters?'

'No,' he answered. 'There is only one woman I would lie with and if I cannot have you I want no other.'

'But you have no heir.'

'That can wait,' he said tersely.

He undid the clasp of his cloak and drew her into the shelter of his body for the fire had died away and he saw her shiver.

She did not resist but stood close to him her hands clasped under her bosom.

'Margaret,' he said quietly, touching her cheek gently, 'if it were not as it is, wouldst thou lie with me?'

'Yes,' she whispered so low he only just heard. 'In God's eyes I am certain it would have been no sin for you and I to have wed.'

Pushing back the furred hood of her green

velvet mantle he kissed the tendrils of hair at her temples.

'You are wise, my sweet Margaret and teach me more of God's love in a sentence than I learnt from monks or nuns during my childhood. When we are apart I shall only have to recall those words to be with you again.'

'Will you have to go soon?'

'Yes, I must not be long absent from Henry.'

'I suppose that must be so, but now that you are come to me again I cannot bear the thought of you going away.'

His arms tightened around her and she was quiet for a long moment. Then she sighed and looked up into his face.

'Do you think it is wise for Henry, my son, to go to school?'

'Do you not think his tutors are sufficient?'

'It is not that so much, but I think he would benefit from the company of other boys. Lacking a father, and you not with us, he has had too much of my company.'

'Was it hateful for you with Herbert in command at Pembroke?'

'I thought at first I should not be able to bear it. I was filled with longing for the days that had gone, but Herbert treated us kindly enough and went out of his way to see we had

216

sufficient warmth and food. When he died we slipped quietly away with the help of your many friends in the neighbourhood and living quietly on my own lands we have been left unmolested.'

'Was it true Herbert tried to force you to sign a marriage agreement with his daughter and your son?'

'Yes, he even left a clause in his Will to that effect,' Margaret said with a chuckle.

'Damned impertinence!' Jasper laughed, 'but he must have liked the boy for there was not much advancement to be gained by wedding into such a Lancastrian family!'

'Yes, I think he did have a strange affection for Henry. It seems extraordinary that he should have died at the hand of Warwick when they had been such close friends and followers of York.'

'Were they so close?' Jasper asked. 'There has been much talk of jealousy and self advancement. Who knows who is one's friend and who one's foe. Would you have been able to conceive of Warwick marrying one of his daughters to Margaret of Anjou's son?'

'That seemed beyond the realms of possibility when we heard the news. I suppose it is true?'

'Quite true! When one remembers how Warwick slandered the Queen in the past it takes much believing, but I was present when Anne and Edward were married.'

'What is Margaret of Anjou's son like?'

'Completely different from your Henry, I should think. He has no great charm and living so much with his mother has become imbued with her ideas of vengeance and intrigue. He has been known to be cruel also. By and large he is not very popular, but he is the King's heir and as Prince of Wales he claims a certain loyalty.'

'What you have said bears out what I think about a mother not being the best person to rear a son and I am glad you think my suggestion of school for Henry a good one.'

'There are mothers and mothers,' Jasper said. 'And by what I have seen of Henry in the short time I have been here you have done very well by him. But let us not speak so much of others, it is of you I would know.'

While they had been talking she had unclasped her hands and put her arms around his waist, resting her head on his shoulder.

'I must be returning, Jasper. Your homecoming has unnerved me more than I should have thought possible and I find now we are together I do not want to be anywhere else. This, after I had begun to believe I had taught myself a discipline, is upsetting to say the least.'

'Discipline?' Jasper asked her.

'Yes, I thought perhaps it would be possible to spend the rest of my days in the pursuit of knowledge and in helping others to obtain it, but one moment in your company was sufficient to tell me this was not all life has to offer.'

'I should think not!' Jasper said indignantly. 'You are much too young to be thinking in that way. You must live now that your existence will be easier.'

'How live?' she asked. 'With you in adultery? No that is not how it must be for you and me.'

She turned away from him looking into the dark which had crept unseen about them.

'Will you ride out with me before I return?'

She disengaged herself gently and pulling her hood closely about her face nodded.

Together they walked slowly back to the house and coming to the cresset light over the garden entrance stood unwilling to part. At last Jasper stooped and kissed her lightly on the brow and opened the door for her to enter.

He spent the night with little sleep, filled with perplexed longings for the wife of Henry Stafford. He surprised himself by realising that although he craved possession of her body he could be content with the mere presence of her being with him. They were bound with deep rooted ties to make them self sufficient, in a state where others became superfluous. From the moment when he came into her room after Edmund's tragic death and she became his in the instant of throwing herself upon his pity they were as one in a marriage owing nothing to the Church. Yet he could not find it in his heart to hate Henry Stafford or even envy him the privilege of taking Margaret to his bed. What she gave her husband in the privacy of the marital chamber was as nothing to the brief exchanges of eye meeting eye.

They rode out together on the morning of his departure to Westminster, talking very little but stopping now and again beside a pool or hushed glade to hold hands and delight in the simple pleasure of being alive and sharing the gift with one another.

Before they parted he told her he was riding into Wales after Epiphany but that Henry had expressed the wish she would come to Windsor to share the first Christmas of his restoration.

She gave him the most radiant smile he had seen since his return and promised to be there with her family.

They parted, buoyed with the prospect of a further meeting.

He arrived late at the Castle on Christmas Eve and supped in his room with several friends he had not seen for the years of his exile but rose early and when he entered the small chapel saw she was already kneeling before the altar.

It was cold in the stone place, his breath hanging on the chill air. Two large new candles burnt at the steps. He remembered as if it were yesterday the night he and Edmund had spent kneeling on the hard ground as they passed the vigil of their knighting. Not for the first time he wondered how he would have contended with the problem of loving his brother's wife had Edmund lived.

He was glad when the Chaplain came in followed by a robed acolyte and the well known words flowed around him bringing their own peculiar peace.

Later they exchanged the gifts they had preserved from St. Nicholas' Day and Jasper was touched to receive from his daughter a cushion she had made for him embroidered with the arms of Pembroke. He had sought among his depleted possessions for a suitable gift for her and had come upon, in the deepest corner of an iron bound box, the necklace he had given her mother almost twenty years before. He had taken it to a jeweller in the Chepe who had burnished it until the gold and stones glowed once more.

Helen was overcome with the magnificence of the jewels and clasped it around her throat with obvious pride and pleasure. Jasper had had more opportunity to watch his child and he saw now the resemblance that had at first overcome him was mainly about the eyes and that in most other respects she took after him rather than Mevanvy. She was a pleasing girl, graceful and sensible with none of the necromancy of her dead mother. Jasper recognised the hand of Margaret in her upbringing and applauded their joint taste in the choice of her wardrobe and the perfection of her manners.

He was equally impressed by his young nephew who followed him whenever he was permitted. Henry of Richmond was likeable and intelligent without being precocious, affectionate towards Jasper and devoted to Margaret. He deferred to his uncle and sought his advice on matters he thought too personal to discuss with his mother. Jasper was flattered and intrigued. The boy made light of his imprisonment at the hands of Herbert and turned the conversation to ask Jasper about his exile in Wales and France.

King Henry, looking better than on his

release from the Tower, wearing a new robe in his favourite blue velvet but without other adornment, acted the perfect host. The feast following the morning's worship was plentiful and well prepared. The Lancastrian Lords summoned to partake of it raised the rafters of the Hall with songs and excited chatter. Jasper found himself placed next to Margaret on the dais and the surrounding noise became a barrier shutting them away from the rest of the world. With difficulty Jasper kept the curtain apart as it threatened to isolate them from their fellow guests and listened with all the courtesy he was able to summon to the conversations of those placed nearby. But he did not permit her to leave the table with the other ladies before he had extracted a promise from her to meet him on the battlements after compline.

He waited beside the man at arms keeping watch, close to a brazier in a corner of the south wall, for some time before he saw her approaching. He felt no anxiety for her lateness in arriving for he did not doubt having given her word she would disappoint him.

Jasper dismissed the soldier telling him he would take his hour of duty and as the man gratefully clanked away Margaret came up to him. She was wearing the same velvet mantle she had worn at Woking but she let the hood fall back as she raised her face for his kiss.

Jasper drew her into the protection of the buttress where the glow from the charcoal fire played on the folds of her skirt and threw shadows on the stone wall behind them. She did not demur as he took the netted band from her hair and it tumbled about her shoulders. His eyes clouded with love he stroked her cheek and ran his hands through the rich tresses, murmuring her name. With a sigh she nestled against him seeking the protection of his strength.

They stayed there, lost to the passage of time, talking very little and then only of the shared past, each lapped in the warm comfort of the others benevolence until they heard the distant clink of metal on the stone stairway of the turret. Without haste Margaret plaited her hair and Jasper pulled up the hood and tied it beneath her chin. He kissed her forehead lightly and she left him as the man at arms returned.

It became their custom over the twelve days of Christmas to meet each evening and they hunted with the other guests when the ground was not too frozen. By unspoken consent they agreed to ride alone on the last day of Jasper's stay.

Before they set out Jasper took his nephew to King Henry's College of our Lady of Eton beside Windsor where the King had been only too happy to find a place for Margaret's son. Young Richmond had made a good impression on his fellow Lancastrians during the Christmas festivities and several of the ladies and younger members of the party gathered at the Gatehouse to bid him good fortune in his new life.

Jasper led the boy to the chambers of the Provost who sent for a clerk to show the new commensale his place in the long dormitory. Henry of Richmond took his leave of Jasper with sincere affection, kneeling to receive his blessing.

When he had gone the Provost turned to Jasper.

'He seems a very fine young man,' he said. 'If his scholarship equals his charm of manner he should do well here.'

'I am glad of that. As you know he is a fatherless boy and his mother is anxious she shall not spoil him.'

'There does not appear to be much fear of that,' William Waynefleet said, smiling. 'Will you accompany his Grace when he comes down here for the traditional Shrovetide feast?'

'If I am returned from Pembroke and his

Grace has no other duties for me I shall come with pleasure.'

Returned to the castle he sent a page to advise Margaret he would await her in the stable yard. He inspected the girths and harness with the groom and when she came helped her to the side-sitting saddle of her mare. He shook his head when the men asked if they were needed and spurring his horse they cantered out over the drawbridge and through the few houses to the rolling wooded hillside.

'Henry was quite happy when I left him,' he assured her. 'If you wish to visit him it will be possible on Shrove Tuesday when the Court will be at Windsor and the King goes to the College.'

There was no wind and the bare trees and bushes stood motionless under a light covering of frost. Once free of the castle precincts they did not hurry until they came into a cleared way leading up to a distant hilltop.

'I'll race you there!' Margaret cried.

'No falling off this time,' Jasper warned her. 'One damaged ankle in a lifetime is enough!'

'I'll be careful,' she said laughing and urged her mare forward. Jasper let her go and then seeing her breast the foot of the rise galloped after her. He drew level as they began the descent on the other side. She reined in and sat gazing out over the grey distance of massed forest. The stillness deepened and the only noise came from the cracking of twigs beneath the feet of the horses. Jasper leant over and pulled Margaret to sit in front of him, holding her closely against him.

'Tomorrow you will be gone,' she said tonelessly.

'Yes, there is much needing my attention; Courts to hold and cases which have been in abeyance awaiting judgement. Rest assured, dearest Margaret, I shall do my best to come back to you, perhaps for Shrovetide.'

She put her head back on his, their cheeks touching.

'Will you say goodbye to me here?' he asked her. 'I could not bear to bid thee farewell before the household.'

He dismounted and held up his arms to help her slide to the ground. The horses moved restlessly for a moment and then stood still.

They stood facing one another until Margaret lifted her face for his kiss. He touched her eyes with his lips and she closed them, breathing deeply.

Suddenly he pulled her to him, his mouth on hers. She moved her head in an effort to evade his caress but his hold tightened. In the next instance as her body stiffened against him he knew she was crying.

Immediately contrite he relaxed his embrace and she swayed against him.

'Jasper, oh Jasper.'

He held her gently until she had recovered a little, comforting her with endearments and soothing words.

'That was unpardonable of me,' he said at last. 'I know you will forgive me, but it was still wrong. It was the thought of parting with you yet again and wanting you so very much.'

'It is I who am to blame,' she answered. 'It is I and not you who needs to seek forgiveness.'

Margaret raised her eyes, their brilliance dimmed with the conflict of emotions she was suffering, and putting her arms behind Jasper's neck, kissed him on the mouth.

Standing away from him they looked at each other.

'Take me back,' she begged.

He called her mount and helped her to the saddle. She sat, dejected and pale, not looking away from him. During the sad journey back through the woods neither of them spoke.

As the small huddle of dwellings came in sight he caught her bridle and pulled her mare close to his horse.

'There is no need for me to tell you if you want my help I shall come at once.'

'No, there is no need. I trust you more than any person in the world.'

He left for Wales on the following morning, before the inhabitants of the castle were stirring.

He had taken his supper alone on the previous evening avoiding a further meeting with Margaret. She had shocked him as they rode into the stableyard by suggesting it would help them both if he found himself a wife. He was glad the yard was full of people as the significance of what she said sank in for had they been alone he felt sure he would not have been answerable for his actions. He was startled by the vehemence of his rejection of her advice and his anger did not leave him until his party reached the hospice of St. Albans.

Weary and dispirited he threw himself down on the straw-filled mattress. In the pervading quiet of the darkness he gradually acknowledged he had been rubbed raw, not with her for the wisdom of what she had said, but with himself for not wishing to admit she was right.

But I shall not marry, he told himself fiercely, while my senses cry out to mate with her. The heir of Pembroke must remain unbegotten as yet.

14

Coming through the narrow street of Pembroke and climbing the sharp mound to the Gate House, Jasper experienced a sense of dismay when he realised he would be alone in his home without those who had previously made up his household.

He was greeted by Sir John and Lady Scudamore who appeared sheepish and decidedly anxious to please. Jasper thought the Lady somewhat stiffer than he remembered and sought in his mind for a reason for her diffidence.

To his delight, he had not been many hours in Pembroke when his friends from Kidwelly, Coedcantilais and the Bishopric of St. David sent servants to say they intended coming to his courts when he held them.

When they came their pleasure at his reinstatement was genuine and unfeigned. Butler of Coedcantilais soon told him the cause of Lady Scudamore's coldness. It appeared Jasper had sentenced her father, Gruffudd ap Nicholas, at an Oyer and Terminer he had held during the last months of his stay at Pembroke nearly nine years ago, and the man had been smarting under the decision ever since.

'It has split the family at Carew and caused quite a feud,' Butler said with a chuckle, which came somewhere from the depths of his rounded belly. 'His grandsons are divided among themselves on the issue. Morgan ap Thomas is definitely sided with Gruffudd, but David refuses to move from his loyalty to you, while Rys professes himself staunchly loyal to his own. It is common gossip Morgan and David have not spoken for years!'

'I cannot imagine brothers fighting among themselves,' Jasper said wonderingly. 'But it is regrettably true it happens all too frequently.'

Bearing in mind the outcome of this previous judgement he made a great effort to give proper hearing to the myriad of cases brought before him.

The days, turning warmer as the Spring came on the west winds, troubled him not at all, for he was busier than he had been for years. It was the nights he dreaded when he retired to the comfortless, luxurious chambers that were his own. He invited friends and stayed up drinking with them until he saw their eyes glazed with sleep and reluctantly had them lighted to their own quarters; but it still was of no avail for his empty bedchamber mocked him with the promise of what might have been.

Lying sleepless he was haunted with fantasies of Margaret in his arms until he was forced to the conclusion that if he did not overcome his longing for her he would go out of his mind.

He was glad when at last the hearings came to an end and he could set out again for Westminster. He found himself almost detesting the home he had once cared so much about.

He made the journey, with a strong escort reinforced by several followers anxious to identify themselves with his banner, at his customary speed. Those new to his methods were soon saddle sore but kept up gamely with the older retainers rather than appear lily-livered.

Arrived at Westminster he found letters awaiting him from Henry at Windsor and from Margaret of Anjou who still delayed her homecoming on one pretext or other. She begged him to keep a strong army at instant readiness to protect Henry should the need arise. She told him she was gradually gaining support from Louis of France, who painfully slowly handed over to her a growing number of troops.

His half-brother's letter pleaded with him to come to him and give him his support. He left at once for Windsor.

Arrived at the Castle he presented himself immediately to Henry and it was with difficulty he suppressed an exclamation of dismay for the King had deteriorated considerably since Christmas. Jasper had not been with him for half an hour before he realised his brother was less capable than ever of reigning. He had no true grasp of the political scene and seemed bewildered by the change in his fortunes. When he spoke of Warwick a confused look came into his eyes. He talked much of his soul and the need for man to become acquainted with God's purpose and showed the only flicker of interest in any other subject when Jasper mentioned the impending visit to Eton for Shrove Tuesday.

'That is why I wanted you here,' Henry said pathetically. 'I needed you to accompany me.'

Jasper left him, saddened by Henry's plaintive belief that once his wife came to join him his troubles would be over. For he honestly thought Margaret of Anjou would take upon herself the problems of government and leave him alone to spend his hours in the contemplation of immortality.

It would have been easier to bear if Jasper could see about his brother men capable of helping him, but he appeared to be surrounded with men of the Church and elderly statesmen who were as much out of touch with the present situation as their master.

Later, over wine, in the anteroom of the Hall, Jasper expressed his anxieties to Oxford and Exeter, only to have them confirm his fears.

'Where is Warwick?' Jasper asked. 'He should be here to bolster the King.'

'He has gone to his estates but is expected to return when the King goes to Westminster later in the month.'

'Have you news of Margaret of Anjou?' Oxford asked Jasper.

'She writes simply to say she is collecting together mercenaries from France and will join the King as soon as she is able.'

'Henry is pitifully eager to have her return. Do you suppose there is any likelihood of him abdicating in favour of Prince Edward?'

'Abdicating?' Jasper reiterated. 'I had not thought of such a thing. What are your views?'

'He so dislikes Kingship nothing would surprise me; but I have never considered he had any particular affection for his son and not having seen him for so many years will not have come to care for him any better.'

'Do you think he really is his son?' Exeter asked with a quick glance over his shoulder.

The other men shrugged their shoulders.

'Had the boy been born during Suffolk's lifetime I should have had grave doubts on his parentage but as it is I think we must give the Queen the benefit of the doubt.'

'Edward must be eighteen years of age now, he would certainly be of an age to come to the throne.'

Before he went with Henry and the Court to the King's College at Eton, Jasper received a messenger from Woking. He bore a sealed missive from Margaret in which she told him she had visited her son during the previous week and thought it unwise to go so soon again to see him.

' 'I am delighted to find him settled and apparently happy in his new surroundings. I wish I could find it in my heart to tell you that I am as glad to be without those I love. The awakening Spring stirs me with troubled longings and it becomes difficult to concentrate on the many tasks needing my attention. God be with you and grant you health and a tranquil mind. Margaret.' '

Jasper thanked the man with a wry smile and penned a hasty reply, telling her he would write further when he had had an opportunity to see for himself how Henry of

Richmond was faring.

At Eton he accompanied the King on a tour of inspection. Many improvements had been carried out since the Founder had visited the place and he was pleased with what he saw. Finishing with the Choir of the Chapel they were led by Waynefleet to the school room to meet the boys.

On his way across the paved courtyard Henry walked with Jasper.

'It is good to discover Edward of York did not curtail my plans here. One would not expect a man so concerned with the vanities of life to be interested in a place of learning, but he might have seen fit to change something because it was my conception.'

While Jasper made some non-committal reply the King went on.

'It will be interesting to see how our nephew is progressing with his studies. I am disappointed his mother is not with us today for the feast but I understand she came down to visit him quite recently. How sad it was our brother died and left her a widow so young. It was, I always think, a great pity the Church's Law precluded your marriage with her for in that manner the fortunes of our two houses would always have remained as one interest.'

Jasper did not reply, turning his head to hide the expression on his face and Henry continued, looking sharply towards him.

'But it was most fortunate you were able to arrange the Buckingham marriage for her, even if the family is suspect of Yorkist leanings since Henry Stafford's nephew, the young Duke, was married to Catherine Wydeville, sister of Edward's Queen.'

'Edward's Queen has given birth to a son,' Jasper interposed hurriedly to change the subject. 'I hear they are to remain in Sanctuary at Westminster. This is surely most generous of you. Would it not be wiser to send them to Bruges to Edward?'

'No, no!' Henry said shaking his head. 'What harm can there be in giving succour to a defenceless woman and a new born babe.'

Jasper was relieved they had now arrived at the classroom because he knew he was not alone in feeling anxiety for Henry's forbearance in allowing his rival's wife to stay in England where it was almost certain she would attract sympathy for herself, her seven-year-old daughter and the new son.

The scholars and commensales were drawn up in lines to receive their royal patron, faces shining with scrubbing and hair neatly brushed.

Henry went down the rows stopping to speak to each boy. When he came to Henry of Richmond he beckoned Jasper to join him.

The Earl of Richmond knelt swiftly.

'How does our nephew progress?' the King asked of the hovering Provost.

Jasper saw a pink flush creep up Richmond's neck as the Provost answered.

'Well enough, Your Grace. He applies himself with diligence and shows a true interest in the acquisition of knowledge.'

Richmond looked up at Jasper who drooped an eyelid in a conspiritorial wink. Jasper saw the child's mouth quiver as he suppressed a grin.

'Then the Lady Margaret may be justly proud of the tuition she has provided for her son. It must be good news indeed for a parent to learn his child applies himself well. I wish it were possible to say the same thing about my own son. From all accounts I judge him to be fond of the sword rather than the pen.'

The Provost, somewhat embarrassed by this confidence of the King, presented another boy and Henry resumed his tour of inspection.

Seated later in the Refectory Jasper was at table with his nephew.

'I am sorry Mother was not here this day to be with us both. Have you seen her since you returned from Wales?'

'No,' Jasper answered, a little shortly. 'But I

had word from her to say she had visited you recently and would be staying at Woking for Shrovetide.'

'She looked a little tired to me,' Henry said as a servant placed a loaded trencher before them. 'But she complained of nothing. Sir Henry Stafford had suffered a bout of the ague. I expect she was tired with nursing him, don't you, Uncle Jasper?'

'Very probably,' Jasper agreed drily. 'Did she say how Helen is?'

'Very well, I think. Mother said she believes she misses me sometimes, but I shall be able to go home at the end of term time,' the boy said naïvely. 'Do you think we shall ever be all together again at Pembroke?'

'Do you like it there?'

'Very much. There is something quite different about Pembrokeshire that sets it apart from the English countryside. Perhaps it was because I was born there it calls me so strongly. Do you agree with me, Uncle Jasper?'

'Yes, I do,' Jasper told him. 'When I was a boy at Hatfield I dreamt of going to Wales and when at last I came there, it was every bit as good as I had hoped.'

They spent the rest of the long meal talking about the far off days of Jasper's childhood. Henry of Richmond listened with particular eagerness to what his uncle told him of Edmund.

'Was my father like you to look at?'

'Better looking, fortunately for him,' Jasper said, laughingly.

'That must have made him very handsome!'

'He loved my mother very much didn't he?'

'Yes, he did and she him.'

The boy was quiet for a moment and then he turned his candid eyes to Jasper.

'Strangely enough,' he said gruffly, 'in my mind my father and you always seem the same person to me.'

'Thank you,' Jasper replied levelly.

On the short ride back to Windsor several of the men of the party complimented him on the youth's bearing.

'Henry of Richmond will be a most useful addition to the supporters of the King,' Oxford told him. 'The throne can do with supporters of his calibre.'

Within the next few days the need of this support was urgently underlined when Margaret of Anjou sent hasty word to tell the English Council of Louis' decision to declare war on Burgundy. The French King could not have chosen a more dangerous moment to make war on a sovereign directly opposed to the reigning King of England.

Messengers were despatched hurriedly to Warwick to implore the Duke to hasten his plans to bring home the English Queen to the support of her husband.

After consultation with Oxford and the other Lancastrian lords Jasper left at the same time for the Welsh Marches to recruit an army to be ready for any emergency. The only pleasure he gained out of the enforced departure was the removal of the dilemma of knowing whether or not to go down to Woking and see Margaret. It was now impossible.

He spent every waking hour riding the length and breadth of Wales rousing support for Henry of Lancaster. He was returning to the hospice in Hereford when news was brought to him of the landing of Edward of York, with his brother, Richard, Duke of Gloucester, in the small port of Ravenspur in Yorkshire.

'Edward? Landed?' Jasper asked incredulously of the courier who brought him the unwelcome tidings. 'With how many men?'

'About two thousand, but from all accounts he is gaining considerable support as he comes southwards.'

'Who is letting him through?'

'His own people in Yorkshire to whom he claims he is but returning to come into his rightful inheritance.'

'What of my lords Shrewsbury and Neville? Why do they not stop him?'

'My lord,' the man said, 'with no disrespect to my lord Warwick, while he issues the orders no man hastens to obey.'

'But that is ridiculous!' Jasper cried. 'If Edward of York is not stopped he will be in London before long!'

He intensified his own recruiting, hoping to hear daily of Margaret of Anjou landing with the strong forces she had been promising. But he learnt with something approaching despair within a few days that not only had she not come but that three Lancastrian forces under Oxford, Montagu and other captains had been outwitted near Newark.

He now sent a strong party under a captain with a chaplain and two of his own squires to bring Henry and Margaret, if she so desired, to the safety of Pembroke.

Word came almost immediately he had done this of the defection of the Duke of Clarence from Warwick to the side of his brother Edward of York. It appeared he had forgotten the promises he had made Warwick when he had married his daughter. With his forces allied to the already formidable ones of York and Gloucester the prospect for the Lancastrian cause looked bleak indeed.

Jasper prayed as he had never done before that his sister-in-law and her son should be allowed to reach the haven of Pembroke.

Sleeping only a few snatched hours during the night, he garnered men to his side and heard with relief of Margaret of Anjou at last setting sail for England. He waited impatiently to receive word from her captains of the place he was to meet up with them.

Before this information reached him he learnt Edward of York had reached London, always enthusiastically Yorkist, and had taken Henry, the King, once more into captivity.

Margaret of Anjou landed in Weymouth on the same day as her ally Warwick's forces clashed with York's at Barnet. Warwick was defeated in a fight carried on in mists swirling in confusion through the opposing armies. Slain, the body of the once proud Earl was carried to St. Paul's and exposed to the public gaze. Edward of York was allowing for no mistakes.

When Margaret of Anjou heard of the rout of Warwick, she, with her son the Prince of Wales, turned for Exeter. Her heralds went before her to bring Jasper and the other nobles who had promised her their support to her side.

Jasper and Edward of York learnt of her

arrival at the same moment and each set out to meet her.

Leaving the temporary headquarters he had set up in the Hospice of Hereford, a scouting party he had despatched east in the night, came into report Henry of Richmond's party coming to meet him from Ledbury. He sent them back to tell the Captain of the force to await him at Hulme Lacy.

When he came to the place he halted only briefly to greet his nephew.

'Is your mother not come with you?' he asked not seeing Margaret.

'Yes, she came with me as far as Ledbury, but she told me to tell you she would not hinder you at this moment and has gone straight to Pembroke.'

'Why did you not go with her?' demanded Jasper.

'My Lord Uncle, I am almost a grown man and my place is with you,' Henry said gravely.

'Honourable sentiments, but I could wish you had accompanied your mother. She took strong protection?'

'Yes, my lord,' the captain assured him, 'I saw to it she was well guarded and had guides versed in the secret routes to Pembroke.'

'Let us pray she goes unhindered and no spy of York's has followed your party. Go you, young Henry, with the Chaplains and remain at the rear of the army unless I give orders for you to do otherwise.'

Henry of Richmond looked swiftly at Jasper and reading what he saw went meekly to the waggons at the train.

Jasper concentrated on encouraging his troops and pushed his private worries to the back of his mind. He spent the day riding up and down among the ranks.

Scouts came to him during all the hours of daylight with confused reports of Edward's and Margaret of Anjou's armies converging on the town of Gloucester, but night fell with no definite news. Under cover of darkness he sent messengers to the Queen and bivouacked his army as best he could.

With the first light he called his captains, a large number of them Welshmen, and instructed them to have their men on the march within the hour.

This done he found his confessor and after receiving the Sacrament, prayed for courage and the safety of those committed to his charge. Before taking up his position in the van of the army he rode to the baggage carriers at the rear. He found young Henry dressed in a suit of light mail, obviously hoping to be included in the fighting force of the day.

Jasper did not hesitate.

'You will stay here, as I told you yesterday,' he said sternly to his nephew.

It said much for Henry's upbringing that, although his face coloured swiftly, he merely bowed his head and said.

'I am in your charge, Sir.'

'There will be plenty for you to do if we engage the enemy,' Jasper told him as he spurred his horse and turned away.

But coming into Tewkesbury Jasper knew there would be no pitched battle on this day. The fields around the village were strewn with the carnage of war. Scavengers scurried through the dead and dying. The fresh grass and scarcely budded trees all bore grim reminders of the slaughter which must have taken place earlier in the morning.

Calling his captains together he sent them back on the Hereford road, telling them to wait until daybreak for him.

He went to the Benedictine Abbey where he found the monks giving what aid they could to the wounded who had flocked to their doors. When he asked for the Abbot he was led to the principle cell.

The Abbot, tall and thin, had only a tale of woe for him.

The Queen's party had arrived on the previous evening, supported by Somerset, Wenlock and many other Lancastrians who had fallen in with her army as it progressed through England.

They had taken up strong positions but Edward, coming with the first light of the new day had a host of overwhelming strength and was supported by Richard of Gloucester with many men from the North.

They had swiftly engaged the Queen's army and in a bloody and ruthless fight over high hedges and deep ditches utterly routed them.

'Where is the Queen?' Jasper asked.

'Fled to the north with Edward of York hot on her heels.'

'And the Prince of Wales?'

'Slain along with most of the other nobles of the King's party.'

'Good God!' Jasper said. 'How was he killed?'

'Some say by Richard of Gloucester, some say by the squires of Edward of York.'

'Who was with the Queen?'

'Only her ladies.'

'Then this must be the end of all Lancastrian hopes,' Jasper said.

He refused the Abbot's offer of hospitality and with his own squires and Henry, who had been waiting for him at the postern, set out for Hereford.

His one thought was to reach Pembroke

and the safety of his stronghold with Margaret's son. He knew the boy was now in immediate danger of his life, for once Edward had succeeded in capturing Margaret of Anjou his next objective would be the Earl of Richmond. The boy was thrown into sharp prominence by the death of the Prince of Wales. To all intents and purposes he was the Lancastrian heir.

Meeting up with his army, he set them free from their obligations to him and ordered their payment without delay.

While they were dispersing he called a parley with his own Pembroke men. He told them to make their way back to their homes and he and Henry would travel with a few picked men.

'I will come with you,' John Morgan of Kidwelly told him. 'It were best if you did not take the usual way through the Brecon hills but struck due south from here to Chepstow and took a ship from there to Pembroke.'

'That seems an excellent suggestion,' Jasper said. 'If Edward has spies left posted about Tewkesbury they will have seen us depart towards here and will naturally expect us to go on the accustomed route.'

It was already dark but Jasper sent for Henry and without alarming him unduly told him they must set out at once. The boy took it calmly enough and left to prepare a bundle of necessities.

Jasper was suddenly filled with the deepest anxiety for Margaret. Spies might already be posting for Pembroke and rousing the Yorkist sympathisers to take the castle. Henry Stafford would be hard pressed to ward them off until his arrival.

He chose a handful of men, old and trusted campaigners, among them his father's groom from Trecastle who had come into his service on Owen's death. He became self appointed body servant to Owen's grandson.

Jasper set out at a good pace and they rode throughout the night. If Henry showed signs of falling asleep in the saddle the groom, constantly at his side, spoke sharply to him and kept him awake with lively anecdotes of his life with the Tudor family.

They came into Chepstow in the cold light of Sunday morning. The steep Quays of the river were deserted but John Morgan made his way to a house set into the hillside and returned with a sleep-eyed boat owner who agreed to take them to Pembroke when he had collected his crew.

The groom and other Pembroke men found quarters for the exhausted horses and Jasper, John Morgan and Henry roused an innkeeper for beer and bread.

It was noon before the captain of the ship pronounced it ready to sail and the party trooped on board and curled up in any convenient place and slept.

The strong winds of the previous days had died away and gentle breezes carried them down into the Bristol Channel. Jasper, awaking cramped and dry in the mouth, looked up at the half filled sails and prayed for a stiff blow.

It was not until the point at Llanwith-Major was reached his prayers were answered and a southwesterly got up.

John Morgan saw him stretch and sit up and came across to join him.

'We were lucky to get out of Chepstow,' he said quietly. 'The groom came back from stabling the horses to say Robert Vaughan's men had been alerted to watch for our coming.'

'How did we escape them?' Jasper asked quickly.

'The groom told the ostler he was one of a decoy party sent out to fool any Yorkists and that you had doubled back on your tracks and were making for Harlech.'

'Good man!' Jasper cried. 'That would strike any Yorkist as feasible and should give us some extra time to reach Pembroke.'

Their progress round the coast seemed

251

painfully slow and the same headlands remained with them for hours on end. They crawled past Worm's head and Carmarthen Bay to St. Govan's head and it was not until they had been at sea for three days they passed through the straits and into Milford Haven.

Jasper posted look-outs in the prow of the boat to keep an hour by hour watch for fires or other signals from the shore. After consulting with the master he decided to leave the boat before it became too conspicuous in the Haven and walk the rest.

The master hove to and let down a small rowing boat. Jasper, Henry and the others climbed down into it and were put ashore. Keeping in the shelter of rocks and bushes they began the long walk to the castle.

Tired and hungry they saw it appearing high above the surrounding countryside in the setting sun of the fifth day.

Jasper told them they must wait until the night had fallen and advised them to rest and sleep if possible.

He shared a very dry crust of bread with Henry and gave him the last of the water in his drinking flask. The boy had behaved admirably during their flight, asking no unnecessary questions and accepting Jasper's decisions without argument.

He grasped the need for secrecy and Jasper was almost certain he understood the reason for it. Jasper was at considerable pains to keep his growing anxiety for Margaret's safety to himself and made no mention of his fears for the ambush of her party.

He gave the order to move off with relief. His thoughts as they crept under the walls of Monkton bridge were a mixture of easement and apprehension for what he would find if they gained admittance. Fortune smiled on them at the portcullis for the man on watch recognised them immediately and calling his fellows admitted them at once.

Jasper took the sergeant at arms on one side and while the others expressed their gratitude for the solidarity of the Castle's thick walls asked him quickly if the Lady Margaret's party had arrived before him. An enormous wave of relief swept through him as the man told him they had come into the stronghold on the previous day.

'Where are they lodged?' he asked.

'In her ladyship's usual apartments, my lord.'

'Will you see food is sent there for us, please. Hot broth would be most acceptable.'

A sleepy page jumped to his feet as Jasper and Henry came down the passage way from the gatehouse to the Tower and opened the door to admit them.

Margaret, sitting in the room with Betsey Massey, ran to Henry and gathered him in her arms. Over his head her eyes met Jasper's.

'Thank God you are arrived,' she said simply.

She looked white and drawn but fighting the tears that pricked at her lids her first thought was for their well being.

'Have you eaten today — or yesterday?'

'Not very much. But food is being prepared for us. How did you fare — were you molested in any way?'

'No, our guide brought us through difficult but little known country and we saw few people.'

'Where is your husband?' Jasper said suddenly.

'Not with me,' Margaret answered quietly.

'By all that is holy, why was he not with you?'

'When your messenger arrived he was absent at Kimbolton on some urgent matter concerning his mother's estate. I knew he was in no danger there and my first thought was to be with my son. Perhaps I should have stayed longer to give the matter deeper consideration but I know you well enough to realise that when you pressed us to return to Pembroke you had good cause for so doing.'

The arrival of servants put an end to the conversation and Margaret watched as they sat down and ate the food set ready for them.

When they were finished Henry rubbed his eyes and begged leave to seek his bedchamber. Betsey Massey bustled to her feet to accompany him. Henry came to Jasper and kneeling took his hand.

'Thank you, uncle Jasper, for all you have done to bring me safely here.'

He hugged his mother and she went with him to the door. She watched until he turned the corner of the corridor and came back into the room.

Alone, Margaret and Jasper stood apart, regarding each other until with a smothered exclamation she closed her eyes and Jasper came swiftly to her and took her in his arms. She clung to him, the tense anxiety of the weeks behind her melting in his embrace. He caressed her cheek, all else forgotten in the joy of their reunion.

'We have known difficult days since we last met,' he said. 'But let us not speak of that now. There will be time enough in the days ahead when the events are not so close. It is enough now to be here with you.'

He lead her to a chair by the fire and when she was seated drew up a stool and sat beside her. He took her hand and she held it against her face, kissing the palm, while she gazed into the fire, unseeing.

When he moved his hand down her neck and let it rest on the curve of her breast she held it there and drew his head to rest on her bosom.

They sat in the dusky room, very still, wrapped in the companionship so peculiarily their own as if the world had ceased to exist. They talked mostly of the days of frustration since they had parted at Christmastide avoiding the harrowing happenings of the immediate past. He had told her briefly of the utter defeat of the Lancastrians at Tewkesbury not wanting to cause her further worry by stressing the position of her son as sole heir, of his half-brother, but her quick brain had seen the implications of the death of the Prince of Wales and other Lancastrian leaders as fast as he had told her.

At last she protested she was utterly selfish to keep him from his rest.

'You look as if you could sleep for days without waking!' she told him.

Reluctantly he raised his head.

'If I could but bed with you I should stay there happily enough. How I have longed to lie in the comfort of your arms. Oh, Margaret, what cruel fate conspired our destinies?'

'I do not know,' she said sadly. 'But let us at least be grateful to whoever has allowed Henry, you and I to find sanctuary together here.'

Her eyes wide she leant forward and kissed him. He stood up and went quickly to the door.

'If I lingered now I should fall asleep in your lap. I'll find your woman and tell her you are ready to go to bed. Goodnight, my dearest heart, as soon as I am awake tomorrow I shall return to you.'

He staggered to his room and was hardly aware of the menservants who hovered about him to help him undress. He slept until the evening of the next day and when he had eaten and called a meeting with John Morgan and Butler of Coedcantlais to discuss the fortifications of the castle and the state of its provisions he went to Margaret's Tower. Betsey told him she was walking on the ramparts with Henry and finding them there he made a slow circuit and then returned to her parlour and talked with them both until he pleaded exhaustion and left them to go to bed.

He had been at Pembroke for three days when the captain of the watch reported David ap Thomas, a nephew of the Steward's lady, wished to have speech with him. Jasper remembered him as having expressed Lancastrian sympathy and after a momentary hesitation had him admitted.

David was a man of medium height, beardless and dark with the melting brown eyes of the Pembroke people.

He knelt to Jasper and with a swift look at the secretaries and captain of the guard turned to Jasper again.

'I have news for you,' he said.

Jasper motioned for the others to leave them.

'What is your news?' he asked.

'My lord, I very much regret to tell you, the King, your brother, is dead.'

'Oh, no!' Jasper cried. 'How can this be? Was he ill — or has some harm befallen him? Edward could not bring himself to hurt his helpless rival.'

'Edward of York might not stoop to murder but his brother of Gloucester is ready and willing to anticipate his wishes as we saw too clearly when he murdered the Prince of Wales on Tewkesbury field,' David answered grimly.

'You are certain of the news you bring? The source is reliable?' David nodded. 'What happened?'

'It is said King Henry was returned to the Tower where he had been confined, as we all know, after the battle of Barnet. Here Richard

258

came swiftly after the Yorkist victory at Tewkesbury (when Margaret of Anjou was also at their mercy having been taken at a nunnery close by) and while the saintly King knelt at his prayers most foully stabbed him in the back.'

'This is an unspeakable atrocity!' Jasper said softly, wincing at the thought of his peace-loving, kindly brother suffering such an unwarranted death. 'Is there other news?'

'Only that Edward has been acclaimed with joy by the citizens of London, especially, so says the common talk, by the women folk who are eager to have the opportunity of lying with the Yorkist once more,' David told him with distaste.

'Is he gaining sympathy around here?' Jasper asked sharply.

'A rising star will always attract supporters, my lord. But rest assured you retain your loyal and devoted followers.'

Jasper regarded him for a long minute and then, going to the door, called for John Morgan and the others to come and hear the sad tidings David had imparted to him.

They expressed disgust at the cruel, unnecessary deed, decrying the act of Richard of Gloucester as tainted with the same horror as the murder of the innocent Thomas á Beckett by the misguided knights of Henry II. It was not difficult to see they were made apprehensive by what they heard, realising they were now become part of a severely persecuted minority. They accompanied David ap Thomas to the gate, very subdued and thoughtful.

Jasper went to break the sad news to Margaret and Henry. They were shocked deeply, each remembering how much they owed to the saintly and kindly man who had influenced their lives directly in the past. As they grieved, Jasper wondered what they could expect next.

He was not kept long in suspense for a week after David's timely warning he was awoken by John Morgan bursting into his bedchamber to tell him the castle was besieged.

15

Dressing hurriedly he went at once to inspect all the gateways and entrances and assured of their impregnability came to Margaret to appraise her of their plight.

She took the news calmly enough.

'We are getting used to being confined here. At least this time I shall have the comfort of you being near at hand. Do we know who has come against us?'

'John Morgan believes it is Morgan ap Thomas, brother to the David who brought us the news of Henry's death.'

'Lady Scudamore's nephew and old Gruffudd's grandson. He is a well known Yorkist and would stand to be rewarded by Edward if he should force us to surrender.'

'We shall be able to hold out as far as food and water are concerned for several weeks if necessary. That is, if we can survive on a very sparse diet of oats and the pipeline bringing water is not discovered by the enemy.'

He looked down at her.

'Life has not been easy for you, my Margaret, has it?'

'Nor for many other women in these difficult and wasted years of strife, but I have been so very blessed in those I love, for none of them have ever played me false or spoiled their honour with treachery or double dealing.'

She smiled at him and the drawn look of anxiety faded from her face. She was, he found himself thinking, one of those rare women who matured with an added grace.

'None could play you false,' he said, and added lightly, 'although my next suggestion will probably give you cause to wonder!'

'How is that?'

'Would it add to your burdens or help you if I moved from the Gatehouse to share your apartments?'

'It would help very much to know you were close at hand to Henry — and me.'

'Then I shall give instructions for my bed to be made up in the small room at the turn of the stair. You may sleep soundly in the knowledge that no one will be able to come to your chamber without accounting to me. Will you promise me something?'

'Yes,' she said a little curiously.

'Neither you or Henry are to go outside this suite of rooms. You must forbid him to walk on the ramparts or go there yourself. A stray arrow would be sufficient to rob me of that I hold most dear. You do promise, don't you?'

'I do,' she said.

'Then I must leave you for the moment but I shall keep you informed of what is taking place.'

Jasper found John Morgan and Butler with the Captain at Arms at the top of the Monkton Tower. They had not wasted their time and archers were posted at each vantage point. Fletchers were handing out extra supplies of arrows while look outs were hidden from the summit of the keep to the peep hole over every gateway.

'How many do you think are stationed across there?' Jasper asked the Captain.

'It is difficult to estimate but as far as I can judge around seven or eight hundred men.'

'So many!' Jasper cried. 'Then we are not going to find it an easy task to send someone for assistance.'

'No, indeed,' John Morgan said. 'The bushes beyond the water are alive with bowmen and Butler thinks they are clearing spaces to bring up some cannon.'

'Thank God then for thick walls.'

'Surely Morgan ap Thomas, for we are now sure it is he who is the ringleader — see his banner fly over there — has bitten off more than he can chew with a siege of this fortress?' Butler queried.

'He is probably recalling how Herbert walked in and made himself master,' Jasper laughed.

'If he is he is at a disadvantage on two scores for on that occasion Lord Jasper was not here and the Scudamores opened the gates for Herbert.'

'Where are the Steward and his wife, by the way?' Jasper asked. 'In the confusion I had not realised I had not seen them this morning.'

'And you are not likely to see them either for their servants report their beds were not slept in last night.'

'So they have gone to join Morgan? Well, we are better off without them. At least we can rest assured we have no traitors in our midst.'

'I have worked out a watch dividing the day and night into three parts so that each of us here can take command for an eight hour stretch. Unless, of course,' the captain added, 'the action becomes fierce when it will be necessary for us all to be on duty.'

'Three parts?' Jasper said. 'Am I not to be counted among you?'

'Well, my lord, I thought it were better if you were on hand to come at any hour — if you are willing, that is,' he added hastily.

'You know I am willing. I should give my life rather than allow the Earl of Richmond to fall into the hands of Morgan ap Thomas.'

The day passed without more than the casual and haphazard release of several arrows which fell harmlessly into the water at the castle foundation.

Before he retired Jasper did a last tour of inspection. John Morgan was in command of the watch and he reported there had been no movement since nightfall.

By the third day the cannons were in position and the castle shook as missiles thudded against the stonework. Several of the stone balls landed in the Outer Ward but there were no casualties.

Disappointed with the results of the cannonade the besiegers began hewing trees from the wooded hills opposite the strong-hold and from the hammering it was obvious they intended to construct a battering ram to use in breaking down the door.

This did not worry Jasper over much for the Gateway entrance with its three massive portcullis was virtually impregnable. He put the castle servants to digging huge quantities of earth and carting it to bolster the other entrance. His chief source of concern was the possibility of the severing of the water supply. It would not be difficult for Morgan ap

Thomas to learn of the whereabouts of the buried pipeline that conveyed the crystal clear water from the springs south of the castle and Jasper could only pray that whoever had installed it would have had sufficient foresight to bury it very deeply.

A week after the siege began Morgan launched the sharpest attack against the fortress, sending forward men with scaling engines and others with the now completed battering rams. Those swimming the river and creeping along the walls from the town met with short shrift as the defenders pelted them with stones, rotting refuse and bales of burning straw.

After several unsuccessful attempts to break down the doors Morgan's men retired to their positions on the further bank leaving their wounded to fend for themselves.

Jasper left his viewpoint on the walls and went down to the cellars where the provisions were stored. The cellarer accompanied him. The fresh food was by now almost finished, each man and woman within the castle having received an equal share while it lasted. Being June the grain stacked in sacks in the granary was depleted but the miller thought by rationing it he would be able to make bread for some time to come. There was no danger of running short of wood as enormous stocks were piled in the yards.

Jasper went to Margaret's rooms happy in the knowledge the inhabitants of Pembroke would not starve for the moment.

The days of the siege had been amongst the best of his life. Living in close proximity to Margaret had assuaged a little of the frustrating desire, never far distant from his waking hours, to possess her completely. The subtle intimacy of their relationship was enhanced by the opportunity to share meals and sit together once the long day had faded. It was almost as if some recompense was given in their ordeal of keeping alive in the face of the enemy.

He and Margaret had been most concerned for the welfare of the young Henry, but he appeared to be unafraid of the besiegers lying so close in wait for him and only grumbled at Jasper's ban on his taking part in the action. His tutors had left the household when he had gone to Eton, but Margaret's chaplain Christopher Urswick had taken it upon himself to devote several hours a day to teaching the boy. Thus occupied he had less time to brood or complain at his enforced confinement.

Margaret was standing at her casement, looking out over the courtyard below, as Jasper came into the room. It was evening.

The sky a translucent blue tinged with the warmth of sunset. A seagull hovered in the still air, turning and floating at the flick of a wing.

Since Morgan ap Thomas had come against them Margaret had discarded the rich velvets and the delicate silks she usually wore and had dressed herself in simple wool.

She was wearing now a robe in green, low over the bosom, without ornament. Jasper was suddenly transported to the solar of Lady Braybrook's manor fifteen years before when he had come to Margaret and his brother and told them they must leave at once for Pembroke.

'You have not worn that dress since you were at Colmworth,' he said.

'You remember?' she answered as the blood pulsed along her cheek bones.

'Yes. I don't think I could ever forget.'

She turned back to the window and watched the seagull, now joined by another, curving across the cloudless sky.

'So Morgan's men have returned to their headquarters while they plot other means of bringing us to our knees?' she said. 'Have we been successful in sending anyone to Kidwelly or the other friendly estates to tell them of our plight?'

'Not yet,' Jasper admitted. 'It would be

certain death for any man who tried to run the gamut of Morgan's lookouts. I think our main chance of receiving help is from our friends hearing of our plight from sympathisers. It is most likely the monks from the Priory will have sent word to Kidwelly and Carew of what is taking place.'

'Why do they delay in coming to our relief?'

'As you know it takes time to amass an army. Spies would tell any would-be helper we are besieged by a huge force and it would take several days to arm and gather together a comparable host.'

He came and stood beside her at the window.

'Do you want to be gone so very much?'

He saw her hands grip the sill until the knuckles turned white.

'It is only for Henry I care,' she said huskily. 'For myself I would stay here and take what came. Death has no fears for me.'

She was very quiet at supper and went to bed early pleading a headache. Jasper and Henry sat talking with her chamberlain until their evening's allowance of wine was finished. Henry went to his bedchamber and Jasper walked with the chamberlain to his quarters and climbed afterwards to the ramparts to hear the report of the watch.

Having made a complete circuit of the castle and assured himself there were no stealthy swimmers or climbers preparing to take them by surprise he said his goodnights and went to bed.

He awoke in the night, abruptly, and pulled on his bedrobe. Quietly opening his door he went to the guarded entrance of the apartments.

The man on duty told him he had heard no unusual noise or movements, but not convinced, Jasper climbed again to the ramparts. He stood with the Captain of the Guard until his eyes grew accustomed to the blackness.

'I have heard nothing, my lord.'

Straining his ears for the slightest sound, Jasper moved slowly round the path he had covered only a few hours before. Nothing seemed untoward and as the first delicate fingers of dawn crept into the east he returned to the Captain and told him he was going back to bed but to call him instantly if necessary.

Before going to his own chamber he went to Margaret's parlour to assure himself all was well there. To his surprise he saw beneath her door the glimmer of a light. Without stopping he knocked and went in. The white and gold brocade curtains of the bed were not untied and she was lying, still in the green gown, on top of the covers. Her face was white and her eyes, in the faint light of the small lamp burning on a table against the wall, dark and enormous.

She sat up in surprise as he entered the room, but seeing it was he, lay back again. He went swiftly to her and took her in his arms.

'My dear! What ails you? Why are you not asleep?'

She lay limp against him but buried her head against his shoulder.

'Your head? Is it that? Shall I fetch Betsey or one of the women?'

'No,' she whispered. 'They cannot help me. No one can. Least of all you.' she said, and began to shiver violently.

'Dear heart!' he cried, anxiety clutching him. He held her closer, running his hand caressingly from the nape of her neck down her spine. In a little she became quieter but the warmth of her body burned into his and her face was damp with tendrils of hair clinging to her cheek and temple.

'Will you go to bed if I help you?' he asked.

She nodded and with trembling fingers he undid the fastening of her dress. He helped her to stand and it fell to the floor. She stood before him in a delicate shift, gossamer fine. She threw off the heavy coverings of the bed and dropped on to the down-filled mattress with her head averted.

In an agony of longing engendered with the intimacy of the moment he fell on his knees beside the bed and nestled his head on her breasts. Half expecting she might repulse him he was surprised when her hands held him fiercely against her.

'Oh, Jasper! Jasper. How can you love me? How can you love me when I am so worthless?'

'You? Worthless? Never was any woman more worthy than you!'

'That is not true! I am a cheat, full of make believe virtue, binding you to me and giving nothing in return. I take your protection, live in your home and prevent you, by adhering to the rules of Holy Church from enjoying that which I would give with my whole heart.'

'Do you think I do not know this?' he said softly. 'Do you not know I love you the more for it? When I came to understand all those long years ago how very much I cared for you, I accepted then the difficulties and the frustrations it would bring. Don't forget I loved you while Edmund was still alive, wanted then to take you to my bed and beget the unborn children that would have been yours and mine. Don't speak to me of unworthiness! If it is a sin to want each other you and I are bound for Hell fire as surely as night follows day. But you told me yourself that you did not believe God thought us wanton. Do you not still believe in His mercy?'

'I do, I do! It is just that I am overwhelmed with self disgust. What is it that prevents me from giving myself to you?'

'Do you really not know?' Jasper said, raising his head and gathering her close. 'Do you really not know?'

She shook her head.

'It is because I will not take you,' he said simply. 'My love for you goes too deep to spoil it with furtive couplings which we, afterwards, would regret. Have you forgotten, chaste Diana, I am old in sin?'

'Mevanvy?'

'Yes, Mevanvy.'

He bent and kissed her parted mouth.

'Now, heart's darling, go to sleep and torment yourself no more with your failings. I shall stay here until you do,' he said hastily as her eyes widened in fear.

Exhausted from the hours of wakeful anguish she took his hand and turning over onto her side closed her eyes.

She was asleep in a few minutes, trustingly curled within the shelter of his arm. He stayed with her until her even breathing assured him she slept and the light in the chamber was dimmed by the new day. Then gently he took his hand away, kissed her naked shoulder and covered her with the bed clothes.

In his own chamber he threw himself down and lay for a long time staring at the small slit that was the only source of illumination.

Almost hypnotised into sleep he was startled by a thunderous knocking on the door.

'My lord! my lord!'

He leapt up and found the Captain of the Guard in a fervour of excitement.

'We are not without friends after all, my lord. The look-out has seen a force advancing from Carew.'

'How does he know they are allies and not reinforcements for Morgan?'

'They fly the banner of David ap Thomas.'

'I shall join you in a moment. Boy!' he called to the page coming to see the cause of the uproar. 'Wake the Lady Margaret's household and tell them to dress, and send to the kitchens for bread and wine and flasks of water.'

The page ran off and Jasper's servant and squires arrived and helped him dress and put on the lightest armour he possessed.

Gaining the ramparts he heard the long,

winding note of a trumpet and saw horsemen cantering down the cobbled street of the town. At a distance behind them came a force of men, numbering in swift assessment between fifteen hundred and two thousand men. As they approached he saw they were armed with pronged forks, billhooks, sickles and other curious implements.

He had a fleeting moment of thankfulness that these were his friends rather than his enemies before, with a blood curdling howl, they fell on the besiegers rising in bewilderment from their blankets and holes in the ground.

In the short space of an hour the battle was raging, fierce and bloody. The onlookers in the castle were unable to help their friends as it was impossible to distinguish one side from the other.

When the noise of battle was at crescendo pitch Jasper saw a small knot of horsemen approach the Gateway. He raced to the portcullis and gave instructions for David ap Thomas to be admitted. As the Welshmen came into the Castle and the great doors fell back into place behind him Jasper put his arm about his shoulder briefly.

'I can never thank you enough,' he said.

'That is nothing, my lord. You and your lady and her son are unhurt?'

'We are very well,' Jasper assured him.

'We have a small boat awaiting at the cavern of Wogan. My men have instructions to cover our departure and prevent my brother from realising what we are about.'

'How many of us can be accommodated aboard the boat?'

'Just the three of you and myself, my lord.'

'What of the rest of the household?'

'Do not fear on their behalf. When we have sent Morgan back to the hills where he belongs we shall see your staff and personal servants are brought into safety.'

'Where do you propose taking us?'

'To Tenby, my lord. The mayor of the place is a friend of mine and he has his instructions to have ready a ship to take your party to France.'

'What can I say to thank you?' Jasper said.

'Will you go to the cavern and I will come to you there in ten minutes.'

He ran to Margaret's apartments and found her sitting in her parlour with Henry, her chamberlain, Betsey and her confessor. Their eyes met across the room as he hurried towards her and took her hand to kiss.

'My lady. Are you and Henry ready to set out on the instant?'

'Yes,' she replied steadily.

Betsey bustled up to her. She had in her

hand a small bundle.

'Alone?' Margaret queried.

'Yes. But we are not abandoning the others. David ap Thomas has pledged his word to look to their safety and escort them to a place where they may rest in peace.'

Margaret put her arms about the faithful woman who had been with her since her childhood at Bletsoe.

'Don't you fret, my dear lady,' Betsey told her. 'The important thing is to get you and your son to a safe place. There is no price on the heads of the likes of me. We'll be together again, one day, don't you fear.'

Without lingering and giving Margaret time to dwell on the fate of those with whom she had shared so much, Jasper hurried her from the room and across the inner curtain wall to the Northern Hall and the cavern beneath.

He went ahead and Henry helped his mother, giving his arm and calling out the hazards ahead. Going down the circular stair he went in front of her guiding her on the uneven and sometimes damp steps.

In the huge vaulted cavern it was almost dark but they followed the shaft of light from the arched entrance. David awaited them here and going after him on the banks of a canal they came to the river where a boat with a sail was held by two of David's men.

Jasper and Henry lifted Margaret aboard and climbed in themselves. David and one servant stepped onto a thwart while the other put one leg across the gunwale and pushed off from the side.

'We are going to row out,' David said quietly. 'So will you, my lady, and you, young sir, lie down in the bows. Lord Pembroke will you take this oar with Thomas here while I take the other with Griffiths. There is a lookout post on the westward side of the castle and when he gives the signal we shall row as quietly as possible.'

Jasper glanced uneasily to the other bank but he could see no sign of movement and guessed the besiegers who had been posted there had taken themselves off to the safety of the thickly wooded hillside. He was relieved when David gave the signal to proceed. The rowlocks had been muffled but the occupants of the small boat saw, as they came to the hazardous stretch of water where they were in full view of their attackers, that the precaution had been unnecessary for the besiegers were too occupied in self preservation to give a thought for the unlikely flight of their victims.

No one spoke as the four men pulled with all their strength to gain the comparative safety and cover of the southern bank.

David called out to Henry and Margaret to keep within the shelter of the bows but watch on either side of the river for a stray enemy who might give the alarm to his companions. After about half an hour of strenuous rowing, when Jasper's hands and back began to ache with the unaccustomed exercise, David professed himself satisfied they had escaped without the knowledge of his brother and his followers.

'Go and join the Lady Margaret and maintain a strict watch,' he said to Jasper. 'While we raise the sail.'

Somewhat gratefully Jasper shipped his oar and took up his place beside Margaret and the boy. She smiled as she made room beside her.

With the square sail rigged and the leeboard out, the easterly wind hurried their progress down the Haven. With every yard they sailed Jasper's anxiety faded slightly and watching Margaret's face he saw the taut uneasiness gradually leave her. David called to Henry to sit with the sailors and learn how to help them manage the boat.

'Where are we bound?' Margaret asked Jasper at length.

'Tenby; David has been thoughtful enough to have a ship already awaiting us there.'

'For France?' Jasper nodded. 'How long will it take us to reach Tenby?'

'That depends on the wind and tide, my dear one.'

She did not reply but leaning back against the gunwale undid the clasp of her hood and closed her eyes. As the wind caught her hair and the sun warmed her upturned face she sought Jasper's hand and clung to it beneath the folds of her mantle. Relaxing his gaze from the banks he looked at her swiftly and his heart misgave him as he saw the tears on her cheek.

16

As the dying sun touched the tranquil waters of the Haven with golden radiance, David told them he thought it wiser to sail through the short night. The two men he had chosen were versed in the shallows and rocks of the estuary and if Jasper agreed they would each take a watch with one of them. Henry begged to be allowed to share in the guard duties and was delighted to be told he was definitely old enough to participate and could take his spell of duty with David.

The anxieties of the morning had given way to lassitude as the day progressed, but after eating the food they had brought, supplemented by more from the ship's locker, all of the little company felt refreshed and almost began to enjoy the sail. The wind still blew moderately from the east and sent them coasting towards the open sea.

Jasper took the first watch with Thomas. When he handed over to David and the others the moon had risen and was ringed with a misty halo.

As he went to the bows to rest he hoped the squally weather this usually predicted would hold off until they were safely in Tenby.

He had made up a bed for Margaret with his cloak and some blankets David had stowed on board. He found as he came forward she was still awake. He threw himself down beside her and she made a place for him on the bundle she was using as a pillow, covering him with the mantle. Without speaking he enfolded her in his arms and she lay against him drawing warmth and comfort from his strength. When he kissed her brow and closed eyes she moved nearer in his embrace, stroking the nape of his neck with gentle fingers.

'So you and I were to spend a night in each other's arms after all,' he said softly. 'Even if it were to be under the eyes of David ap Morgan, two Welsh sailors and your son!'

'My son,' she whispered. 'Poor Henry, deprived of his father before his birth and now to be bereaved of his own country. Do you think Louis will receive him well?'

'There is no reason why he should not. He is first cousin to Edmund and myself, at war with Burgundy and therefore no friend of Edward's. He should look upon the surviving Lancastrian hope with great favour.'

'Supposing in the future he should make his peace with Edward?'

'We shall have to face that when we come

to it. Edward will be too busy consolidating his own throne before he thinks about foreign alliances outside those with his sister in Burgundy.'

She fell quiet and Jasper thought she had gone to sleep when she took his hand and held it to her mouth. She kissed the palm folding the fingers inward with the same gesture he had made when they met after his last prolonged exile in France.

'Your hands taste of the sea,' she said lightly, as he moved restlessly. She turned over to lie on her face. 'I am glad not to have to sleep on a wooden deck every night of my life! Although,' she added, head averted, 'if it were under the same circumstances I should never again ask for a down-filled mattress.'

She sat up, running her hands through her hair, faintly visible in the moonlight against the backcloth of the square sail. The wind was almost dead but the strong tide, turned in their favour, carried them progressively westward. Now and then the call of a curlew broke the stillness but otherwise the gentle slap of the water against the hull was the only sound. In the stern David talked intermittently with Griffiths and Henry.

Jasper pulled himself against the gunwale and touched the curve of Margaret's cheek with his hand.

'So the sole dress you now have to wear is the green one Edmund gave you. We shall have to set about finding a sempstress in France who will fashion you a new wardrobe.'

She said nothing as he touched her neck and bared shoulder but rested her head against his.

'You will be able to find tutors for Henry won't you?' she asked.

'There are bound to be other exiles living at Louis' court who will be only too glad to use their time giving instruction to your son. Margaret, you must have given thought to the fact that Henry, being the only male heir of the Lancastrians, is pursued by Edward not only because of his obvious opposition to a Yorkist on the throne, but because Edward thinks he has a very real chance of wresting that throne from him. For that reason alone he will be a special pupil!'

'I should not be honest if I did not admit to thinking of it, but Henry is not yet fourteen years of age and I do not see myself as another Margaret of Anjou — fighting for her son's place in the world.'

'There are other means of saving England from the Yorkist yoke than by bloodshed,' Jasper said musingly. 'Time is on our side and while we are in France — '

'We?' she interrupted him.

'You, Henry and I.'

She lifted her head and kissed him on the mouth, not withdrawing as she usually did after a brief touch of the lips, but lingering while her arms tightened about him. At last she drew back and sighed deeply.

'Jasper. Very dearest Jasper, I am not coming to France with you and Henry.'

'Not coming!' Jasper cried. 'Margaret! I cannot face months, perhaps years of separation from you again! I cannot go and leave you in danger!'

'You can and you must,' she said quietly, lying back on the makeshift bed.

He bent over her appalled at the prospect of banishment without her then with a groan put his head on her breast clinging to her with desperate urgency.

'If I stay it will take longer for the Yorkists to realise Henry and you have disappeared. You must have a liaison with your home interests and I must be on hand to fight for the safe keeping of Henry's and my estates. If we are all absent we shall be faced with the future prospect of no where-withal to live. Besides that,' she said very low, 'I have a husband.'

Jasper turned his face into her bosom.

'I think we have both almost forgotten that fact in the events of the last month,' she went

285

on. 'But I must come back to earth from the Arcadia we have shared and use any talents I might posesss for the survival of those I love more than life — or personal happiness.'

'If you can bear to part with me, how can you think of letting Henry go away from you?'

'It is almost the same as sending him to school, but I have the added reassurance of knowing that you will be with him. There is not any fear in my heart for him on this account alone.'

'And our love?'

'We have always known its cruel restrictions and now we shall have to take it to ourselves as part of our existence and draw upon it to sustain us. It is better for us both, perhaps.'

'Only perhaps?'

'Only perhaps.'

'You and I do not seem to have had a great deal of sleep during the last two nights. I can see the dawn breaking already.'

'I shall not sleep now,' Margaret said. 'Do you think there is any of the wine left?'

Jasper went to the stern to find the flask and found David anxious for the weather they might expect when they came into the open sea.

'I hope the Lady Margaret has a good stomach for this windless dawn will blow up into a stiff breeze by midday,' he said.

'I think I shall rather enjoy it,' Henry said. 'Won't you, uncle Jasper?'

'We shall see,' Jasper told him wryly. The weather seemed to him at this moment the least important trouble they had to face. Returning to Margaret he caught himself thinking he wished the boat would capsize and thereby end the unendurable prospect of parting with her again.

They sailed well within the lee of the wild coastline but rounding Linney Head the fitful sunshine of the morning was lost in low clouds scudding in from the south west. Light rain began to fall as the sea grew choppy.

In hurried conference Jasper and David decided to brave it out if Margaret proved a good enough sailor to stand the buffeting the small boat was already beginning to take.

She had joined them earlier for bread and some of the delicate cheese David had provided, but when the worsening conditions made it necessary to shorten the sail and stand off the land, she saw she might be inconveniencing the men as they strained at the sheets and returned to her position in the bows. Here she was afforded slight cover but Jasper watched helplessly as wave after wave broke against the ship's side and sent a deluge of water over her.

Henry went to sit with his mother and talked with her in an effort to divert her attention from the dangers of sailing in an open boat. He took off his own short cloak but she would not wear it and made him put it on again.

'I have the blanket and a thick mantle, thank you, sweeting. Keep your cloak for yourself otherwise you will be arriving at Louis' court in a very sorry state!'

She told him, as calmly as she was able, of the decision she had made to remain in England. Henry bit his lip and stuck out his chin in a gesture reminding her disturbingly of Jasper and his father. She had seen both brothers do the same thing when they had received news that upset them.

'Let us hope we shall not have to remain in France overlong,' he said at length, then looked at his mother swiftly. 'Uncle Jasper is coming with me, isn't he?'

'Of course,' Margaret reassured him.

By late afternoon the rain was beating down and the sea had become really rough. As they rounded Saddle Head and made for St. Gowan's the boat was wallowing from crest to crest. All the occupants were drenched. Jasper had fought his way to the bows and with Griffith's help lashed Margaret and her son to the standing rigging. She had thanked him with the intimate smile she kept for him and he had stooped and kissed her swiftly on her brow. Her hair and face were soaked with sea water and rain.

'Who tastes of sea water now?' he said in her ear above the crashing of the waves.

Stackpole Head was almost invisible as they came in by the jutting rocks but immediately they felt the benefit of the protection it afforded. Within the small bay the water was calmer and the rain lashed down from behind. Two hours later the wind dropped and pale sunshine scattered the remaining clouds.

As the sun set they came in sight of Caldy Island and before dusk gained the haven of Tenby harbour.

Lookouts had been posted to watch for their arrival and willing hands pulled them to dry land. They were greeted by Master Thomas White, mayor of the port, who David presented to them as the donor of the ship to carry them to France.

'We have been much concerned for you, my lady,' he said to Margaret. 'When David's men came and told us to expect you within two or three days and we saw the weather we doubted if you would survive!'

'Thanks be to God we are well, as you see Master White.'

'No doubt you will be glad of some hot food and a change of clothing before you set sail,' the mayor said kindly.

'Thank you. We shall all be delighted to accept your generous hospitality and if I may I shall ask the added boon of a room in which to spend the night.'

'There is a cabin set aside for you on board my lady, and if the ship is to sail with the first light — '

'But I am not going with my son and the Lord Jasper,' Margaret told him quietly, avoiding Jasper's eyes.

'Well, then, of course we have ample room to accommodate you, my lady,' Thomas White hastened to tell her.

With their soaked clothing clinging to them they followed the mayor to his commodious black beamed house and saw with pleasure his wife had had the forethought to light a fire in the hall. She led Margaret with pride to a spacious, well appointed bedchamber where servants kindled driftwood in the hearth.

A scullion staggered in with two great copper ewers filled with hot water which he emptied into a bowl set in front of the fire.

When he had gone Mistress White showed her linen towels and said she would return presently with a warm robe.

Margaret thanked her gratefully and

stepped out of the cumbersome, sodden dress. She knelt down in the bowl of water and washed herself, revelling in the soothing comfort. She was wrapped in the towels when the mayor's wife returned with a chamber robe and a linen shift.

'We have supper ready for you in the parlour,' she said. 'But if you prefer it it would be no trouble to bring it here for you.'

'No, thank you,' Margaret said. 'I shall come down in a few minutes to be with the others.'

Jasper and Henry, dressed in borrowed garments also, waited for her with Master White and David and they ate a simple meal of soup and roast capon.

'Our clothes have gone to the bake oven to dry out, Mother, have yours?' Henry asked Margaret.

'Yes, I think they have,' she said. 'It is not much concern if mine are dried out by the morrow but I hope yours will be.'

'Master White told me I could keep these, anyway.'

They were politely interested in the conversation of their host and hostess during the meal but neither Jasper or Margaret were conscious of their surroundings. They were hardly cognisant of the physical suffering they had endured during the past days. Jasper did not take his eyes from her face, and when Mistress White rose from the table saying they must be longing to seek their bed, he said quickly he would escort Henry to the ship and return to speak with David ap Thomas and the Lady Margaret, for they had much to discuss before sailing on the morning tide.

Margaret went with Henry to collect together the pitifully small bundle of his possessions. She found herself almost unable to speak as he knelt to receive her blessing. Kneeling beside him she gathered him into her arms and hugged him to her.

'Don't cry, my darling,' she said as her own eyes brimmed and her throat ached with love for him.

'Oh, Mother. I wish you were coming with us! If only we knew how long it would be before we are together again. You will send messengers to me, won't you?'

'Of course I shall. I know I don't have to tell you to obey Uncle Jasper and not forget the love of God which will comfort you whatever may befall.'

She busied herself drawing the strings of his shoulder bag, and, arms about his shoulders, went down to the parlour. He turned to blow her a kiss as he went out of the door with Thomas White and Jasper.

Mistress White bustled into the room with a tray set with tankards and ale.

'I'll take these to your room,' she said with a swift look at Margaret.

Margaret followed her to the chamber stifling the burning sensation of misery welling through her. She helped the kindly woman draw up some chairs to the fire and was standing gazing into the flames when David knocked on the door.

Mistress White declined their offer of a mug of ale and went out.

'Sit down, my lady,' David said, and pouring some ale, passed it to her.

Several times he started a conversation but it seemed as if all topics were bound up in the personal tragedy she was enduring and he looked up gratefully when Jasper came in.

'Asleep the minute his head touched the pillow,' he assured Margaret as she raised enquiring eyes to him.

He sat down beside her and took her hand.

'It were best, I think,' he said quickly. 'If you were to go to your estates in Devon. Torrington is almost due south of here across the Bristol Channel. I have spoken with Master White and he has agreed to put you aboard one of his vessels when they next leave for Bideford.'

'And if you will,' David said to Margaret. 'I

293

shall escort you there and wait with you until members of your own household are able to come to you.'

Jasper looked gratefully towards him.

'That is what I hoped you would say.'

'Thank you, David,' Margaret said.

The dark haired Welshman rose.

'Good night, my lady. I shall wait upon you in the morning. You and Lord Jasper can rely upon me to ensure contact is not lost between yourself and the young Earl.'

Jasper accompanied him to the room where he was to sleep and thanked him for all he had done in procuring their escape and bringing them safely to Tenby. David made light of his share in the raising of the siege and promised he would do everything in his power to safeguard Margaret as well as find messengers to convey their letters to France.

When Jasper came back to Margaret's chamber he found her, as David had, standing at the hearth. Coming up behind her he clasped her under the bosom, drawing her gently to rest against him. With a small sigh she relaxed in his embrace, covering his hands with her own. For a time they watched the fire flicker into ashes, each thinking the same unbearable thoughts of the separation now so terribly near.

'Can you believe,' he said at last, 'there are

people in the world forced to live with those they find intolerable while you and I, who belong together, are constantly torn apart?'

She shook her head.

'Life must have some other purpose for us than the gratification of the senses. That is the only reason I can find for the cruelty taking both you and my child away from me.'

Jasper kissed the top of her head and the smooth skin behind her ear.

'I have thought much of giving you some token of my love, but when I search in the few treasures I was able to bring from Pembroke, there is nothing adequate. In fact wherever I looked there would no jewel worthy of you.'

'You have already given me your heart and that I prize more than the riches of the East. I shall wear your love proudly and secretly in my breast and thank God, every day, for all you have meant to me since Edmund died.'

Jasper's hand tightened at her waist, holding her to him until she could scarce breathe.

'Oh, Jasper, I am filled with despair for life without you and Henry! What shall I do with my days?'

She broke away from him and moved restively about the room from the curtained windows to the bed. Jasper watched her in desperate helplessness.

'You must be very tired,' he said.

'Not in the body; in the spirit perhaps. I think I slept a little today once we came into calmer waters. You should go to your rest, for you have much before you.'

'I have the entire time of my exile in which to sleep and dream. Any hours between now and the morning are yours.'

She spun round to look at him, her eyes wide with remembered and unknown pain.

'Dearest,' he said, 'if I were to stay with you as I did our last night in Pembroke you would not know the moment of our parting.'

For a moment he thought she had not heard him.

'Come then, that is best. I shall go to bed for to prolong the agony will not soften it in any way,' she said in a tight, hard voice.

In a gesture of acceptance she threw off the borrowed robe and climbed into the bed.

Jasper turned back to the fire, fighting the desire sweeping through him. 'Oh, God,' he prayed, 'don't let me weaken now. Don't let me take her and make it worse for us both.'

He leant his head, wearily, against the carved mantel piece fighting for the control that had been his for so long. As he shut his eyes all he could see in his mind was the almost virginal beauty of the woman he loved, her face strained and her head held high.

When he had recovered some of his calm he went to the bed and found her propped against the pillows watching him. He sat beside her his eyes on hers.

She sat forward.

'Will you unbind my hair?'

He took out the pins, the tendrils curving round his palms still damp from the sea and rain. As her hair fell about her she put her arms about his neck and drawing him to her kissed him fiercely. With a murmur of hopelessness she released him and fell back into the pillows.

Jasper slid his arms beneath her shoulders, baring her bosom and resting his head on her breast.

He never knew how long they stayed like that, talking in whispers of the bonds that joined them. He tried to instil her with an optimism he was far from feeling himself, forcing her to look to the future and the possibility of their reunion. He comforted her with the knowledge Louis' court was not at the other side of the world and that he would come to her if danger threatened her even if his own life was forfeit.

'Heart's darling,' he said, 'go back to England and take up the duties of your rank.

Learn again the craft Edmund taught you as a great landowner. Pick up the threads of scholarship and prove that in that beautiful head lies an intellect surpassing most men of this wasted generation.'

'Forget I am a woman, you mean.'

'You could never do that. You are womanhood at its best, strong, forbearing and — loving,' he whispered.

She touched his cheek and found her fingers wet with his tears. She said nothing but her eyes filled with great drops, trickling down her face to mingle with his. Her arms held him closer as she willed herself not to break down.

'Go to sleep, Margaret. I am here.'

Lying on his stomach beside her he kissed her and smoothed her brow murmuring gentle words of love until at last, when sleep almost overcame him, he felt her relax and knew by her regular breathing she slept.

Very gently disengaging himself he drew back the curtains and stood once more at the bedside looking down at her drawing her image to retain in his heart. Kneeling he kissed her breasts and covered them then swiftly touched her mouth with his own.

Without a backward glance he wrenched open the door and closing it softly behind him went down the staircase and let himself out of the sleeping house.

At the quayside the double watch challenged him and stepped aside to allow him aboard. He stumbled to the cabin where Henry was curled in the opposite bunk and without removing his clothes threw himself down on his own pallet and was instantly asleep.

He did not wake until the dusk of the following day. Slowly he returned to consciousness with the knowledge the ship was dipping to a heavy sea and that somewhere in the region of his chest it was as if bonds of iron were crushing the life out of him.

He wallowed in misery as the little vessel laboured in the swell, until no longer able to support the torment of his thoughts, he swung himself from his bunk and climbed with difficulty to the deck above to find his nephew.

17

It was the Spring of 1483. The month April. The beauty of the warm day and the forest stretching out beneath him touched Jasper with an almost physical hurt as he stood at his small window high in the walls of the Tours d'Elven, part of the Fortress of Largöet in the Dukedom of Brittany.

It was now more than twelve years since he and Henry, Earl of Richmond, had left Tenby in the ship of Thomas White to seek asylum at the court of Louis XI of France.

Perverse winds had forced the Master of the vessel to abandon hope of landing on the French coast and seek shelter south of the treacherous promontory of Finisterre. He had brought the ship into the harbour of Le Conquet where, with reluctance Jasper had sent word to the Duke, Francois II, begging permission to remain in exile.

This he had done against his better judgement for the Duke was an unknown quantity who might be in sympathy with Edward, now firmly ensconced on his English throne. Coupled with this danger was the remoteness of the Duchy which made communication with England difficult. Jasper comforted himself by allowing this second disadvantage to be helpful in that Henry was safer because of it.

Duke Francois had granted the exiles asylum but had decreed they should be kept under restraint while in his country. Jasper and Henry had been escorted from Le Conquet to the walled town of Vannes where they had been housed in the Chateau de l'Hermine.

Brittany had struck the two homeless Lancastrians as a counterpart of the Wales they both loved. The clear light, craggy and indented coastline and rolling countryside were as familiar as their own. Megaliths and dolmens stood in rows commemorating the ancient religions of the two peoples who at one time had common ancestry. Henry had had no difficulty in understanding the peasants who had thronged about them when they came ashore at le Conquet for they spoke the Celtic brogue of the native Welsh.

All would have been easier if Francois II had been more kindly disposed towards them but he was a man full of his own importance, vain and small minded. Jasper had been right to doubt his aid, for Francois lost no time when they first came before him of reminding his prisoners — for so they found themselves

— of the treaty he had signed with Edward almost three years previously. Magnanimously the Duke promised not to divulge their whereabouts to the King of England but regretted he had no other course open to him but to restrict their freedom.

Jasper and Henry were put aboard a fishing boat and taken across the gulf of Morbihan past the small, wooded islands of D'Arz and Moines through the narrows between Locmariaquer and Arzon to the Chateau of Suscinio.

Jasper could still remember the hopeless bitterness he had experienced when he first saw the formidable castle as they came upon it from the surrounding forests. It resembled Pembroke but lacked the friendly huddle of houses at the gate and the monastery across the creek. At Suscinio the moat was filled by the sea which broke on the desolate beaches beside it.

Jasper was reminded of the fear he had once expressed to Edmund of spending his life incarcerated and his apprehension did not leave him once inside the eight towered fortress, for it was well fortified and manned with a large force of soldiery.

He had no time to think of his own plight, however, for he kept as cheerful a countenance as he was able to bolster his nephew, who, by this time was beginning to show signs of the strain to which he had been subjected.

Looking back on those difficult and frustrating years Jasper recalled his main preoccupation seemed to be in helping Henry combat the second imprisonment of his short life. Jasper was grateful for this task for it prevented him from dwelling on his separation from Margaret. Where his own feelings were concerned he made every effort to try and look to the future and a possible reunion, rather than dwell on the past and what might have been.

He prayed with steadfast sincerity for the woman he loved so deeply, that her life was as tranquil as possible and they would be spared to meet again. In the first two years of their stay at Suscinio they had received no letters from England. If the Duke had kept his promise to keep their whereabouts from their enemies he had not told their friends either.

Jasper comforted Henry with the certainty of Thomas White's captain returning to England with information about the approximate destination of his passengers. When once this had been passed on to Margaret she would lose no time in sending messengers to France with instructions to penetrate into the wilds of Brittany and seek out the hiding place of her son and brother-in-law.

Henry received some indifferent tuition from the chaplain of the household but Jasper grieved for his intelligent brain deprived of the training it deserved. He pleaded with the Seneschal for tutors to be send from Rennes or Vannes to teach the boy but could obtain no satisfaction. The only boon the man would allow was an occasional ride on the deserted beach and a swim in the Atlantic breakers on a summer day.

Jasper felt at his wit's end for Henry's future, when help came from an unexpected quarter. Francois visited the castle with his wife, Marguerite and his minister of State, Pierre de Landois. Jasper loathed de Landois on sight. He was a cringing, sharp faced man who clearly showed his disregard for both of the exiled Earls. He treated them as not worthy of his interest and when Marguerite would have lingered to speak with the lonely boy hurried her away.

However, not long after this monks arrived for the sole purpose of giving lessons to Henry and Jasper guessed it was the Duchess who had used her influence with her husband to gain this small concession.

This happier state had not lasted, for when Henry was seventeen years old, orders had been sent from Rennes for the two prisoners to be separated. Jasper had never forgotten the look on Henry's face as the news had been broken to them. The boy, filling out now and losing the awkwardness of puberty, had striven to control the despair he felt, but had turned to Jasper with his eyes widened in horror. Jasper's heart had misgiven him as he had a swift vision of the boy's mother looking at him in the same way when something had occurred to frighten or distress her.

He had comforted the boy with as much reassurance as he could muster and promised he would communicate as often as they were allowed.

Jasper had been removed to the fortress of Josselin twenty miles to the north east of Vannes while Henry had been taken to Tours d'Elven where they were both now in residence.

Fortunately the Malestroit family who owned the Tours were well disposed towards their young prisoner and furnished the small chamber given to him as comfortably as they were able with a clos-lit, a commodious cupboard and a small table. The roof of the chamber was high and vaulted but the only daylight came from a slit aperture in the thick walls. They made no objection to uncle and nephew corresponding and sent messengers fairly frequently between Josselin and Largöet.

Jasper was relieved to read of Henry's acceptance of his new environment and the more relaxed atmosphere prevailing.

Looking down now over the miles of forest to the west and south of the place, Jasper knew there had been little chance of Henry escaping, and the Malestroit's realising this had lightened his sentence as far as they dared without incurring the displeasure of their Duke or his hated Minister, de Landois.

Whether it was their influence, or again, that of the Duchess, Jasper had not been able to discover, but in 1476 he had been allowed to leave the castle of Josselin and share with Henry once more the burden of exile.

For burden it certainly was. Looking back over the years since he had been forced to leave his native country Jasper wondered how it was he had not gone completely out of his mind. Always an active man he kicked against the confining pressure of the stone walls about him. He would gladly have forfeited rank or title to return to Pembroke and live as a simple gentleman as his father had done at Trecastle. And he would have given the remaining years allotted to him to have held Margaret in his arms again.

Henry had been given permission to receive letters from his mother and wrote as often as her couriers could come across the

Channel. During the last year her husband Henry Stafford had died and Jasper had longed to go to her. Only the thought of what might happen to Henry in his absence had restrained him.

Her letters were a source of strength to them both, for she hoped when she wrote them Henry would be able to share them with Jasper. They contained no hint of possible anxiety for herself and were filled with loving concern for their health and spiritual good. She exhorted her son to put his trust in God and pray for the fortunate outcome of his privations. She made no bones of the fact that Edward was now fairly well received by most of the Lancastrian lords who, without a leader, decided to sink their differences and try to live in some kind of harmony. She went seldom to court herself but had taken Jasper's advice and looked to the multifarious duties of her great estates and spent her time journeying from one to another up and down the country.

Jasper moved to the other small window of his room and looked below to the wide lake where he could see the boat from which Henry and a servant were fishing. Watching his nephew Jasper smiled affectionately as the young man caught sight of him and waved. Jasper thought, as he had done many times

307

before, how like Edmund Henry had grown and realised with a thrill of dismay he was the same age now as his father had been when he died. He moved impatiently away from the open casement and crossing the landing went into the narrow solar and sent a page for wine.

Jasper was now fifty-one years of age. As Owen's had done his hair was greying at the temples but was still thick and luxuriant. His body showed the effect of the discipline he imposed upon himself for his shoulders were held back and his spine straight. He dreaded the softening that might result from the restricted life and exercised daily to keep his stomach taut and his muscles in good trim. He pushed himself to this as lethargy was never far distant and there were times when nothing seemed worth the effort involved.

Yet, always at the back of his mind was the hope of a possible happy outcome to the trials he and Henry had suffered for so long, and if and when this day ever dawned and they were permitted to return home, he wanted to be fit and ready to make a new life.

Only once since Edward had retaken the throne had insurrection threatened its stability. This had been when the Earl of Oxford had captured St. Michael's Mount off the Cornish coast and held out there for six months before being overcome and banished to the castle of Hammes in France. It was not so much of rebellion Jasper thought but of Margaret, at last managing to persuade someone, perhaps Bishop Morton or another influential prelate, to remove the attainders on her son and himself and be granted safe conducts for them to return.

Jasper recognised his hopes as sanguine, but he occasionally allowed himself the pleasure of indulging them. It was common gossip in the Malestroit household Edward was sinking into carelessness of his duties as a sovereign and living more and more for sensual delights. He had had many mistresses but over the last few years Jane Shore, the wife of a London goldsmith, had become his constant companion. Those who had seen her and came to the court of Francois spoke of her wit and kindly nature but shook their heads over Edward's preference for her when Elizabeth Wydeville, his wife, far outshone her in looks. It was said the Queen bore with her husband's infidelity with remarkable forbearance and kept her children, Elizabeth, Edward and Richard and the other small daughters mostly at Ludlow, where they were looked after by the Governor of the castle, Sir Richard Croft and his wife Eleanor.

In other respects the Queen had nothing of

which to complain, for Edward had showered honours upon her brothers and sons by her first marriage. It was whispered the Wydevilles were the true rulers of England and Edward was content to allow them and his brother Gloucester to perform the tasks he was too indolent to carry through.

However the government of the realm was executed Edward retained the loyalty and affection of his people who admired his handsome looks, outstanding height and penchant for women of all classes.

Jasper was about to send for some more wine when he heard the distant note of a horn. He went quickly to the stair leading to the ramparts and looking down on the gatehouse saw men hurrying to work the mechanism of the drawbridge. Henry had disappeared from the lake and Jasper watched as he reappeared in the small courtyard beneath. Leaving his viewpoint he climbed down the stone stair to join him.

'Who comes?' Henry asked him.

'Perhaps Jean de Rieux, our host, is returned earlier than expected from Vannes.'

But it was not the Lord de Malestroit who rode across the wooden bridge under the stone canopy. It was an envoy from Francois and his Duchess bearing a rolled parchment for the exiled Earls.

Breaking the seal, Jasper read with disbelief the short note summoning them to spend Easter in the Château de l'Hermine at Vannes. He turned speechless to Henry and handed him the letter.

'By all that's wonderful, Jasper!' Henry cried. 'It cannot be possible we are to leave here! Perhaps we are dreaming!'

'Dreaming or not,' Jasper said drily, 'we'll lose no time in accepting. The letter says we are to return with you now,' he said to the envoy.

The man nodded.

'My lord thought you would be able to set forth without hindrance as you have not many posesssions to gather together.'

'True enough,' Jasper answered, with a touch of irony.

Jasper and Henry went in together to the octagonal Hall for the midday meal, still dazed by the news.

'What can have changed Francois' mind?' Henry said.

'Perhaps he is suffering with another attack of madness and Marguerite has acted without his knowledge!'

'But the letter was written in his own hand.'

'So that disposes of that theory,' Henry said slowly. 'Of course, it might be a trick of some kind!' he added despondently.

'We have been here too long for any trick to be played on us. If Francois had wished to rid himself of us, he had dozens of methods open to him. No, I choose to look optimistically upon the extraordinary change in our fortunes and thank God He has influenced our jailor to give us a different place of imprisonment if nothing else.'

'At least we can look forward to a different diet at Vannes. This Lent we seem to have eaten nothing but eggs and soupe maigre!' Henry said.

They rode out on to the Vannes road with the good wishes of the inhabitants of the Tours d'Elven still ringing in their ears. At intervals they would look at each other and smiling, shake their heads unable to believe they were really leaving the place where they had stagnated for so long.

The narrow track crossed heath and skirted woodlands until beyond the deserted moors of Lanvaux they could see the breath-taking vista of the Bay of Morbihan, now hazy in the cooling sun as it sunk in front of them.

It was almost dark as they came to the narrow gateway of the city and clattered over the cobbles to the entrance of the Château de l'Hermine. The officer of the watch led them immediately to the chambers of the Duke.

Here, Francois and Marguerite received them and presented their daughter Anne. Jasper saw Marguerite's warm smile for Henry and guessed the reason for their release from Largöet was mainly at her instigation. The Duke and his wife still had only the one child and it could be they saw a possible union in the exiled Earl of Richmond and the little Anne.

Francois looked fatter and more bloated than when he had made a brief visit to Largöet some months before and Jasper had not been in his company for long before he realised the man was far from well. He was full of complaints of Louis, King of France, who, now sinking into his dotage, shut himself up in his fortress of Plessis-les-Tours where he saw no one but soothsayers and doctors. Affairs of state he dealt with between bursts of prayer when he prostrated himself on the floor of his chapel and refused to move. Francois moaned it was impossible to deal with a fellow sovereign who shut himself away from public life. He held out no better prospect for the future as it was generally believed the King's heir, Charles, was foolish and headstrong.

'But he has been very kind to the exiled Queen of England?' Jasper began.

'You do not know Margaret of Anjou is

dead?' Francois said incredulously.

'No,' Jasper answered. 'News does not always filter through the thick walls of the Tours d'Elven!'

'The lady died last year. In complete dejection,' Francois said with what Jasper could only describe as relish. 'Her father neglected her when he took a young bride and she existed on the meagre pittance handed out to her by her cousin Louis.'

'Poor woman,' Jasper said slowly. 'Misguided she certainly was but she suffered also. Are there messengers come from England for us, I wonder. My Lord?'

'All that have come for the Earl of Richmond have had their letters sent to Largöet,' Francois said, testily. 'Now we have waited long enough for you. Let us go down to supper.'

As they sat at the loaded boards Jasper and Henry exchanged glances. Maundy Thursday it might be but there was no apparent sign of fasting for silver dishes were piled high with spider crabs and lobster, while servants handed them dishes of the delicate poulards farcis and oysters for which the district was famous. Jasper was pleased to note Henry did not over-eat of the splendidly prepared meal and exercised considerable restraint. Stomachs shrunken with the fare of Elven could not be expected to deal with such food.

During the weeks following their arrival in Vannes, Jasper and Henry took up gradually the normal life of the Château. For the first time for years they were permitted to walk freely in the narrow streets of the city and go down to the port to watch the fishermen land their catches.

It was pleasant also when the day was over to sit in the salon to hear musicians and sometimes watch a play performed by the troupe of mummers attached to the castle. Jasper watched with pleasure as he saw Henry indulge in several mild flirtations and discovered also he had not lost the art of charming a smile to his listener's face. He knew if he had wanted it many of the ladies would have been only too eager to make assignments with him but he laughingly protested, when Henry expressed concern for him on the matter, that he was getting too old for romance.

'No, Jasper, that I could not believe.' Henry said looking at him keenly as they walked together from the Cathedral St. Pierre where they had heard Mass.

For a little while they continued in silence across the Place.

'You love my mother very much,' Henry asked quietly, 'don't you?'

'Yes,' Jasper answered steadily. 'I have loved her since the day you were born — perhaps even before. There has been no other woman for me.'

'Not even Helen's mother?' Henry said quickly.

'No. I make no excuses, but I was young then and the Lady Mevanvy was very desirable.'

His mind went back to the far distant days in Pembroke and he could see Mevanvy standing at the fireside with the child suckling at her breast while he chaffed with impatience to possess her. He caught only the end of what Henry was saying.

' — and my mother loves you also.'

'Yes,' Jasper answered him simply. 'She turned to me quite naturally when your father died and our affection for each other grew as you and she lived in my home. We knew from the outset it was hopeless to think of marriage or living together and we accepted the blessing of companionship and shared interests.'

'And now?' Henry prompted. 'Now that Henry Stafford is dead?'

'There is still no hope for the Law of Holy Church forbids any marriage such as ours would be.'

'I am so very sorry,' Henry said. 'For it

would be the best thing in the world for the three of us!'

'Oh, well!' Jasper replied lightly, 'We are indulging ourselves in flights of fancy, for your mother is separated from us by the Channel and the barrier of our attainder, and I do not know,' he added almost to himself, 'if she still loves me!'

18

The next morning Jasper and Henry were sent for to present themselves with all haste in the Duke's private parlour.

They came into the room to hear an excited hubbub of conversation. Francois beckoned for them to come to him and they pushed their way through the throng. Standing at the Duke's side was David ap Thomas.

Quickly making greeting to Francois Jasper gripped David by the hand.

'David! by all that's wonderful! How are you come? What news do you bring?'

'My lord — news of all kind. But first are you both well?' He turned to Henry with a questioning air.

'I'm forgetting in my joy at seeing you that you do not recognise my nephew after all these years.'

'I do not forget you, David ap Thomas,' Henry said taking the Welshman's hand and bowing his head. 'If it were not for you, Jasper and I would be but memories by this time! My mother? Is all well with her now in her widowhood? Do you see her often?'

'I serve her when I can, my Lord. She sends her loving greetings and the news she has been quietly married to Thomas, Lord Stanley.'

Henry looked quickly at Jasper who as quickly turned away and gazed woodenly over the heads of the people crowding the chamber. For a moment he heard nothing as a burning sensation spread through his stomach. He forced himself to a control that made him dig his nails into the palms of his hands.

'Lord Stanley!' Henry was saying. 'But he is a Yorkist and so I hear, a minister of Edward's.'

'The King is dead!' David cried.

'Edward — dead? When did this happen?' Jasper asked glad to talk of other matters than his own hurt.

'About four weeks ago. Of late he had taken to drinking deeply and indulging a vast appetite for food and — '

'Jane Shore?' Henry prompted drily.

'Yes, indeed,' David answered smiling. 'So when he was struck with excruciating pain in the stomach he had no resources on which to fall back and although he fought against death he was too weak and succumbed.'

'So his son is now King. England has a child upon the throne once more. I suppose that will mean the Queen's family and Richard of Gloucester will act as a combined Regency?'

'No,' David said slowly. 'What has befallen is the cause of the excitement in this room.

'Let us beg permission from the duke to go to our quarters where we may sit in peace and hear all David has to tell us,' Jasper said.

A few minutes later, with tankards and a jug of cyder on a table beside them, they sat and listened to David's story.

'It appears when the King died the Prince of Wales was at Ludlow with his uncle Lord Rivers, while the Queen was in residence at Westminster with her other children. A hasty Council meeting was called and Edward's Will read and discussed. Richard of Gloucester was absent in York but his friends Lord Hastings and the Duke of Buckingham were both present and it became immediately obvious to them that the Queen's family were anxious to abide by a former Will made by the late King in which he stated he wished the upbringing of his sons to be in the hands of the Rivers — Wydeville party and to ignore a later Testament instructing Richard to take over the protectorship. Buckingham set off without delay to intercept Richard, who would be coming south, to advice him to secure the person of the new little King to use as a bargaining hostage against the Queen and her relatives. It was known to Buckingham that the boy, Edward, had been notified in Ludlow of his coming into his inheritance and would be also making for London.'

'But surely Richard did not need to have possession of the boy to carry out his dead brother's wishes?'

'One would have thought not, but it seems Richard has other plans than to make himself Regent.'

'Surely not aiming at the throne for himself?' Jasper asked.

'Nothing less,' David told them grimly.

'Does Buckingham realise Gloucester's purpose?'

'Who knows? My lord Buckingham is not an easy man to understand, so I am told.'

'He is a cousin of mine,' Henry said slowly. 'I should have thought he was a Lancastrian to the bone. But did he not marry one of the Queen's sisters?'

'Yes, the Lady Catherine Wydeville.'

'Could she not have influenced her husband to support her sister's child? But, be that as it may, what happened when the young King came south?' Jasper asked.

'His party, under the command of Lord Rivers, went through Northampton and en route for Stony Stratford was halted by

Buckingham and Gloucester. Gloucester spun some story to the little Edward about it being necessary for him to have the protection of the strongest barons of his realm and took over from Rivers, who mysteriously disappeared.'

'Poor little devil,' said Henry. 'I know how bewildering it is to have older people change the course of one's life. Where is Edward now?'

'In the Tower; where Gloucester has placed him while he plans the next moves in his bid for the throne. The Queen, horrified at the sudden change in her brother-in-law and the antagonism between him and her family, has taken herself to Sanctuary at the Abbey. She is not alone in her dismay for no one is certain of what is afoot. The Wydevilles are not over-popular, but neither is Gloucester.'

'Is it your opinion only that Gloucester is aiming for the throne?' Henry asked.

'Most people think he is seeking to become Regent only. That is not what I believe. If he seriously intends to support his brother's son he should have had him crowned by now.'

'And this has not been done?' Jasper said quietly.

'No. There has been no mention of a day even.'

'It would appear as if Richard of

Gloucester is following the example of his father and elder brother and making a bid for power with the support of his immediate circle and intimates. It bodes no good for the welfare of the realm when those ruling it are divided, I did not think I should live to see the day when Yorkists would fight among themselves,' Jasper commented grimly.

'There is the possibility,' David said quietly, looking at Henry, 'that when a house is divided among itself then is the time for better men to step in and claim what should be theirs.'

'How could this be?' Henry replied after a momentary hesitation. 'We are penniless and prisoners of the Duke.'

'Stranger things have happened,' David said smiling.

'Tell me of Wales and the news from Pembroke,' Henry said.

Jasper pushed back his chair and went to the door.

'Forgive me, but there is a matter needing my attention. I shall rejoin you later.'

He felt suddenly as if the ceiling of the room was pressing down upon him and that he must escape before he heard David speak of Pembroke and arouse the nostalgia of the days he had spent there with Margaret.

Margaret! Although he had known within

his heart once her mourning days were over for Henry Stafford it would become necessary for her to think of remarriage he had hoped desperately she would not. He had known as he entertained these fond hopes the uselessness of his cause for it was right and proper for her to take another husband to safeguard the tremendous inheritance she possessed. He wished for the hundredth time she was penniless and of no importance, unbound by the ties of property and free to do as she wanted.

He pictured her in the simple green dress when she sat beside him in the boat as they sailed down the Haven and made for Tenby. What did she look like now? How could he ask David what the years had done to her?

He came out into the clear sunshine, warm with the westerly wind blowing gently from the sea. Without knowing where he was going he walked slowly to the city wall and leaning his back against it stared, unseeing, across the roofs to the distant bay.

How could she marry Thomas Stanley? Surely he was old enough to be her father? Don't delude yourself, he reminded himself grimly, you are almost old enough for that yourself!

Oh, God, he prayed, don't let me lose my sense of humour as well as my freedom.

Almost in answer to his thoughts he heard, floating up from the moatside, where a group of women were washing their family linen in the lavoir, a little burst of laughter.

Looking down he saw several townswomen, kneeling to their task with their arms to the elbow in the water, chattering and conversing gaily. He watched them, as with high white coifs nodding they scrubbed at garments and rinsed them. Something about the mundane labour restored his equanimity and he was soothed by its very ordinariness. One woman in particular attracted his attention. She was dressed as the others in a full skirted dress with a laced bodice of which she had released the strings to give her ease of motion.

Jasper was looking at the rounded fullness of her bosom when she happened to glance up at him. She did not flinch under his gaze but returned him look for look until at last she smiled and resumed her washing.

He moved away leaning his arms on the wall's parapet concentrated on the steady stream of passersby beneath him. When he looked again towards the lavoir the woman had gone. Unreasonably disappointed Jasper began to walk slowly back towards the Château. At the corner of the street by the shop where he and Henry had seen townsfolk buying the town's famous lace-fine pancakes he came face to face with her. She smiled again and this time Jasper smiled back and leaning forward relieved her of the heavy basket of wet clothes she was carrying on her hip.

'That is much too heavy for you,' he said, impulsively.

'But I am more used to carrying burdens than you are,' she replied.

'Let me have the pleasure of helping you this once. It is not often I have the opportunity of assisting pretty women.'

She chuckled and darted a quick look at him.

'You do not know if I am pretty or not. You have not seen me properly.'

'I watched you at the lavoir and that told me enough!'

They walked through the narrow passages between the overhanging houses exchanging pleasantries until she stopped before a fish shop.

'This is my house,' she announced with a defiant pride.

Opening the door she put out her arms for the basket. Jasper had a glimpse of a small courtyard beyond the interior of the shop. The well scrubbed boards were bare and the place empty.

'Let me help you hang the clothes in the

garden,' he heard himself ask.

The woman regarded him without speaking and then stood back to allow him to precede her. Jasper heard her shut the door and bolt it after them.

In the small yard at the rear of the dwelling it was warm, and shut away from the crowd bustling in the street outside. Jasper put down the basket and together they threw the garments and bed linen over the line. As they met in the centre he bent over her and kissed her hard on the mouth.

She held out her hand and led him towards the staircase that went out of the courtyard into the upper rooms.

'Come and I shall offer you the hospitality of the house.'

Unhurriedly she pulled forward the only chair in the neat living-room and he sat while she brought pewter mugs and drew cyder from a small barrel in the dim corner.

'Your husband — he is a fisherman?' Jasper asked her.

'No. I am a widow, my man was killed fighting in the wars between the Duke and the French. I live here with my mother and one brother. He is the fisherman and they are down at the quayside now sorting the day's catch.'

'But you will marry again, won't you?'

'Perhaps,' she replied. 'I am in no hurry to become a slave too soon. I have enough to occupy myself here with the family to cook for and the sewing I do.'

She gestured towards a pile covered with a piece of cloth.

'No man is too anxious to wed with me for I have no dowry now.'

'How fortunate for you,' Jasper murmured.

'Fortunate?' she echoed, but did not press the point. She had drawn up a three legged stool and sat opposite him.

'You are an Englishman, are you not? The Earl from across the Channel who has been the guest of Duke Francois for so many years?' Jasper nodded. 'Is that why you are so sad?'

'Do I look sad?'

'Yes. But I do not believe it is on account of your imprisonment. May I ask if you have a wife?'

'No, I have not.'

'I see.'

She began, without haste to unpin the starched headdress. Jasper stood up and crossed to the tiny casement. Below in the yard the linen flapped lazily in the breeze. When the woman came up behind and clasped her strong arms over his chest he was tempted to cry out to her to leave him in peace but suddenly he turned and pulled her against him.

When she led him to the inner door he followed, almost in a dream, and lying on the bed watched as she stepped out of the homespun dress. He closed his eyes on the sight of her naked body, as he was thrown back to the room in the Mayor of Tenby's house and his leave-taking of Margaret.

She came in beside him, comforting him with the warm softness of her flesh. Jasper shut out the thoughts threatening his reason and tightened his arms about her.

When it was finished she lay beside him, stroking his back until at length she kissed his forehead and swung herself off the bed. She laced up the bodice of her dress and plaited her hair. Jasper did not watch her.

'Come,' she called gently, 'my family will be returning presently and I must prepare food for them.'

Jasper rose unsteadily from the bed. He felt slightly light headed, abstracted and low spirited. He did not notice when the woman left him and went into the other room.

When he came out she was busying herself with setting the table. She smiled and he went to her, taking off a signet ring he always wore on a little finger. She took it and held it to the light of the casement.

'The arms of France?' she said questioningly.

'My mother was a Princess of the house of Valois,' Jasper said quickly.

She came back to him and gave him the ring.

'I do not need payment. I offered you the hospitality of my house and I gave it willingly. If I have eased your sadness a little that will be my reward.'

She did not accompany him when he went down the stairs and let himself out into the street. He hurried back to the Château perplexed and still depressed.

He knew the inhabitants of the castle would be eating their midday meal but the thought of food revolted him. He climbed hurriedly to his chambers. The page who saw to his needs was awaiting him.

'Why are you not at meat?' Jasper demanded.

'The Earl of Richmond said I was not to go down until I had handed you these letters.'

The boy took up a roll of parchments and gave them to Jasper. His heart thudded in his breast as he recognised the seal of Richmond.

'Thank you,' Jasper said kindly. 'Go down now. I am sorry to have kept you waiting.'

The door closed behind the child and Jasper broke the seal with trembling fingers. It was the first letter he had received from Margaret since his exile began.

'My dear,' she wrote:

'I do not believe my other letters to you have been delivered for not once in those I have received from Henry has he ever made mention of them.

'When word came to us you had been removed from the Tours d'Elven and David said he would come again to Brittany and try to see you, I resolved to make one further attempt to contact you.

'He will have told you of my marriage, although I could have wished to tell you myself. You do not need me to labour the point of the necessity for such a step, but I want you to know that when I made the contract I vowed also an oath of chastity.

'May Our Saviour and the Virgin keep you in Their Blessed care.

Margaret.'

Jasper sat for a long time staring at the parchment in his hand then threw himself on to the bed and buried his head in his hands. In that moment he tasted the most bitter dregs life had to offer.

19

By the late summer of 1483 the Court of Francois Duke of Brittany had taken on a new face for the English exiles. No longer were they regarded as quasi-dangerous refugees but had assumed a potential importance that resulted in a betterment of their lot.

During the months after Jasper's visit to the house of the woman of Vannes there had come several Englishmen who were unable to stomach the new regime of Richard of Gloucester. The first had been Sir Edward Wydeville who had been Admiral of the Fleet but had had his command spirited away from him by followers of the Protector. A brother of the unhappy Queen of Edward, he had had with him on board his ship a small part of the late King's treasure, and when it became obvious of what Richard intended to perpetrate he brought it to Henry and offered it to him with his loyalty.

Edward Poynings followed a little later and brought with him the full and hideous story of Gloucester's usurpation of the Throne.

He had set about the business with a

determination matched only by its uncaring brutality. Nothing was sacred in his bid to have complete power.

Henry and Jasper listened in horrified fascination as Poynings told how he tricked the unsuspecting and ageing Archbishop Bourchier into begging Queen Elizabeth to give up her second son, Richard, Duke of York, to alleviate the loneliness of his brother in the Tower. Much against her will the unsuspecting Queen allowed the child to go out of Sanctuary in Westminster and by September she had not seen either of them again. The once beautiful woman had become half crazed with sorrow and anxiety and lived with Elizabeth and her other daughters in perpetual fear.

She had much cause for concern for Richard had systematically ridden himself of the Wydeville family. All her brothers except Sir Edward and Lionel, Bishop of Salisbury had been beheaded.

When Richard of Gloucester finally took his nephew, son of the dead Clarence, into captivity in his own household it appeared as if the way was clear for him to assert his rights to the throne.

Men watched, unbelieving, as he blackened the names of his brother's widow and his mother when he described them as adultresses to honour his own birth.

The late King, his brother, he claimed, had not been his father's son but the child of an unknown, fathered on his mother when she was alone and unguarded in the early days of her marriage.

If this was not sufficient to discredit Edward's claim to the throne Richard struck at his two sons' claim to inherit by raking up the illegality of their parent's marriage because Edward had been already betrothed to someone else at the time of the marriage.

'Half stupefied by what they heard, and intimidated by the vast army Richard commanded to attend him at Westminster, the Council consented to him taking the Throne,' Poynings told Jasper and Henry. 'At this time there was no whisper of his murderous intentions towards the sons of Edward and he had, after all, the support of Buckingham, the Nevilles and Hastings.'

'What do you mean by murderous intentions towards Edward's children?' Henry asked sharply.

'I hope I may be wrong,' Poynings answered him slowly, 'but there is growing anxiety, especially in the South of England that some disaster has overtaken them.'

'Can no one find out the truth of the matter?'

'At one time they were seen playing bows and arrows and other boyish games in the confines of the Tower but for some months now no one has caught a glimpse of them or been allowed to visit their chambers.'

'The man must be possessed!' Jasper cried. 'How can he hope to rule a land by putting to death the innocent sons of his own brother! Are his supporters blind?'

'Not so much blind as seeking their own glory. It could be, of course, they thought when they first helped him it was better to have a strong man behind the young Edward and begging your pardon, Sir Edward,' he said turning to the Admiral, 'the Wydeville family had their enemies.'

'Too true,' Sir Edward agreed sadly, 'and I curse my helplessness in not being able to go to the assistance of my sister's children. I cannot understand how Catherine, my sister, who is married as you know to Henry Buckingham, does not use her influence to speak for them.'

'A woman has to have extraordinary powers to sway a man when he has made up his mind,' Jasper said. 'Has she children of her own?'

'Yes, she also has two small boys. One would have thought this sufficient to rouse her sympathy.'

'She probably has no idea of what is afoot and lives in seclusion at Kimbolton or another of Buckingham's residences.'

'It may be she keeps silent as many do for fear of the consequences. Since Richard turned on some of those who helped him to power nobody is certain of the future. The business of Hastings and Morton is perhaps one of the most mystifying happenings of the usurpation.'

'You have mentioned this before; what happened exactly?' Henry asked.

'No one is quite sure. Perhaps the whole matter hinged on Jane Shore — '

'Edward's mistress?'

'Yes. It would seem she was also a favourite of Hastings and when the King died she was reluctant to return to the quiet life of a city goldsmith's wife and accepted Hastings' offer of a place in his household. Richard of Gloucester had wind of this and was afraid the King's erstwhile mistress would be able to sway Hastings to sympathy for the cause of the Queen and her children. Almost at the same time he received information from some of the hundreds of spies he employs, of Bishop Morton's compassion for the helpless consort. Richard called a meeting of the Council to be held in the Tower and when it was assembled accused Hastings and the

Bishop of treason and without giving Hastings time to make any explanation, had him bundled outside and beheaded. While the astonished company were recovering their wits he handed Morton over to the charge of Buckingham and had him despatched with a strong force to Buckingham's house in Brecon.'

Jasper remembered the long-off day when he and Edmund had stayed at this same manor while the present Duke's grandfather had been making a bid for the loyalty of the Herberts to the Lancastrian cause. It was a strange turn in the wheel of fortune when a Buckingham stood so strongly behind a Yorkist usurper. Not for the first time Jasper wondered about the character of the young man who commanded such a vast and important inheritance. It was certainly obvious he had no leanings to the party of his mother's Beaufort family. What could make a man desert those for whom both his grandfather and his father had died? A strange nephew for Margaret indeed.

But it was to appear as the clear light of the Brittany summer turned into the fullness of autumn that the Duke had had time to reflect on his highly questionable actions.

Jasper and Henry, returning from a visit to the Isle au Moins where they had halted briefly at the shrine of the Spanish saint Vincent Ferrier and swum in limpid water, found Margaret's most trusted adviser Reginald Bray waiting impatiently to speak with them.

Reginald Bray, tall and elegant, bowed over Henry's hand and clasped Jasper by the arm. It was twelve years since they had met.

'The Lady Margaret?' Jasper asked quickly. 'Is she well?'

'It is of her I must speak,' Bray said, glancing over his shoulder to the crowded room. Pierre de Landois hovered in the background apparently listening to the conversation of some of the men who had accompanied Bray but wearing the over-attentive look usually associated with eavesdropping.

'Let us go to my rooms,' Henry said.

When they had closed the heavy oak door behind them Jasper reiterated his question.

'She is in good health; but still sadly missing her son and her late husband's brother,' Reginald Bray answered. 'At the moment however she sees for the first time since she parted with you a faint hope of having you restored to her.'

'How can this be?' Henry cried. 'It may be we are collecting followers here who would be prepared to help me in a fight for the throne, but I am without money and cannot hope to amass an army when across the Channel we would be up against the formidable armies of Richard's supporters!'

'But it is of this very subject I bring news of the greatest importance. During the last few weeks the Lady Margaret was making a pilgrimage to the shrine of Worcester Abbey and quite by chance happened to fall in with Henry, Duke of Buckingham.' Jasper and Henry exchanged glances. 'The Duke was making a journey from Brecon where he has as his prisoner John Morton, the Bishop of Ely, who had been confined there since Richard of Gloucester accused him of treason. It would appear the young Duke was in some state of perplexity and persuaded the Lady Margaret to accompany him to a nearby manor, where he had friends, to talk with him.'

'Tell us of Buckingham,' Henry said. 'To us in Brittany he would seem to be the enigma in the complex situation in England.'

'I would agree with you,' Bray said. 'Most of us have put his conduct down to youth and a desire to be associated with the new order prevailing. I think it was mostly a matter of time before he saw the error of his ways.'

'And this he has done?' Jasper asked.

'Yes. While Morton was a guest in his

house at Brecon, it came to the Duke's notice that a strong wave of feeling about the late King's sons was sweeping through the southern Counties of England and that several nobles were preparing to make an attempt to storm the Tower and find out for themselves what had befallen them. Perhaps it was this that touched the Duke's conscience or more probably it was the persuasive tongue of the Bishop, but which ever way it was Buckingham decided he had had sufficient of Richard's devious and cruel ways and he became determined to put right at least part of the evil with which he had been connected.'

'This was the matter he talked over with my Mother?' Henry enquired.

'It was. Your mother was his uncle's widow and there is no doubt he would have heard of the reputation she has acquired for wisdom and the sensible deportment of her life under difficulties, and he put his problem before her. Uppermost in his mind was the tremendous necessity for England to have a strong, just king who would heal the sores of the last twenty years of conflicting government.'

'Did he not see himself in this role?'

'This must have crossed his mind but apparently he discarded the idea as he felt himself inadequate for the task.'

'But he considered Henry was the proper person,' Jasper said quietly.

'Exactly!' Reginald Bray said turning to Henry. 'My Lord, I bring gold from your mother and important plans for the joining of whatever armies you are able to bring and those of the Duke of Buckingham. He is certain your combined forces should be able to overpower Richard and take the throne from him.'

Henry shook his head disbelievingly.

'It seems impossible. I have been exiled here for so long that no one can have any idea of my character or strength.'

'My lord, the fact you are the remaining Lancastrian heir and son of the Lady Margaret is enough for most people. Coupled with this the reputation you enjoyed in your short youth at the English court and what has filtered home during the years here has convinced people you are the man England seeks.'

'What of Stanley?' Jasper said without expression. 'As a confirmed Yorkist he would be in opposition to his wife's hopes for her son?'

Reginald Bray turned to Jasper.

'As you know, my lord, my Lady is a woman of great charm and exceeding courage. If you add to this a brain which would do justice to a man of much learning and education it should not be difficult for you to see when she chose her new husband she was looking, even then, to the future.'

Jasper smiled.

'It would appear the Lady Margaret has not altered very much over the years!'

'Indeed not. We, who have been privileged to serve her during these long years of hardship and personal grief, can only admire her for the way in which she has conducted her life. She spent her time quietly at her manors, interesting herself in charities and the advancement of learning. It has been said no one who made supplication to her has ever been turned away without comfort or help. It is she who has put forward the idea which I think you will agree should prove the key stone of any bid you may make for the English throne, my lord,' he added to Henry.

'And that is?' Henry prompted.

'Your marriage with Elizabeth of York, the late King Edward's daughter and eldest child.'

'By all that's Holy! My lady mother certainly thinks of everything! But what of the lady? and how does the Queen Dowager reconcile her Yorkist background with a wedding for her child with me?'

'I conveyed the idea, personally, to the Dowager and she greeted the suggestion as a drowning person clutches at weeds. She is so completely unhappy that she is willing to give support to any sane person who will help her. The life she lives in the Sanctuary of Westminster is confining and frustrating to say the least.'

'So if I am willing, I have a bride!' Henry said laughingly. 'What do you think, Jasper?'

'Knowing your mother she would not have put forward the suggestion if she did not think Elizabeth would please you as well as be suitable, so I think, most strongly, you should accept.'

'We are forgetting the girl,' Henry said. 'Do you know her, Sir?'

'If I remember correctly she is fair of face as are all the Wydevilles. Delicate rather than filled with the lusty life of her father, but nevertheless pleasing. She must be about nineteen years age. A very suitable consort, my lord.'

'We rush on too fast,' Henry smiled. 'Let us hear the plans Buckingham has for us.'

By the time Bray returned to England with Henry's acceptance of the schemes proposed to him, the Breton court was preparing to help the new aspirer to the English throne with all its power. Francois, seeing himself as

King maker, devoted his failing energies to making available any information which would be of service to Henry and Jasper. He told them where to recruit mercenaries and sent emissaries to the sick Louis asking for his aid in helping the young Tudor.

Sir Edward Wydeville set out for St. Brieuc to make ready his two ships for a landing on the Devon coast to link up with the rebellion Buckingham hoped to launch by the beginning of October.

The two exiled Earls became the centre of interest. Old supporters and friends redoubled their efforts to assist them and those who had regarded them warily before now found them of particular concern. Only Pierre de Landois kept his distance and on more than one occasion Jasper heard him advising Francois to have nothing to do with the attempted invasion.

It was obvious this new activity at the Breton castle of Vannes could not be concealed from Richard of Gloucester and when he sent Sir Thomas Hutton, on what was described as a visit of Courtesy to the Duke of Brittany, no one was deluded. However, any request he made to the Duke was not complied with and Henry and Jasper went on unhindered in their task of preparing to go to England.

They left Vannes on a still October morning full of hope for their return to England.

In the ships of Sir Edward, and others chartered from fisherfolk, they sailed down the narrow inland harbour of St. Brieuc out into the open sea buoyed with the thought of their homecoming.

Jasper had not allowed himself to think of the delight of seeing Margaret, but once aboard the sturdy ship he could no longer shut out the joy the very thought of her brought to him. He lived again the brief hours of happiness they had shared, their brevity serving only to underline their true delight.

'Oh God,' he prayed. 'If it be Thy Will let me see her again. I have served the penalty of loving another's wife. Grant me forgiveness and a chance to spend the remaining years of my life in the orbit of her friendship.'

In calm seas and with favourable winds they sailed into the harbour of Plymouth; dropping anchor and flying the signals agreed with Bray. But although they waited all day no boat came to welcome them as had been arranged and by nightfall Sir Edward decided they had better put out to sea and make for Poole, the second rendezvous decided upon.

They dropped anchor once more and this

time were rewarded with the sight of several long boats making spider's progress across the bay.

One look at Reginald Bray's face, as he made the difficult climb up the rope ladder thrown over for him, was sufficient to convince the news he brought was not good.

'Something is amiss?' Henry asked.

'Everything,' Bray said tersely.

'What happened?' Jasper asked as they crowded down into the Master's small cabin.

'Whatever Richard's popularity, he is still able to command a large army and by fair means or foul he stationed men up and down the country and put to flight all those who were hoping to join up with Buckingham.'

'Their forces were inadequate?'

'Against the enormous bands Richard had called to arms, yes. Buckingham soon heard of this falling away of Dorset and Courtney and all the others who had been behind him and turned alone to face Richard. His effort met with no success and Buckingham escaped from the fight which was sharp but very bloody and concealed himself in the house of a servant of his. Here he was either discovered by spies of Richard or betrayed by the servant in whom he had placed his confidence. No one seems to know the truth, but whatever happened Richard had him dragged out of hiding and refused to see him before putting him to death in Salisbury market place.'

'Richard appears to be a man with no compassion,' Jasper said heavily when they had absorbed the news and began to realise it entailed the dashing of their hopes. 'Has Henry's mother escaped his wrath?'

'It is early days to know what will be the outcome of the business but I can only tell you Buckingham died most courageously, refusing to implicate anyone in his plot. He bore full responsibility for the rebellion and sent word to Richard to say that if he had failed he trusted others would be more successful in unseating him from the throne to which he was not entitled.'

'You do not think the matter is ended here then?'

'Most certainly not,' Bray replied. 'If anything the revolt has brought others out against Richard and I am convinced you have but to wait, my lord, and opportunity will present itself again. In time the real nature of the man who calls himself Richard III will be revealed and in this will be his undoing.'

20

Jasper and Henry returned to Brittany and the Château of Vannes and before long saw the truth of what Bray had told them.

All the months following the reversal of the Buckingham rebellion brought more adherents to Henry's cause. Richard of Gloucester had become the most hated and despised ruler.

Apart from their loyalty the men who found their way to Vannes brought welcome news of Margaret to her son and Jasper. No letters were received from her and the Englishmen confirmed she was penalised by an act of attainder and confined to a remote manor on one of her husband's estates. Lord Stanley had been given the task of keeping her in virtual imprisonment and appropriating her inheritance. Despite these hardships she lived in daily thankfulness for the courage of Buckingham who had knelt to the block without disclosing her part in the disastrous revolt. Although pressed to give up the names of those involved with him he had refused utterly to implicate others.

'We have much to be thankful for to Henry

of Buckingham,' said Jasper gruffly when they had been told of the matter. 'He proved he was a man of honour despite what had gone before.'

The situation at Francois' court had changed completely from the distant days of 1471. The Duke, although failing in health, had allied himself with Henry of Richmond and assisted them as far as he was able. His ships guarded the Breton coast and became a source of anxiety to Richard. He refused to entertain Richard's ministers and sent more emissaries to France, where Louis was now dead, on the English Earl's behalf.

His spies, and the English men coming to Henry's side, told of Richard's concern for the support his rival was obtaining and the huge measures he was taking to counter any invasion. Money was literally being wrung out of a populace reluctant to part with it.

In a ceremony at Rennes Cathedral a solemn Mass was celebrated and the betrothal of Henry and Elizabeth of York formally declared. At the same time the loyalty of Henry's followers was proclaimed in a statement where they accepted him as a future sovereign.

By the Spring of 1485 Richard was desperate as he saw how the wind blew from Brittany and fluttered his kingdom away from him. He recognised the frailty of his hold and sought to strengthen it by any means. Strange stories came to Vannes of his courtship of his niece, Elizabeth of York.

'Incest! Apart from the fact she is my betrothed,' Henry cried to Jasper. 'How low can a man stoop to grasp power!'

'That we shall find out when Warwick's daughter, Queen Anne, proves a stumbling block to his designs.'

They did not wait long to discover the depth of Richard's iniquity for in the beginning of April word came of the death of his wife. Moulded in a fragile beauty Queen Anne had never recovered completely from the death of the heir to the throne in the previous year. Her short life had already seen the killing of her first husband and the loss of the child, on whom she doted, was a sadness she could not overcome.

When at Christmas, she had seen Elizabeth of York dressed in the same extravagant robe as herself and guessed both had been gifts from Richard, she had withdrawn from the company pleading sudden illness. In the following weeks she had taken to her bed and become so ill the physicians despaired for her life. She died in March.

The most bitter antagonists of Richard did not mince their words and said outright he had poisoned the woman whom he no longer desired, while the more charitable claimed he had broken her heart with his outrageous behaviour with his niece.

Growing clamour against the King for his conduct forced him to make official and public denial of any dishonourable intentions towards Elizabeth of York.

'What manner of girl am I contracted to marry that she can not recognise the fact her uncle is hot to lie with her?' Henry said to Jasper when they were told the news.

'If I were you, I should be generous and think her so innocent she did not understand his actions,' Jasper told him reassuringly. 'Of one thing you may be certain this last outrage will send supporters flocking to you.'

This was proved abundantly true as each week brought more followers anxious to throw in their lot with the exiled Earl of Richmond. All brought proof of the melting of Richard's sympathisers and the urgent need felt throughout the country for the return to stable government.

The only drawback to Henry's cause seemed the health of Francois. At first, carried by the enthusiasm for his share in his one-time prisoner's hopes for the future, he had recovered a zest for life but lately he was attacked with bouts of sickness and pain. It was during these times he was a source of anxiety, for he was inclined to relinquish his authority and despite the efforts of the Duchess to prevent it, would hand over the making of decisions to Pierre de Landois. These opportunities were seized with delight by the unscrupulous minister who had no more liking for Henry and Jasper than they for him.

When Francois made up his mind to go to some medicinal baths on the borders of the Duchy and France, Jasper and Henry said they would be glad to escort him to the place. They were only too pleased to help him obtain a cure.

They left him in the care of the monks who lived close by the therapeutic springs and rode home to Vannes.

When they came into the chambers, pleasantly tired with the ride in warm April air they discovered a priest of Margaret's household, Christopher Urswick sitting there.

'Thank God you are come!' he said when he had greeted them.

'Did you think we had gone?' Henry asked.

'I thought perhaps I had arrived too late with the warning I bring from Bishop Morton.'

'Bishop Morton? from England?'

'No from Flanders. Since the rebellion of

the Duke of Buckingham he has been hiding there. Your friend, David ap Thomas, was present at Southampton when a deputation from Richard, the King, headed by Dr. Thomas Hutton left the port to come here. He discovered the doctor was to offer Duke Francois all the revenues of the earldom of Richmond — your lands, my lord — if he would give up his two prisoners to be conveyed to England.'

'Has he consented?' Jasper asked sharply.

'He knows nothing of the offer. He had already left for the borders when Hutton arrived. Hutton does not realise I arrived hard on his heels and am hidden here, but I am able to tell you he has had an audience with de Landois and by all I can hear the minister is only too anxious to comply with Richard's wishes.'

'Doubtless,' Henry said drily. 'He hopes Francois will not recover and with the Lady Anne of Brittany still a child he can forsee a very pleasant future for himself with his nest lined with Richmond gold. What do you suggest we do, Jasper?'

'Send Christopher Urswick at once to the court of the French King and beg the boy to allow us to safe-conduct into his realm where we can wait while we complete our plans for the invasion of England.'

'That would be best, I agree. Would you do this for us?' Henry asked the priest.

'Of course, my lord. I shall leave immediately so that the minister may have the smallest opportunity of finding out I have even arrived. What will you do?'

'I think it would be best,' Henry said, after a moment's thought, 'if my uncle and some of the entourage left very quickly afterwards — '

'Great God!' Jasper exclaimed, 'I shall not leave you now at the very moment when danger threatens you!'

'Yes, you will,' Henry said smiling. 'There has hardly been a moment when danger has not threatened me during my life and throughout all those years you have guided me and kept me safe. Now that I am come to man's estate and am looked to to take upon myself the rule of England, I want to ensure above everything you are safe. What would my mother say,' he added softly, 'if I were to slink away and leave you to an unknown fate?'

'That need not arise if we were to go together,' Jasper said hastily, refusing to meet Henry's eyes.

'But we cannot go together. I think it best if we split up and I make it known in the Château you are returning to Francois with some documents of which he had special

354

need. As far as we know, Pierre de Landois is ignorant of the fact we are aware of Hutton's visit, but it would make him instantly suspicious if we left en masse. It would not take him any time to gather sufficient troops to apprehend us on some excuse or other. No, my dear Jasper, we are safer if we travel separately.'

Surprisingly the priest agreed with Henry and despite Jasper's protests and doubts for the wisdom of the scheme the matter was settled.

The page who waited upon Henry was sent to the kitchens for food while Henry went personally to the rooms of some of the Englishmen quartered in the castle and told them to prepare to leave secretly and quickly for France. Most of them expressed concern at his decision to follow later but he overruled their uncertainties and made a rendezvous for them with Jasper.

When it came time for him to depart Jasper found himself almost unable to speak.

'Do not fear for me, Jasper. I give you my promise to set out tomorrow and if it makes your journey any easier I have asked Sir Edward and several of the others to remain here a little longer to fox de Landois further.'

'That is some comfort, at least,' Jasper said heavily. 'But I like it not, my son, to betray my trust and go without you!'

'You have never betrayed your trust and I ask you to put your faith in me now.'

'Very well. We make for Anjou and Langeais, is that right?'

'Quite right. It is at Langeais the young King Charles has set up his household and I am sure he will take us in and give us refuge.'

Henry came to Jasper. Before the older man could prevent him he had knelt and taken his uncle's hand.

'Thank you, mon pere-oncle for your loving kindness. God be with you, until tomorrow.'

Jasper rode with the verve of his youth until those who accompanied protested they were exhausted and begged to be allowed an hour at least in which to ease their aching backs and sleep. They found a barn, half filled with straw, and sunk gratefully into the odorous comfort.

Jasper was unable to sleep, hagridden with the anxiety of leaving Henry to outwit de Landois alone. He snatched brief dozes punctuated with recriminations for allowing his nephew to override him.

Avoiding Nantes they came to the monastery where Francois was prepared to receive them. Urswick had passed through on the previous day and the anger Francois had experienced with his Minister had encouraged a speedy recovery. Highly incensed at what he had learnt, Francois had given orders for his Captain of Arms to return to Vannes with sufficient men and horses to effect the evacuation of all the Englishmen sheltering in the town. He left Jasper in little doubt of the punishment he would mete out to Pierre de Landois for the peremptory manner he had employed in acting on his own without first consulting his overlord.

Encouraged by the support of the Duke, Jasper and his party crossed the border and came to the ancient fortress of Langeais.

The huge château with its rounded bastions towered above the narrow city streets and presented a formidable aspect to would-be attackers. Once inside however, much of the military impression gave way to a more gracious mode of living as the Englishmen were led to the presence of the young King of France.

He received them in state sitting on a high backed, gilded chair, his sister Anne of Beaujeu close beside him. He was a pale youth, weak featured but dressed elegantly. Jasper had not been two minutes in the audience chamber before he realised the boy had little mind of his own. Charles made much of the cousinly relation existing between Jasper and himself but apart from this turned continually to Anne, deferring to her opinion which she gave readily but with a proper degree of hesitation. By the statesman-like quality of her advice and the searching brilliance of her eyes Jasper knew this air of simplicity was affected, probably for his benefit. Anne of Beaujeu appeared to be a fitting offspring of the late King Louis of France.

The formalities over, Jasper and the handful of men who had accompanied him, were allotted newly completed apartments overlooking the square courtyard. After they had eaten he slept dreamlessly in the silk sheeted bed.

When he awoke the gnawing anxiety for Henry reasserted itself and he rose hastily and sent a servant to Anne's seneschal asking for an interview with the Duchess. It was a waste of time to brood on the dangers his nephew might be encountering and he found himself wishing, as he had done continuously during the thirteen years of his exile, that Fate had dealt more kindly with those he loved more than life. He could see, as he stood gazing out of the leaded window, not the broad reaches of the Loire as they wound away from him but the rocky coast of Pembroke and Margaret's face aglow with pleasure as they rode together and she held out her arms for him to help her dismount: where was she now? how was she facing imprisonment and the loss of her freedom? Was Stanley treating her with the proper regard her gentle nature and high spirit needed?

Jasper turned away from the casement, suddenly tired and furious with his inability to do anything to aid her.

'I am old,' he thought. 'The years have drifted away with our lives, robbing us of joy.'

The servant returned to say the Duchess awaited him and Jasper followed him, praying fervently the most influential woman in France would be continuing her father's policy of supporting the cause of the Earl of Richmond against the usurping King of England. It seemed imperative he must go back to England.

He found Anne sympathetic, and when he raised the question of the loan he had been negotiating on Henry's behalf, she cut short his polite probings and stated her brother's Council were putting the promised amount at their disposal. Jasper experienced an enormous sense of relief. With money, and the increasing number of English and Welsh who had flocked to the banner of Richmond, his chances of calling Richard out were enhanced considerably.

The Duchess told Jasper the Court were leaving for Paris in the near future and she gave him sources from which he could set about collecting mercenaries and chartering ships.

He was glad of the work this entailed for it was to be almost a week before Henry came to the Château of Langeais.

Jasper greeted him with obvious relief and after clasping him in a quick embrace hurried him off to learn of the journey he had made through Brittany and across the border into France.

Christopher Urswick joined them in Jasper's chamber and he volunteered to return to Francois to discover the fate of the many English still remaining in Vannes.

He was back in Langeais in four days and stuttered with excitement as he told of Henry's great fortune in leaving Vannes when he did, for Pierre de Landois had had almost immediate information of his intention to go to the court of France, and had sent after him a large force to bring him back as a prisoner to Vannes.

'I am fortunate indeed!' Henry cried. 'But what of the others?'

'They should arrive here tomorrow. As you

know, Duke Francois sent money and instructions for them to come to you completely unimpeded, so Pierre was forced to remain in the Château de l'Hermine and sulk as they made off. Those in Francois' entourage do not fancy Pierre's lot when the Duke returns to Vannes himself and metes out punishment.'

By common consent those already at Langeais went to the chapel of the Château and Urswick offered thanks to God for Henry's deliverance.

Almost two hundred and fifty of Henry's followers rode into the castle during the following day and Christopher Urswick and several picked men set off soon after for England. He had instructions to meet up with David ap Thomas and travel with him into Wales to contact John Morgan and those others who would be prepared to throw in their hand with Henry.

As the summer approached and the French court took up residence in Paris, mounting excitement gripped the exiles. From all the reports Urswick managed to smuggle across the Channel it was obvious Richard was a worried man. He had abandoned the pleasures of London and the dubious wooing of his niece and lodged himself with a strong army first at Kenilworth and later at

Nottingham. He sent out Commissions of Array warning his nobles and gentry to have men ready to leave for any place in the country at an hour's notice.

Henry and Jasper winced as they read a copy of the Proclamation Richard had circulated through the breadth of his Kingdom condemning Henry and his mother.

'The said rebels and traitors,' so ran the document, 'have chosen to be their captain one Henry Tudor, son of Edmund Tudor son of Owen Tudor, which of his ambitious and insatiable covetise increaseth and usurpeth upon him the name and title of Royal Estate of this Realm of England. Whereunto he hath no manner, interest, right, title or colour. As everyman well knoweth, for he is descended of bastard blood, both of the father side and the mother side, for the said Owen the grandfather was a bastard born and his mother, daughter unto John, Duke of Somerset, son unto John, Earl of Somerset son unto Dame Katherine Swynford and of her in double adultery gotten. Whereby it evidently appeareth that no title can or may be in him.'

'What do you make of that?' Henry asked with distaste as he put the roll of parchment down. 'There is some truth in what he says — '

'He forgets *his* mother springs from the same stock as yours so that in blackening her name he dirties his own,' Jasper said drily. 'Think of it only as proving to you he is a desperate man and acts accordingly.'

'It would appear the sooner we land upon the shores of our island the better,' Henry replied.

By the middle of July all possible preparations were completed and Jasper and Henry bid farewell to their host Charles and his sister, finding it difficult to express their gratitude for the many favours and boons they had granted them.

In Harfleur they inspected the ships and men who had been enlisted in their service. Jasper noted the condition of the boats outstripped that of the troops, who looked to him dirty and ill disciplined. In private he impressed upon his nephew the need to issue orders to his captains insisting upon daily routines and close regard for the precious weapons they had managed to scrape together. Jasper prayed, when they landed in Wales as they intended, friends had been able to rally better troops than these for otherwise their case was doubtful.

Word had been received of those nobles most likely to assist them, but both were uneasy of the stand Margaret's husband would take when war was declared. They had information Stanley was accepting gifts from Richard and keeping his wife as closely guarded as he had been instructed by the King.

Christopher Urswick now rejoined their party with Bishop Morton and from Hammes castle, where he had been kept prisoner since his unsuccessful rebellion on St. Michael's Mount, came John, Earl of Oxford bringing with him the best equipped soldiers so far to join Richmond.

Heartened by this Henry's party set sail from Harfleur and with favourable winds and calm seas breasted the tip of Cornwall and set their course northwest for the Milford Haven.

Unmolested, the little fleet gained the protection of the Haven and dropped anchor off Dale harbour.

Before they climbed down the swaying rope ladder to the longboat waiting to put them ashore Henry turned to Jasper.

'So we are come home, Jasper.'

'May God go with you and if He will grant you the high destiny you seek.'

21

It was an extraordinary gathering who waited on the shore to greet them.

Above the splash of the oars Jasper could hear from afar the tempestuous beat of drums and loud cheering. As their boat scrunched on the shingle many willing hands dragged them to dry land. Familiar faces mingled with those unknown.

David ap Thomas pushed his way to the forefront of the crowd and knelt to Henry who embraced him and raised him to his feet. A man on a magnificent charger advanced as the thronging people fell back to allow him free passage. As he came up with Henry he descended from his horse and prostrated himself on the damp beach.

Henry regarded him with astonishment until the man begged him to walk over his stomach and proceed inland. Still confused, and somewhat selfconsciously, Henry complied and then turned and helped the suppliant stand.

'Thank God you are come, my lord, and I am able to greet you in this manner!'

'You do me singular honour,' Henry said to

him. 'To what do I owe this expression of your loyalty?'

'Perhaps to my stupidity. I am called Rhys ap Thomas — brother of David and Morgan — and in the past I made the foolish boast you would not enter this country in any effort to claim the throne except over my belly — '

'I see,' said Henry with a twinkle.

'Fortunately the good Bishop of St. David's gave me dispensation when I came to my senses and he absolved me from my vow in this manner. Now you see before you a most loyal and devoted servant. Will you do my family the honour of spending your first days at Carew Castle?'

'Willingly, Rhys ap Thomas.'

The crowd watched as Henry stood back while the Welshman sprung to his saddle; then drew in their breath sharply as the newly arrived Earl knelt and folded his hands in prayer.

'Judge me oh God and plead my cause against an ungodly nation. O deliver me from the deceitful and unjust man — '

'For thou art the God of my strength — ' the crowd took up the psalm and their voices rang in the warm summer air.

Henry bowed his head and kissed the earth of his birthplace and when David ap Thomas led forward a horse, mounted and waved his followers after the disappearing figure of Rhys.

Jasper watched this loyal display with growing optimism and when a mount was brought for him found himself the centre of a knot of men and women, all eager to grasp him by the hand and show their pleasure at seeing him returned to his own land. So many spoke at once it was difficult to unravel what was said but the gist appeared simple enough and that was Henry would have no difficulty in recruiting an army with which to challenge Richard of Gloucester. Most of those eagerly clustering around him offered their own services and said they would present themselves at Carew on the following morning.

As he saw Pembroke across the narrow strait before they reached Carew Jasper grasped fully the truth of his ended exile. Nostalgia flooded through him shutting out the clamour of the day's events and curling round his heart as he thought Margaret and he stood on the same soil for the first time in these fourteen dreadful years. He wondered how long it would be before word would reach her of her son's home-coming and determined to make his first duty, when they came to the castle of Rhys ap Thomas, to despatch a messenger to Stanley's estate.

He did not doubt David had already thought of this and sent men off with the news as soon as Henry's fleet had been sighted off the Pembroke coast but he wanted to ensure she had word quickly, and from him.

At Carew a strong band of supporters waited to greet Henry, Jasper and the Earl of Oxford. Rhys presented them and led the way to the hall where a banquet had been prepared in honour of the occasion.

On the following morning Henry held a Council and listened while all the available information about the deployment of those loyal to Richard was made known to him. It was soon obvious the success or failure of the mission hinged upon the support or emnity of the Stanley family. Those who presented Henry with facts and figures thought they were safe in promising the help of many Welshmen who could be recruited as he marched upon England, but did not hesitate to state their misgivings should the Stanleys help Richard as Richard expected they would. He had during the last year been loading them with gifts and money. However, Margaret's marriage with Thomas Stanley could prove the turning point of the argument and bring over the brothers to Henry.

Later in the day Jasper was called to the courtyard of the castle to find scores of Pembroke men ready to express their loyalty to him. Heartened by this show of strength Jasper called them into some kind of order and followed Henry on the road to Haverford West.

Before leaving, Henry had issued a proclamation in which he called for the support of all true subjects to rally to his aid in claiming his throne. At Haverford West he was kept busy enrolling those who answered his call.

While he was so engaged Jasper snatched a few moments to visit the Priory of the Grey Friars and pray silently at the tomb of Owen for victory for his grandson.

The army, considerably strengthened since it had first landed, set off for Cardigan on the morning of the 4th August. It had almost reached the town when a scout brought in reports of one of the Herberts marching against it with a considerable force.

Henry pushed on for Cardigan, refusing to be alarmed by what he heard sending other men back to Carmarthen to find out if the report was true.

He was rewarded by the discovery it was a false alarm and by the arrival of Richard Griffiths, who commanded much influence in the Principality. Griffiths brought with him a well disciplined band and news of others like himself waiting to join Henry of Richmond on his journey into England.

At Cardigan Henry and Jasper, who took with him the Earl of Oxford, separated. They agreed, if they took different ways to Shrewsbury where Henry intended to cross the Severn, they stood a greater chance of rallying more men to the Banner of the Red Dragon Henry had adopted as his own.

As he put mile after mile of Wales behind him Jasper's spirits soared. The lassitude and the burden of advancing age he had felt during the latter part of his exile vanished as the daily exercise renewed the vigour of his body. He began to feel confident in the success of Henry's campaign.

This was heightened as the army with Oxford and himself grew by the hour and the stories of Richard's misrule multiplied.

At Shrewsbury on 13th August he fell in again with Henry who now had behind him several thousand soldiers and mercenaries. Henry had taken up a position outside the town because the Chief Bailiff, Sir Thomas Mytton, refused to grant them access.

When the morning dawned Mytton sent word to say he had put down the drawbridge and would receive Henry with pleasure. Wary of a trick Henry, accompanied by Jasper and Oxford, entered Shrewsbury and far from being thrown into custody were given the Bailiff's blessing and a small body of men fitted out by the townsfolk.

At Newport, the first Englishman came to express his devotion to Henry and pledged his five hundred men to give every assistance. He gave Henry news of the Stanley family and said they had closely shadowed the swift march Henry's army had made across Wales and Sir William was encamped close by at Lichfield while Lord Thomas was not far off at Atherstone.

Henry and Jasper silently thanked God as this information was given them as they realised here was undeniable evidence of which way the Stanley family intended to show their loyalty. Considerably encouraged they were able to encompass information of the huge effort Richard was extending to counter any attack Henry made.

Richard had sent to London for the Great Seal upon the strength of which he called to arms the men of Northumberland, Yorkshire and Norfolk. He left Nottingham for Leicester.

Henry set up his headquarters at Atherstone when he heard where Richard had encamped. He had not been long in the place when his mother's husband came secretly to him.

Although he made no promises of assistance he told his stepson he and Sir William Stanley were suspected by Richard and he, Lord Thomas, had been forced to hand over his own son, Lord Strange, as a hostage for his own good behaviour.

'My mother?' Henry asked. 'How is it with her?'

'She is well, my lord, and prays hourly for your safe deliverance and success. She awaits you at Collyweston.'

'I pray to God we may be with her soon,' Henry said, as he accompanied his stepfather to the back of the inn where he had left a groom with horses. 'Whatever the outcome of the battle ahead tell her I have never ceased to love her or thank the Almighty for her care and goodness towards me.'

'So, she is at Collyweston,' Jasper said quietly, when Henry told him. 'How she longed to go to her manor there when she and your father were first married. Thomas Stanley must be fairly confident of the outcome of this affair if he has relaxed his vigilant guard on the Lady Margaret to permit her to reside in one of her own houses.'

With the news that Richard's force was

advancing towards him Henry moved from Atherstone to encamp on the moors before Shenton. With him were Jasper and the Earl of Oxford, backed up by all those who had taken up the call of the Red Dragon.

The morning of 22nd August was misty with the promise of Autumn but by the time the sun had broken through Henry could see the army of Richard drawn up against his on a nearby hilltop. Spies reported Northumberland and Norfolk flanking the banner of the Boar.

Other scouts sent by Jasper and Oxford came back to tell of the armies of both Stanleys stationed behind and to the side of Henry, keeping out of sight of Richard.

In hasty consultation Henry, Jasper and Oxford decided to move forward, wheeling as they did so to face south and rid themselves of the hazard of the fast rising sun in their eyes.

Richard, mounted among his foot soldiers, saw the move and straightaway gave the order for a volley of arrows. Under their cover he shouted at his men to press straight for the groups around Henry. In seconds the battle was engaged and Henry looked with horror as his Standard Bearer was over thrown and the flag of the Red Dragon lay in the dust beneath the horse's flying hooves.

Jasper rallied the men who were temporarily discomfited by this early setback. Out of the corner of his eye he saw Oxford's men pressing back those of Norfolk and encouraged by this he waved those about him forward, calling to them to mass about Henry and protect him from Richard's obvious design to strike and kill.

He was rewarded with the sight of some stalwart retrieving the banner and Henry surrounded with a shield of lances.

Norfolk's men now made a fainthearted attack, following not too quickly behind the men of Richard's force who were wading into Henry's. For some time the fighting became close and desperate and then Jasper sensed a wavering on Richard's left. Looking in that direction when given a momentary respite he saw with great relief the flag of Sir William Stanley fluttering next to Oxford. Glancing hurriedly to his own left he saw with something approaching astonishment Richard's flank was almost unguarded. Northumberland had chosen to remain neutral and had not given the word to his men to follow Richard.

Jasper was recalled to the action by the braying of a horn and the sight of Richard standing in the stirrups of his horse and urging his men onward. A lance struck at him and then another and he went down. In the confusion following Jasper heard a tremendous cry of triumph go up from those surrounding Henry as Richard's army broke its ranks and started a headlong flight away from the scene of the fighting.

Henry's army followed until it came up with the forces of Lord Stanley moving towards them. Jasper saw Margaret's husband, portly and leonine headed, advance towards Henry who had dismounted. As the two met the elder brought from his cloak a golden diadem; kneeling, he proffered it to Henry.

Looking around him Henry hesitated momentarily but a roar went up from the victorious army standing by and he took the crown and placed it on his mailed head.

A great weariness came over Jasper.

'Where did you come upon this?' he heard Henry ask Stanley.

'I caught a plunderer escaping with it.'

'He must have been swiftly at the side of the dead Richard,' Henry said slowly. The young man looked, Jasper thought, slightly bewildered at his quickly gained triumph, but Henry showed no signs of hesitation as he gave instructions for the host to kneel and thank God for their victory.

'We make now for Leicester,' he told his

captains when the prayer was finished. 'Let there be no plundering or despatching of the wounded of either side. Collect together our prisoners for sentence to be passed in Leicester and make a tally of our dead as well as those of Richard.'

He turned to Jasper.

'My Lord Jasper, will you go first into the city to prepare the way for us?'

Jasper looked at him gratefully.

'At once,' he said.

He took with him David ap Thomas and a small band of Pembroke men. At the castle he gave the tidings of Henry's victory and bade the Steward make preparations to meet the new King and his followers when they arrived that night. He heard the man agree to provide food and lodging for those of the army who would accompany Henry and followed the servant who was detailed to show him his allotted chamber. He declined offers of food and when the door was closed, allowed his squire to remove his coat of mail and the leather jerkin beneath it. When he had sat to have his boots pulled off he fell sideways on to the bed and slept.

The squire came to arouse him several hours later to say Henry had come and was awaiting him in the hall. Jasper doused his head in cold water in the garderobe and dressing hurriedly went down stairs.

Henry saw him approach and breaking away from the men crowding round him drew Jasper into the circle and presented him first to Lord Stanley and then to others he had not met before.

'Your son?' Jasper enquired of Stanley.

'He is safe and well, I thank you. Richard gave the order for his execution as he left to do battle but apparently no one had the heart to carry it out.'

'Our casualties are light,' Henry told Jasper. 'I grieve for any whose blood was shed, especially for Sir William Brandon, my Standard Bearer, but I think we may count ourselves fortunate to number our fallen as about a hundred.'

'That is good news indeed,' Jasper cried. 'How many did Richard lose?'

'Perhaps a thousand. No one is quite sure.'

'Who retrieved the Standard?'

'Rhys ap Thomas. He is to be knighted in the morning before we set out for Colly-weston.'

Jasper turned away as he found to his dismay his eyes were filling with tears.

'My Lord Henry,' Lancaster Herald called at this moment, 'pray be seated for your dinner is upon the table.'

Jasper moved away but Henry restrained him.

'You sit with me,' he said.

Jasper ate little during the meal and talked less, listening to the excited talk around him which increased in volume as the wine flowed.

The gruesome description of Richard's body being brought to Leicester naked across the saddle of a pony hardly touched his conscious mind for he could only think that with God's blessing he would be reunited with Margaret on the following day.

'I am foolish as a youth in love,' he chided himself. But he knew his love bore no comparison to the hot, fickle passion of the young. It had grown with the years, binding her to him, giving him the strength to endure the hardships of his exile.

Suddenly unable to encompass any longer the noise and excitement he made his excuses and walking down to the river threw off his clothes and swam in the cool water. The strokes were leisurely, sending him through the river without haste so that he was wrapped in a blessed calm. As his eyes became accustomed to the dark he lay on his back, making occasional movements with his hands, drawing comfort from the serene arc of the night sky and sensing the myriad scents of August. He felt refreshed and reinvigorated and when he climbed the bank dried himself on his undershirt and pulled on his tunic and hose. He returned to the castle and went unseen to his room. He waved away his squire's concern for his wet clothing and sent a page for wine.

He sat close to Henry when, on the following morning the King meted out rewards and punishments. The latter were few and restricted to three men who had been closely allied to Richard. Only these were to suffer death. Northumberland who had survived the battle and asked to be numbered among Henry's followers was accepted, while Surrey, heir of Norfolk who had fallen, was sent to the Tower to await Henry's will.

There was a murmur of approval for this leniency and Jasper realised Henry was not courting favour but exercising the wisdom he had gained in Brittany and France. His own life had been in danger for so long he recognised the boon of what it held.

At last the business of the day was finished and Henry announced he was taking a small contingent only and going to Collyweston to see the mother he had not set eyes on for fourteen years. Although the business of the realm was pressing and his presence in London was needed urgently there was not a voice raised in protest. Short shrift would have been given to anyone daring to question this decision, Jasper thought.

It was obvious from the brisk pace Henry started out with that he was as anxious to reach Collyweston as Jasper. Henry had sent word to the Steward at Higham Ferrers, where Richard had sent Elizabeth of York for safe keeping, to bring his future bride to Collyweston.

They covered the fifteen miles from Leicester swiftly, arriving at the slate roofed manor house before sunset.

Cantering up to the steps before the front entrance they saw a group of people gathered. Jasper strained his eyes to pick out Margaret from among them.

He recognised her long before she moved to the front, her straight back and slim figure unaltered with the years. It was impossible to tell if her face showed the strains she had suffered from a distance but once abreast of the doorway Henry reined in and leapt from his horse gathering her in his arms. Jasper watched, his throat tight, as Margaret buried her face on Henry's shoulder and clung to him.

He slid down from his stallion and stood waiting quietly until Henry disengaged himself and stepped back.

Jasper and Margaret faced each other.

With a stifled cry and oblivious of those about her she came to him and putting both her hands on his shoulders she kissed him, her tears wetting his cheeks.

'My dear,' she whispered, 'thanks be to God you are both come home to me at last.'

22

He found the excitement at Collyweston easy to bear after the feverish rejoicings at Leicester.

He had absented himself in the beautifully appointed room Margaret had given him, realising with pleasure this was the first time he had been her guest. The room was expressive of her personality, the walls covered with tapestries and the bed upholstered and hung with the brocade he had given her as part of her dowry at Pembroke. He was quite happy to stand at the window and looked across the well tended garden to the valley beyond. He knew Henry had much to tell his mother and he was well able to wait until she was ready to speak with him. He was glad Lord Stanley had elected to come to Collyweston the next day, pleading the necessity of seeing to the proper burial of Richard whose corpse had been exposed to the public gaze all of this day to prevent any future case of wrong identity.

He went down to supper when it was announced and found her household assembled. He and Henry were presented to each one.

At the last Margaret stopped before a youngish woman, somewhat carelessly dressed in apricot silks.

'Catherine, Duchess of Buckingham.'

Startled, Jasper looked more closely. He saw a pale round faced girl, with a slightly defiant air. So this was Edward's sister-in-law, widow of Buckingham. She appeared so obviously nervous he smiled and was rewarded with a quick upward quirk of stiff lips.

Margaret had placed him on her right hand and Catherine on his other side. The meal was chosen with care and served on gleaming silver and napery. It was typical of the order pervading the house.

While he ate with relish what was put in front of him and talked with both of his neighbours he longed to be able to look at Margaret, holding her face between his hands and searching behind the well remembered features for the truth of all she had suffered. When he had come down to the parlour he had looked at her swiftly and seen, now the tears had dried, she was still beautiful, with that fineness of bone that never lost its appeal. Her hair was hidden under a lace edged wimple and he could not judge if it were white at the temples as his own.

Although the meal went on for what seemed hours he enjoyed it. This was what he had dreamt about in Brittany, and in two days he and Henry were leaving for London. Not one precious moment must be wasted.

But at last it was finished.

Henry took his arm and together they walked round to the garden.

'Can you believe we are really home?' Henry asked him.

'Not completely,' Jasper answered. 'So much has happened since we landed in Dale I find my mind is unable to encompass it all.'

'One thing stands out above all others and this I shall never forget — '

'Don't speak of it,' Jasper interrupted him swiftly. 'Anything I did, I did as if it were for my own.'

'Without your encouragement I doubt if I should have lasted my first winter in Vannes. Also there is the other matter overlooked by most but which carries great weight with me. I think any other man but yourself would have seized the opportunities we have been given to advance himself and push me behind.'

'But that was impossible!' Jasper cried. 'Your right to the throne descends much, if not completely, from your mother and has little to acknowledge from Edmund.'

'Thrones have been won on frailer grounds than those,' Henry answered. 'Anyway, my honoured Jasper, my debt to you is unpayable, please accept my loving gratitude as the best token I can bestow.'

'Thank you,' Jasper said smiling.

They had returned to the house and Jasper climbed, somewhat reluctantly, to his room. Once more he returned to the casement and stood gazing out into the warm blackness. Here and there, far below, a light flickered in the dark and to the south a beacon glowed. He watched, leaning against the window frame until a small sound caused him to turn round.

Margaret was sitting in the chair at the foot of his bed. Wordlessly he went to her and buried his head in her lap. She caressed his hair, her fingers, soft at first but gaining strength until he heard her sob and fall against the back of the chair.

'Don't cry,' he whispered. 'Our time together is so short. Talk to me, tell me all that has befallen you while I have been away.'

'Where do I begin?' she said trying to still the tears clutching at her throat.

'From the moment we parted at Tenby.'

She leant forward and took his face in her hands.

'Let us go into the garden. Just at the moment I cannot bear the trammel of walls around us.'

'First let me look at you,' he pleaded.

He brought her under the candelabra and as he had wanted, looked down at her. She returned his stare, unblinking, until he caught her to him and held her close.

'We have aged together,' she said very low. 'You look as Owen did; perhaps more handsome than when you went away. Infinitely more dear, if that were possible.'

'But you are more beautiful. Lying in those damnable clos-lit of Brittany I tried to conjure up your face but it was difficult to capture more than a fleeting memory of how you looked. Come then, lead me to your garden.'

Once outside the house he put his arm about her waist and she moved closer to him making no effort to elude him. She took him to the garden limit where a dewpond glimmered in the starlight.

'Before I was taken to Lathom,' she said without self pity, 'this was my favourite place. Sit here on this seat where I have thought so much about you and Henry.'

Her head on his shoulder she began to tell him of the long ago days when David ap Thomas had taken her in one of Thomas

White's ships to Bideford and escorted her to Torrington.

'I was ill for months. I suppose looking back, I was worn out with anxiety and the news my mother was dead did not help. Henry Stafford came to Devon and was kind and considerate. He saw to all my affairs until the first shock of my grief was over. Then, bearing in mind what you had said to me, I began to take an active part in the management of my estates. It was this saved my reason. I forced myself to understand the accounts and the repairing of outmoded houses and barns. Later I found again some delight in study and learning, but it never held me as it had done before. Women are strange creatures, are they not? They live by their emotions and their actions are coloured by them.'

'However strange, I would not have you altered,' Jasper said huskily. 'What happened when Henry Stafford died?'

She did not answer at first but then said quickly.

'My first reaction was to throw in everything my life had become and join you and Henry in Brittany. But just at this time, if you recall, Edward died also and the resentment to Richard began almost immediately. Reginald Bray came to me and suggested that as I should marry again I might choose Lord Stanley. Perhaps Bray realised I was thinking about coming to you and he knew this was not the right thing for me to do. I considered what he said in the light of cold logic and decided to marry Thomas. He was recently widowed and it was not difficult to persuade him I would make a suitable bride.'

They were both quiet until Jasper broke the silence.

'How did he take the matter of your vow of chasity?'

She sat up beside him and took his hands in both of hers.

'Do you really want to know?' she asked.

'Are you laughing?' he parried swiftly.

'A little,' she replied. 'I think he was pleased!'

'Impossible!' Jasper cried. 'How could any man not want to lie with you?'

'You are forgetting all men are not as virile as you,' she whispered.

'Just as well,' Jasper growled.

'You do not remember I am forty-four years of age,' Margaret said quietly. 'And used by now to living an almost nun-like existence. When all that a woman holds most near to her heart is taken away from her, whether it be a child or a man, she is forced to find interests other than these. As you know my estates became my life and then when Richard saw fit to take these from me only God seemed to be able to help me.'

'Those days of 1483 were terrible for Henry and me before we heard what Richard had done to you.'

'They were anxious times for me on your behalf also because when it became known an attempted landing had been made I was shut away before I could learn what had befallen. Jasper' — she moved away from him — 'I owe my life to Buckingham — '

'I know!' he cried fervently. 'His initial allegiance to Richard was unbelievable but he exonerated himself and by suffering death without disclosing your part in the rebellion he has put us for ever in his debt.'

'It is of this I would speak,' Margaret said slowly. 'Do not be angry with me — '

'I could never be that. I count myself blessed that opportunity has been given me to look upon your face once more. There is no room for wrath in my love for you.'

'Thank you.' She paused. 'I find it more than difficult to say what is in my mind, but it must be done and the sooner the easier for us both. Will you help me repay my debt to Buckingham?'

'Gladly, for it was he who gave me the

gift of seeing you here, like this. What would you have me do? Take his sons as my wards?'

'Yes; and ask Catherine Wydeville to be your wife.'

'Margaret! what are you saying?'

'She is lonely, bewildered — and she has a most kind heart.'

'But I do not know her!' Jasper cried. 'How can I think of marriage when you are beside me after all these wasted years?'

'Very dearest Jasper.' She used the old familiar endearment and picked up his hand from where it rested on his knee and turned the palm to her mouth kissed it. 'It is easier now, perhaps, than later. By what happened yesterday on Bosworth field you are become the King's uncle and I, the King's mother. Much will be expected of us. We are neither of us young — ' she stopped as he moved irritably 'and I refuse to spend the rest of our lives being a stumbling block to your happiness. You *must* have a home and family life and Catherine is the first woman I have known who genuinely puts the thought of others before herself. If you cannot see, at the moment what I am striving to do for you, think about it.'

'I admit to being completely stunned but — '

'As I ask you, you will give it thought, won't you?'

'Yes. You have asked me to do so little for you since the day Henry was born that I shall not reject the idea out of hand as my first resentment told me.'

'In all the years since Edmund's death I have loved only one man. Nothing will change that, nothing can. You are part of my life, the sharer of my dreams. Now that you are come home my heart cries out to take care of you and share our lives; but it cannot be and I cannot bear you should drift into lonely old age.'

'Don't speak any more about it now,' Jasper said heavily. 'Speak of yourself to me.'

'I have told you the bald outline and the stresses and strains making up the day to day existence is no secret to you for you underwent the same trial. I would listen rather to your part of the exile in Brittany; how Henry stood up to the new life and grew to manhood without me. But first you have not mentioned, except in passing, Helen's marriage. You are happy I allowed the wedding when you were not here to give your consent?'

'Of course. She could not be asked to wait for an unknown number of years to marry. You like this William Gardiner?'

'He seems to be ideally suited to her and is well spoken of by those who know him well. She has settled down to being the mistress of his household with ease. I have sent word to her of your homecoming and perhaps you will find time to visit her.'

'Of course. I have been a most unsatisfactory parent and had it not been for you Helen would have been deprived of any family life. Are there children of the marriage?' he added suddenly.

'No, you are not yet a grandfather, Jasper!'

'I think Henry expected Elizabeth of York would be coming here to meet with him. Is there word of her arrival?'

'Yes, she is arriving on the morrow. Let us pray that the marriage will be acceptable for them both and in their union will be an end of this useless strife.'

'Henry was nonplussed concerning the rumour of Richard's courting of her. Was there truth in the matter?'

'Who is certain of what goes on in the mind of another? I was not at court, of course, at the time and what I know is only from hearsay but there are those who will tell you she was definitely acquiescent to Richard's wishes. I pray most earnestly, for Henry's sake, there is no truth in this and that Elizabeth will help us all by making him

392

a faithful wife and Queen.'

The moon rose over a bank of trees filling the secret garden with pale light. Jasper turned to Margaret and touched the pleated linen coif that came down over her cheekbones.

'May I take it off?'

She nodded and helped him find the pins that bound her hair. When it fell about her shoulders he pulled her to him and cradled her head on his shoulder, gently stroking her face.

'Somehow, it doesn't seem to matter so much our love has known no consummation. Perhaps in the differing facets of caring for another it is not necessary to express it by bedding. I have possessed you in a look more surely than any man who had a wife or mistress. Oh, God, why was I not born first and died in Edmund's place?'

'Don't talk like that,' she said huskily. 'Where would I have comfort and understanding without you?'

They stayed together, talking quietly until the dew began to rise. Jasper carried her to the house and stole into the shuttered rooms with her beside him. At the door of her chamber he bent and kissed her swiftly on the brow.

'No more than that,' he said. 'But with it

goes my heart, beloved Margaret.'

He did not sleep, hearing the cockcrow and the sounds of the day's awakening below him. He was surprised he did not feel any sense of tiredness and when his squire came to rouse him, dressed with care and sat down at the window to await his nephew's bidding and think over what Margaret had said to him.

He was filled with a strange contentment such as he had never known before. 'If this is middle aged love,' he thought, 'would to God I had known of it before.'

He found he was able to think without passion of Margaret's proposal for his marriage with Catherine Wydeville. In the morning light it seemed a small thing to give his name and protection when Buckingham had given his life for Margaret in Henry's cause.

Henry sent for him before he was able to dwell on the matter and made it plain to him he did not intend to make decisions without Jasper beside him. While they were talking together Lord Stanley rode in from Leicester and before noon the party of Elizabeth of York was announced.

Margaret joined them in her parlour and he looked at her swiftly, expecting her to be heavy eyed with lack of sleep, but she was serene and composed giving him the full depth of her smile and then going unhurriedly to bid her future daughter-in-law welcome.

Jasper saw the girl as she entered the room and realised she closely resembled her aunt, Catherine, but as Margaret presented her to Henry he could see, although her features were similar, she was wan and lacked vitality. The fullness of her robe hid the lines of her body but the slender throat did not speak of sturdy hips and Jasper hoped she was capable of childbearing. It would be a tragedy if Margaret and Buckingham had worked for this union only to discover there could be no heir.

Elizabeth of York, now accompanied by Henry, made her curtsey to Jasper and he was struck with pity for her air of self depreciation. Henry shared his compassion for he was treating her with great courtesy and encouraging her almost as he would have done a child. It was not difficult to imagine how Richard had played on her affections. For Henry's sake Jasper hoped his future bride would prove more spirited than she looked.

Her face lit up for the first time when Catherine of Buckingham came into the room and she broke away from Henry to go to her aunt. With relief, Jasper saw the reserve melt in both women and a little warmth come into Catherine's expression.

Several hours afterwards Henry and Jasper set out on the first stage of their journey for Westminster.

Margaret and the other women did not accompany them but were to leave Collyweston later to take up residence in London for Henry's Coronation.

As they rode south Jasper had ample opportunity to consider his nephew in his new status as King of England. Since the battle of Bosworth Jasper had thought only of Margaret and had been detached from the change in Henry's fortunes but now he regarded the young man quizzically, seeing an almost tangible growth. Thinking back he realised this had already been apparent in his handling of the prisoners after the victory.

In London, his faith in Henry's ability grew as he watched the new sovereign putting the affairs of his state in order and making the arrangements for his Coronation and marriage. He had always believed Henry bore within him the spark which singled him out from his fellows and endowed him with the gift of leadership and he now gave thanks to God his trust had not been misplaced.

The Coronation was arranged to take place on 30th October and the first Parliament of the reign immediately afterwards.

Before this date Margaret, with Elizabeth of York and her mother and Catherine, Duchess of Buckingham, came to Westminster and were given their own apartments. The Palace was thronged with those men who had come to Brittany to give Henry their support; while those who had been loyal to Richard kept away, hiding in their estates. Although he pushed on with the business of his kingdom Henry did not lose sight of the possibility of Richard's erstwhile henchmen banding themselves together and rebelling against him, and gave instructions to Oxford, Sir Edward and Poynings to keep armies in a constant state of vigilance.

Four days before the ceremony in the Abbey Church Henry called Jasper to him and invested him as Duke of Bedford in gratitude for what Jasper had meant to him. He told his uncle that after Parliament met he would set about restoring to Jasper the Earldom of Pembroke and the other manors and holdings which had constituted his inheritance.

Later Jasper went to speak with Margaret in her chambers. As he entered, her ladies and Betsey Massey, still her faithful handmaid, made their curtsies and left them.

'You always did imbue your women with

tact,' Jasper said, as he sat opposite her before a roaring fire. 'I have only to come to your parlour and they flee like frightened rabbits.'

'I am sorry if I am mistaken in thinking you wished to speak with me alone!' Margaret told him, raising an eyebrow and smiling. 'I have only to ring this bell and they will return at once.'

'Heaven forbid!' Jasper cried hastily. 'When it is possible to find an hour in the day when we are free to be together do not let us ruin it with fluttering ladies about us.'

'So now I see the illustrious Duke of Bedford sitting at my fireside. You still only look like Jasper Tudor to me — as you always will. Henry tells me he wishes to restore the Earldom of Pembroke to you.'

'Yes, that is so, but I care not whether I ever return to the castle again. Do you know, sweeting, there is a legend that nightingales do not sing in the County?' he added as an afterthought.

'No, I did not realise that! Is it perhaps because they knew they were wasting their time as far as we were concerned?' she asked with a chuckle.

'That could well be the reason, but David ap Thomas told me it was because his namesake Saint David was disturbed by them when he said his prayers and begged our

Lord to forbid them near his country!'

'A charming legend either way; but seriously, Jasper, do not refuse the Earldom, you have been deprived of enough in your time and it will be a most useful heritage to hand to your son.'

Suddenly the warm chamber was very still. Jasper looked at Margaret, unblinking, until smiting the arms of his chair with clenched fists he stood and went over to the window.

'You flatter me,' he muttered. 'Besides, I have a son already — Henry. There is no need for other.'

Margaret left the fireside and came beside him, looking down on the grey river surging in the fullness of high tide.

'You have thought about what I said to you of Catherine Wydeville?' she asked gently.

'I have.'

'And you will do it?'

He turned to her, the life drained from his face.

'For you — yes.'

'Then it is settled.'

Neither of them spoke, lost in the dark web of their tangled emotions until Jasper gave a mirthless laugh.

'When we look back, it seems you and I make a habit of choosing spouses for one another. I can only trust your judgement is as good for me as mine for you when I brought Henry Stafford to your bed.'

Margaret recoiled, her eyes widened and the pupils black with pain.

'Don't look like that!' he cried. 'I spoke in jest, my dearling.'

'I know,' she replied very low, 'It is foolish of me to behave so stupidly when what we are discussing is my own idea. Come,' she said, striving to lighten her voice, 'tell me what you think I should wear for the Coronation.'

He stayed with her longer than had become their daily custom, unable to tear himself away from her in what he knew would be possibly the last meeting they would have before he was committed to Catherine of Buckingham.

When, at last, he rose to leave her she had recovered her composure but as he kissed her lightly on both cheeks he knew by the swift rise and fall of her bosom and the grip of her hands as they clung to his arms she was controlling herself to the limits of endurance.

Every fibre in his being longed to enfold her close to him and carry her through the open door to her bedchamber beyond but he forced himself to step back and cover the racing of his pulses by kneeling to her.

She put out her hand to him and he took it and turning the palm held it to his mouth.

'I have not forgotten that other meeting,' he said as he folded her fingers and stood up. 'Keep my love in your heart for always.'

He went quickly from the room and made his way to the chapel close to his chambers. He spent more than an hour on his knees, praying as he had never before prayed, for strength in this crisis of their affairs.

That evening, he sent a page to ask the widowed Duchess of Buckingham if she would receive him.

He found Catherine with her brother, Sir Edward Wydeville and some other friends listening to a musician playing the hautboy. She came to greet him and he begged her to allow the entertainment to continue. Obviously pleased she signed for the man to continue.

While the clear notes filled the room he studied, covertly, the face of the woman he was to marry.

She was as unlike Margaret as well thrown pottery from exquisitely carved jade but Jasper was ready to admit she looked an agreeable woman. She was dressed more becomingly than at Collyweston and as she listened to the music her features were relaxed and her mouth curved. It was her very softness caused Jasper to shift uneasily in his chair. Somehow it would have been easier if the woman had been high spirited and mettlesome, a touchstone for the anomalies of his character rather than someone with an air of such pliancy.

When the other guests departed he stayed behind, awkward with what he had to say and was considerably relieved when Sir Edward also lingered.

Taking his courage as a shield he spoke quickly.

'I am glad you are here, Edward, so you may know I am come to ask your sister to be my wife!'

Catherine looked up at him, startled.

'My lord! I had no thought of this!'

'But this is most wonderful news,' Edward Wydeville cried. 'There is no one I can think of who is better able to take care of you, my dear.'

He looked at Jasper.

'I am quite sure my sister will be honoured to accept your suit. Is that not so, Catherine?'

Jasper sensed her hesitation but she answered quickly.

'Yes, yes, of course. I am aware of the singular honour you pay me, my lord — '

'Jasper,' he corrected gently.

'Jasper,' she echoed.

They were married in the first week of November. A quiet ceremony attended by members of both families.

At the feast Margaret gave for them afterwards Jasper drew Margaret into an alcove and handed her an engraved glass of rare crystal. It was filled with wine. At this bidding she drank from it, his eyes never leaving her face, and handed it to him. He drained it and while she looked at him, perplexed, threw the goblet against the wall behind her where it shattered with a sharp explosion and lay in pieces on the floor.

Margaret gasped and her hand went to her mouth. She saw with something approaching awe Jasper's eyes were full of tears.

'Don't speak!' he said quickly. 'All that has been between you and me, I offer as a libation. All that might have been is in God's keeping. Go to your task of helping Henry as the King's mother and rest assured I shall always be at hand if he need me. Be certain also I shall fulfill my new responsibilities with honour. But look not for heirs, my dearest love, they stay unborn — in you.'

We do hope that you have enjoyed reading this large print book.

Did you know that all of our titles are available for purchase?

We publish a wide range of high quality large print books including:
Romances, Mysteries, Classics
General Fiction
Non Fiction and Westerns

Special interest titles available in large print are:
The Little Oxford Dictionary
Music Book
Song Book
Hymn Book
Service Book

Also available from us courtesy of Oxford University Press:
Young Readers' Dictionary
(large print edition)
Young Readers' Thesaurus
(large print edition)

For further information or a free brochure, please contact us at:
Ulverscroft Large Print Books Ltd.,
The Green, Bradgate Road, Anstey,
Leicester, LE7 7FU, England.
Tel: (00 44) **0116 236 4325**
Fax: (00 44) **0116 234 0205**